Gender Rolls

By Xine Fury

ISBN: 978-1-967029-07-5

Contents:

Session Zero

"Is there anything more beautiful than a fresh character sheet?" the man in white asked. "It's a clean slate. Nothing but potential. From here on out, anything can happen." As he spoke, he handed the new player a piece of paper along with a pencil and a handful of dice.

"Sure," the player said, though she didn't sound like she meant it. She scrutinized the blank sheet, perplexed by some of the options. "I guess I'll start with my name..."

"Actually, you don't fill in that one," the man said, stroking his long, white beard. "A couple of the veteran players will come up with a name for you."

"That's silly," the player said.

"Well, your character won't even be able to speak coherently for the first few levels," the man said.

"What if I don't like my name?" the player asked.

"Don't worry, you can change it at level eighteen."

"Sounds kind of arbitrary," the player said. "What about my stats?"

"Roll three six-siders for each stat. In order, no rerolls."

"That's harsh," the player said. "There's no point buy

option? Or some sort of standard array?"

"Nope, everyone rolls the same way," the man said. "It keeps things fair."

"But that's the opposite of fair," the player said. "What if I get crappy stats, and the other people in my party end up with loads of eighteens? I'll never get a chance to shine."

"You'll just have to make up for it with smart gameplay."

"I'm going to be stuck with this character for eighty-plus levels," the player said.

"Closer to sixty," the man said. "There's a history of heart disease in your family." He pointed to a bit of text in the "background" section of her character sheet.

"Oh, great," the player said. "So I could be going into this game at a disadvantage right from the start. Why should I keep playing if I don't like my character?"

"Because there are no other games," the man said, his arms stretched wide. The player looked around at the rows and rows of empty tables, stretching into infinity in every direction. "It's this or nothing."

"Fine," she said, and started rolling some dice.

"Not bad, not bad," the man said appreciatively. "I see a couple of sixteens in there, and nothing below ten. You'll do pretty well. Now roll for starting wealth."

"And *that's* supposed to be fair?" the player asked, studying the table of income brackets. "The players who roll a hundred start with nearly unlimited wealth. Why would they even play the game after that? They could just retire right away."

"That hardly ever happens," the man said.

"Whatever," the player said, rolling. "Thirty-four."

"Not too bad," the man said. "Lower middle class. You won't starve, but you will have to work for your meals."

The player filled out a few more fields, then studied the sheet closely. "Only one hit point... no skills yet... speed's just one square, zero armor class... Wow, this game is brutal at first level."

"Yeah, those veteran players really take care of you for the first few sessions. They practically spoon-feed you. Did you remember to roll for sex?"

"I can't just pick?"

"Nope," the man said.

"But I already know I want to be a woman," the player said.

"Great," the man said. "Most people haven't thought that far ahead. You can go ahead and put an 'F' in the gender field. But you still have to roll for sex."

"If I have to play this character for a lifetime, shouldn't I be allowed to play the character I want to play?"

The man paused, leaning forward on the wispy white gaming table. He looked lost in thought for a moment, then stood up straight. "I'll make you a deal," he said, raising his index finger. "Since you have such a strong preference, you only have to roll to see if your sex matches your gender. The odds are in your favor. Just don't roll a one."

The player took a deep breath, then closed her eyes and rolled the die.

"...Crap."

The Opposite of Magic

"Claw!" the beast roared as it took a swipe at the nearest fighter. Enaj, noble knight of the Deromra Legion, ducked beneath the monster's claws and attempted to reciprocate with a slash of his own. Though his sword glowed with an aura of Lacigam energy, it still bounced off the creature's metallic scales.

The monster was the only one of its kind, having been created by an evil bio-alchemist. It had the head of a k'calb raugaj, the massive body of a raeb-krahs, the wings of a d'lab elgae, and the stinging tail of a d'nas noiprocs – all nonsense words to those of other realms, but in the land of Asu it was one of the most frightening combinations imaginable. With a near-impenetrable hide, razor-sharp claws and teeth, and a deadly tail stinger, it was a beast right out of a dark nightmare.

Fortunately, it wasn't very bright. "Sting!" it shouted, as it jabbed at Enaj with its stinger. It had a habit of calling out its moves before it made them, as if its head had to issue verbal orders to its own body. And that might not have been far from the truth. The creature had the brain of a raugaj, and that brain wasn't used to having such a mismatched form. Having only been created the day before, it hadn't had much time to get used to all its parts.

As Enaj ducked away from the stinger, his partner Rehsa stepped out of the shadows and fired three arrows from her bow. All three bounced off the monster's scales, but it got the thing's attention. The creature charged at Rehsa, who ducked back into the crevasse she'd been using as cover. This gave Enaj a moment of respite while the creature peered into the crevasse.

A few seconds was all Enaj needed. "Rewop!" he shouted, and his sword glowed even brighter. Then he rushed forward and sliced off the creature's tail.

"Owie ow ow ow!" the monster shrieked, then turned back toward the fighter. "Bite," the creature growled before opening its jaws wide.

Enaj couldn't pass up the opportunity. "Lunch is on me," he quipped as he thrust his sword towards the monster's open mouth.

But the blow didn't land. The monster made an unannounced swipe with its right paw, knocking the sword out of Enaj's hand and cutting his arm badly. Then it pounced on the fighter's chest and bared its teeth. "Trick," the monster purred with an evil gleam in its eye.

Another three arrows bounced off the creature's armored rump as Rehsa attempted to distract the beast. But this time the monster ignored her. Holding Enaj down with its paws, it once again opened its mouth wide and went for the fighter's face.

A small orb of green flame suddenly hit the monster in the eyes, and it winced in pain. It took a few steps backward, releasing Enaj from its grasp. The beast looked around for the source of the attack, spotting the caster just as another magical projectile hit. "Hurt!" the monster bellowed, backing away.

Rolling to his feet, Enaj risked a glance over his shoulder to see where the spell had come from. The Grand Sorcerer Drahcir stood on top of a large rock, his graying beard frizzing from the magical power he emanated. Peeking out from behind his blue robes, his young apprentice Mada nervously played with her pigtails as she watched the scene unfold.

"Nice of you to finally join us, Drah!" Rehsa shouted, nocking another three arrows.

"Yes, well, your directions left out a few turns," Drahcir replied. As he spoke, he began to generate another fireball in his palm. Mada watched his gestures closely, taking mental notes.

The monster looked from one opponent to the next, calculating its odds. "Fly!" it shouted, spreading its wings. It leaped into the air but came crashing right back down, its wings unable to support the weight of its body. As it attempted to hobble away, the four humans converged on it. Drahcir's next fireball knocked the creature onto its back, and Enaj thrust his magic sword into its unarmored belly. "Die..." the creature moaned, then went limp.

"It is good to see you," Enaj said, patting Drahcir on the shoulder.

"And just in the nick of time as always," Rehsa added, laughing. "Sometimes I think you hide until the most dramatic moment."

Mada moved to Enaj's side and examined his wounds. "I'll have you fixed up right quick," she said, rooting through her pack for some magic salve.

While his apprentice patched up the fighter and Rehsa gathered up her arrows, the wizard bent over the dead monster and squinted. "There," he finally said, noticing the creature's eyes. They were two different colors, but only because one wasn't an actual eye. Drahcir reached forward and plucked the glowing stone from the creature's eye socket. He studied the stone closely, frowning.

"What is it, master?" Mada asked, wrapping a cloth bandage around Enaj's rapidly-healing arm.

"I'm not quite…" he replied absently. He gazed at the stone for a few more seconds, then stood up. "I must return to my tower immediately."

"You sure?" Enaj asked. "We're about to go back to town to claim our reward. Don't you want your cut?"

"Keep it," the wizard said. "Use it to get some better armor. I might not be there to save you next time."

"Safe travels," Enaj said, bowing. Then he and Rehsa returned their attention to the creature's corpse. To claim the bounty, they would have to lop off a few pieces as proof. By the time they looked up again, the wizard and his apprentice were long gone.

"Tracy! Over here!" Adam waved at his friend, motioning for her to come over.

Tracy stood fourth in line at the coffee counter, sandwiched between two businessmen talking loudly on their cell phones. She shook her head at Adam's invitation, gesturing towards the counter. *I don't want to lose my place in line,* she mouthed silently. Then Adam held up two cups of coffee, and Tracy understood. She left the line and joined her friend at a little table next to the window.

"How'd you know I'd be here?" Tracy asked. Outside the window, the horde of annoyed-looking pedestrians picked up speed as it started to rain.

"It's Monday," Adam said. "You always start the week with a double espresso." He slid the extra drink over to Tracy.

"Thank you," Tracy said, taking a long sip. "What do I owe you?" She set her drink down next to a small glass vase that held a single red flower.

"Please," Adam said, rolling his eyes. "Like you didn't buy me a hundred coffees back in college. So how's life?"

"The usual," Tracy replied. "Likes, shares, comments, death threats… sometimes there's cookies."

"Death threats?" Adam asked.

"As of yesterday's livestream, I am officially the fourth most famous trans woman in Fresno," Tracy said.

"Wow, you think they make a greeting card for that?" Adam asked.

"My channel has nearly a million subscribers. I even get recognized on the street now and then. I'd get the occasional death threat even if I wasn't trans. It comes with the territory. Surely you get death threats at the hospital?"

"Now and then," he admitted. "Mostly from those 'Covid's just a hoax' patients."

"Sounds fun," Tracy said. "You ever 'accidentally' jab 'em in a tender area when giving them a shot?"

"I assure you I am always the consummate professional," Adam said.

"Chicken," Tracy said.

"At least I have a real job," Adam said, winking. "So tell me, what did you say to piss off your viewers this time?"

"Nothing big," Tracy said. "I was interviewing some

transphobe about bathroom laws. She kept saying there should be guards at the doors of public restrooms, to do genital checks on anyone who looks too manly. So I – very politely, mind you - pointed out that if the guards were going by faces, she'd get stopped before I would."

"Politely, huh," Adam said, flashing a sarcastic smile.

"When have I ever been rude?" Tracy asked, gesturing towards herself with mock offense.

"So you have a million subscribers and it's just trans content?" Adam asked.

"No, I report all kinds of things," Tracy said. "You really should watch, I post news segments pretty much all day long. On the walk here I uploaded a video on that white rhino thing."

"White rhino thing?" Adam asked, running a hand through his hair.

"Do you ever watch the news?"

"Get me a job where I have ten minutes to myself now and then, and… I still probably wouldn't," Adam admitted. "Tell me about the damn rhinos already."

"They've been endangered for years," Tracy said. "But the past couple of weeks they've been disappearing in rapid numbers. Like, hundreds gone overnight. No corpses or anything. Some people are blaming poachers, but there's no way they're this organized."

"Weird," Adam said.

"But it's more than that," Tracy continued. "Remember the thing with the bees?"

"Didn't that turn out to be climate change?" Adam asked.

"Maybe," Tracy said. "But strange things are happening all over Earth, and I'm starting to think it all ties together. There's this new plant disease that has botanists stumped.

Trees just seem to wilt and die overnight. The strange part is, some animals are dying of the same symptoms. What if the rhinos are 'wilting' and turning to dust?"

Adam didn't look convinced, but he didn't say anything.

"And there was that passenger jet that crashed over the ocean last week," Tracy continued. "They found the wreckage, but not a single body. Where did the passengers go?"

"Washed out to sea, surely?" Adam offered.

"All of them?" Tracy asked. "Their seatbelts were still fastened. They even found some clothing. You're telling me not one body would have stayed tangled in the wreckage?"

"So what's your theory?" Adam asked, leaning closer.

"I think they disappeared before the crash," Tracy said. "I think that's what caused the crash – the pilot vanishing, I mean. And I think it's connected to everything else that's been disappearing or dying lately."

"So you're a conspiracy theorist now," Adam said, leaning back with a concerned expression.

"Wait until you see how it ties in with the lone gunman," Tracy said. When she saw her friend's expression, she added, "Just kidding. Seriously. It's just this one set of stories I think are tied together. I'm not about to start wearing a tinfoil hat or anything."

Adam looked at his phone. "I'm late for work," he said. Seeing Tracy's expression, he added, "No, I mean it. I'm the last person who would ever call you crazy. Remember that time you walked in on me with the stuffed seahorse? Everyone has quirks. But right now I really have to go."

"Thanks for the coffee," Tracy said. She reached out and they held hands for a moment, then Adam turned around and rushed out the door.

Tracy took another sip of coffee. When she set it back down, she noticed the flower in the vase had wilted.

"Master, where does the magic come from?" Mada crouched on her knees next to a bucket of water, scrubbing the floor of Drahcir's study.

"We've been over that many times," the wizard said, studying the stone through a spyglass. A large tome took up most of the space on his desk, and it was open to a chapter titled "Magic Artifacts."

"Yes, I know, but…" the apprentice said, pausing to find the right words. "You've spoken about invisible lines of mystic energy that run through the air, and you've talked a lot – a *lot* – about how tugging on a line causes an effect on the other end of the line. And you've told me all about how these were first discovered, and who figured out how to use them. But none of that really tells me what magic *is*. Where does the energy come from? Who put it there?"

"You're not ready for that yet," Drahcir said, squinting at the book's small print. After a few more moments of struggling to read the text, he held the spyglass over the page.

"Then when?" Mada asked. She sat up for a moment, squeezing her rag out into the bucket. "I know the basics. I've cast my share of spells. I know I have a long way to go, but surely I'm ready to know where the magic comes from. Maybe if I understood more about how it works, I'd be better at using it."

Drahcir looked up from the book and gave his apprentice a long, meaningful appraisal. *Maybe it is time to let her in on the secret,* he thought. Finally he closed the book and put the stone in a little box, which he then placed on a shelf. Giving Mada his full attention, he nodded and said solemnly, "I dunno."

"Huh?" Mada asked, cocking her head.

"We don't know where the magic comes from," the wizard said. "None of us do, not even the grandest and eldest of us."

"Are you being serious?" the apprentice asked.

"Yes," he replied. "And that's why this conversation must remain a secret. People already distrust magic users. If they knew we were so irresponsible as to use powers we don't even understand, they'd lynch every last one of us."

"If it's irresponsible, then why do you do it?" Mada asked.

"Because others do," Drahcir replied. "That monster we fought today? Sent by an evil wizard. And without our help, Enaj might not have survived. Sometimes the only thing that can stop evil magic is good magic. Without people like us, the evil wizards would have taken over the world by now. Or destroyed it."

"Oh," she said, looking disappointed. "So they have no idea at all? About how magic works, I mean."

"We have theories," Drahcir said. "Some think it comes from some all-powerful supreme being, but that doesn't answer the question so much as moves it. Where did the supreme being come from? How did *he* get the magic? Rubbish."

"So where do *you* think the magic comes from?" Mada asked.

"I believe it comes from alternate dimensions," the wizard said. "Parallel worlds. When we pull on the magic lines to cast a spell, it yanks that energy from another realm, a world similar to ours but in another plane of existence."

"That makes sense," Mada said. She looked lost in thought for a moment, then very concerned.

"What troubles you?" Drahcir asked.

"If you're stealing this energy from another world," she asked, "then what happens to that other world?"

"It's nothing to worry about, my dear," the wizard replied, laughing. "If I'm right, then there's an infinite number of parallel worlds, and only a handful of them would have given birth to civilization. The vast majority of them would have no life on them whatsoever. Wherever the energy comes from, trust me, no one is suffering from its loss."

"Hello, faithful viewers! Welcome to today's episode of 'Tracy Leaves the House!' Today I've picked a location suggested by one of my viewers. Even though I'm a little bit uncomfortable with enclosed spaces – seriously, I couldn't come out of the closet fast enough – I'll be exploring Fresno's cave system with my good friend, Asher! Say hi, Asher!"

"Hi!" Asher waved into the camera, smiling.

"Regular viewers will remember Asher from our segments on kayaking, and that camping episode with the unfortunate marshmallow incident. But Asher's eyebrows have grown back and now he's ready to be on camera again. Asher's an advanced spelunker with years of caving experience, and he's just itching to get me underground. With a bit of luck, he might even take me back to the surface when we're done!"

"We'll see," Asher said with a big grin.

"Now obviously I won't be able to broadcast this segment live. So in a minute I'm going to cut the feed, and I'll post a full video tonight with the highlights of my caving adventure. Don't miss it!"

Tracy switched off the camera and clipped it onto her vest. As she stood in front of the cave entrance, she felt an involuntary shudder.

"Second thoughts?" Asher asked, patting her on the shoulder.

"A little, yeah," Tracy admitted. "But I've already promised my viewers."

"I could take your camera in," Asher offered. "You could add a voiceover in editing, they'll never know the difference."

Tracy shook her head. "Thanks, but that's not how I do things. This channel is all about new experiences and facing fears. I'll be fine."

"Then if you're ready, let's head on in."

Despite her uneasiness, Tracy was having a great time. The natural cave formations were absolutely beautiful. As she held up her cell phone to capture one particularly phallic-looking stalactite, she noticed Asher performing an odd ritual. His lantern sat on the ground by his feet, and he stood in the center of the passage, holding out his phone, rotating in a slow circle.

"Taking a panoramic shot?" Tracy asked.

"It's this new caving app I'm trying," Asher said, showing her his phone. "Whenever I get to a new passage, I scan it and it adds it to the database. That way if we get lost I can use the app to lead us back out."

"Is there a chance of that?" Tracy asked. "Us getting lost, I mean?"

"Nah, I know this route by heart," Asher said. "But good cavers don't take chances. It only takes one wrong turn to get completely disoriented. Don't wander off."

"Understood," Tracy said.

They pressed on, taking turn after turn, often ducking low or shuffling sideways to get through a particularly cramped passage. Every now and then Asher would stop and take another scan. After another hour, the narrow tunnel opened up into a huge open chamber. The light from their lanterns didn't even reach the ceiling, and a natural waterfall trickled down the far wall. Five more openings appeared around the chamber's circumference, almost evenly spaced like spokes on a wheel.

"Incredible," Tracy said, taking it all in.

"This is why I brought you," Asher said. "When you mentioned caving, I had to show you this room."

"Nature is… wow," Tracy said, shaking her head. For once she was at a loss for words.

They sat on a rock and enjoyed lunch together, chatting about some of the sights they'd seen on the way in.

"It smells so clean in here," Tracy said. "And it's the perfect temperature. I should think about a cave next time I'm looking to move."

"I thought you didn't like tight spaces," Asher said.

"It would be a challenge, sure," Tracy said. "But I think it'd be worth it. Have you been through the other tunnels?" She indicated the other openings.

"I'll never explore them all," Asher said. "Each one branches and branches and branches again. It would take a lifetime to see everything."

"What's that glow coming from that one?"

Asher squinted in the direction she'd indicated. "What glow?"

"I thought I saw…" Tracy said, then became silent. "Hold on," she said, standing up. She walked across the chamber and peered down the tunnel in question.

"Don't wander off," Asher reminded her, climbing to his feet. He gathered up his gear and followed her.

"There!" Tracy said, pointing down a tunnel. The passage curved in the distance, and a faint yellow light undulated from somewhere beyond the bend.

"Huh," Asher said.

"Is that a 'huh' as in, maybe I found something you didn't know about?" Tracy asked.

"Could be a lantern," Asher said. "I didn't know any other cavers had found this passage, but you never know."

"Maybe it's another way back to the surface?" Tracy offered.

"Doesn't really look like sunlight," Asher said.

"Let's go check it out," Tracy said.

"Slow down," Asher said. "Let me get another scan first. I feel kind of..." Then he started screaming.

Tracy turned around and gasped. Asher's skin was rapidly turning black. Right before Tracy's eyes, the blackness spread until it covered his entire body, right down to his eyeballs. His screams suddenly stopped as fissures formed across his face. Then he collapsed into a pile of black dust. His clothes crumpled to the ground, now empty. His lantern and phone clattered loudly as they hit the stone floor.

I'm not seeing this, Tracy thought. *This is a dream. That could not have just happened.* She backed against the cavern wall, then slid to the floor, hugging her knees. *Wake up. Wake up. Wake up.*

Hundreds of explanations whirled through her mind, and every one of them felt straight out of sci-fi. Maybe they'd found some sort of flesh-eating insects. Or maybe they'd triggered an ancient curse. It could even have been some weird new disease. The near-darkness of the cave made everything seem possible, and she thought she saw strange shapes moving on the far side of the chamber, where the lantern's light didn't quite reach.

"Doesn't matter," Tracy said aloud, then found herself offended at her own callousness. But it was true. Right now it didn't matter. She could mourn Asher later, but at this moment she was in a survival situation. She couldn't remember all the twists and turns she'd taken to get here. She wasn't even sure which of the chamber's six tunnels they'd entered through.

Asher's phone, she thought, and crawled over to where it had landed. The screen was smashed, and she didn't know his PIN anyway. *Surely he had some sort of paper map as backup,* she reasoned. Reluctantly she approached his clothing, afraid that whatever killed him might be contagious. *Get over it,* she told herself. *Whatever just happened, you won't be able to stop it anyway.*

She opened his backpack and found, among other things, some paper maps depicting the local cave systems. Unfortunately, they weren't a lot of help. None of the routes looked like the cave she was currently in, and she wasn't even sure which entrance they'd started from. The good news was that Asher's pack held plenty of survival gear – a few days' worth of food, as well as batteries, rope, pitons, and some other tools.

Her cell phone didn't get reception this far underground, but it occurred to her that she'd announced her plans online. When she didn't post the update she'd promised, would anyone come looking for her? *At least water won't be a problem,* she thought, eyeing the waterfall. But did she have enough food to last until help arrived? Would it be safer to stay here in the chamber, or start searching the passages?

There's no way I'm going exploring, Tracy thought. But what if help never came? She had to at least consider being proactive. She had Asher's gear. She could take it slow, marking which passages she'd tried, keeping a line that led back to this chamber. Maybe she'd be able to recognize the passage that had taken her here. Then she could keep marking the walls, looking for familiar landmarks. She'd taken plenty of video on the way in, maybe she could watch it and see what turns they'd taken.

But first she wanted to check out that passage with the yellow glow. If there was any chance it led to the surface, then it was worth a look. She rummaged through Asher's pack, pulling out a mallet, a piton, and a spool of white nylon cord. She hammered the piton into the wall next to the passage and attached the cord. Then she clipped the spool to her belt so it could play out behind her as she walked.

It still took a few turns before she found the source of the light, and the spool ran out a few feet before the final passage. She unclipped the spool from her belt and wrapped the end around a stalagmite, then peeked into an opening to her left.

The entire room was bathed in the yellow glow. It was a roughly rectangular chamber, maybe twenty by thirty feet. The rock formations in this room didn't look like they'd formed by accident. Several long, flat slabs of stone flanked the room's sides, looking like benches. At the far end, a vertical block rose from the ground like a preacher's podium. In fact, the more Tracy thought about it, the more the room looked like a primitive church.

The glow came from behind the podium, and Tracy immediately stepped forward to investigate. Embedded on the other side of the rock was a small yellow stone, about the size of a marble. It gave off a massive amount of light, so much that Tracy had to partially cover her eyes. She placed her hand on the stone and found that it didn't give off any heat. Then she noticed a couple of words carved into the podium.

D'LROW TFIHS

"D'lrow T'fihs?" Tracy read aloud, her hand still touching the glowing stone.

As soon as the words were out of her mouth, she felt a bizarre vibration all over her body, like the tingle she felt whenever her foot fell asleep. The walls of the cavern melted away, swirling toward Tracy before exploding outward until only blackness remained.

Mada slept soundly on a burlap mattress, in the same room where Drahcir kept his cleaning supplies. She was having a pleasant dream about baby tibbars and nettiks when a loud crash woke her up. Curious, she rolled out from under her blanket and got to her feet. She fiddled around in the darkness until she found a broom.

"Lacigam Torch," she said, making an arcane gesture with her other hand. The broom transformed into a torch, illuminating the small room with magical fire. Then she put on a plain robe and set out to find what had made the clatter.

More noises led her to Drahcir's study. She opened the door and saw a confused-looking woman stumbling around the room. She was a young adult with green hair. And she was completely nude.

"Madam?" Mada said, holding the torch out in front of her.

The strange woman ducked behind Drahcir's desk, peeking out with a panicked expression. "Erehw eht kcuf ma I?" she said.

"I don't understand you," Mada said.

"Od uoy kaeps hsilgne?" the trespasser said.

"Lacigam Translate," Mada said, wiggling the fingers of her free hand.

"Please," the intruder said, looking exasperated. "It's been such a weird day. Is there someone here who—"

"I understand you now," Mada said. "Why are you here?"

"I got lost in a cave, and somehow wound up here," the woman said. "So where exactly is here?"

"This is the tower of the master wizard Drahcir," Mada said. "If you'll come with me, madam, I'll show you out." Tracy carefully stepped out from behind the desk, and Mada saw her full body for the first time. "Or, *sir*, I mean," Mada added. She held her hand up in front of her eyes, blocking her view of the intruder's nakedness.

"Madam will be just fine," the woman said. "Or even better, call me Tracy. And you are?"

"My name is Mada. I can't send you out like that, let's find you a robe or something..."

"Why does this look like a medieval castle?" Tracy asked. "I didn't know Fresno had any castles."

"What's Fresno?" Mada asked.

"Okay..." Tracy said. "What city do *you* think we're in?"

"This is Onserf, and always has been," Mada said. "Least it's been called that as long as I've been here."

"Never heard of it," Tracy said.

"See for yourself," Mada offered, gesturing toward a window. While the visitor approached the window, Mada stepped into an alcove where they kept some spare clothing.

Tracy stood at the window and froze. It was well after sunset, maybe even closer to dawn. But between the full moon and the torches that lit each street corner, she could easily make out the details. The town below looked right out of a renaissance festival. Stone houses with thatched roofs lined the streets, and a guard in period-appropriate armor rode a horse down the street.

"How did I get here from a cave?" Tracy wondered out loud.

"I'm not sure how you got here at all," Mada said, handing Tracy a robe. "Not only do we keep the doors locked, but Master Drahcir keeps an Aura of Aversion around the tower to deter thieves."

"Aura of..." Tracy started to ask, but shook her head. "I'm not a thief, I'm just very, very lost."

"I believe you," Mada said. "Most thieves don't work naked. Maybe I should wake my master and..."

Just then the entire room lit up, as wall sconces illuminated all around the study. Seeing Mada clearly for the first time, Tracy gave her an odd look. "You remind me of a friend of mine," she said. "But he's—"

"What's all the commotion?" came a man's voice. Drahcir entered the study, still in his sleep clothes. His eyes widened when he saw Tracy. "You!" he barked. "But that's impossible... how can you... Who *are* you?"

"This person was wandering around your study," Mada explained. "I don't think she's a thief, but she doesn't know how she got in."

"She doesn't belong here," Drahcir said, frowning in confusion. He moved towards his desk, never taking his eyes off of Tracy.

"Of course," Mada said. "I was just about to show her out."

"No, no," Drahcir said. He picked up a pair of spectacles off of his desk, then used them to study Tracy more closely. "I mean, she doesn't belong in our realm. Her aura is all wrong."

Tracy looked from Drahcir to Mada in confusion. "Is this some sort of prank?" she asked, but they ignored her.

"Come, Mada, take a look," Drahcir said, and handed her the spectacles. She looked through them and gasped.

"It's green," Mada said, and Drahcir nodded. "Master, there's more. I think she might be some sort of shapeshifter. I saw her naked, and she had a… you know… man's part."

"That's it, I'm out of here," Tracy said, heading for the door.

"Lacigam Lock," Drahcir said. He raised his hand and the door slammed shut in Tracy's face. She attempted to push it open, but it wouldn't budge.

"I'm afraid I can't allow you to leave quite yet," Drahcir said. "Not until I determine if you're dangerous."

"Oh, I'm dangerous," Tracy said, marching toward him. "And you're about to find out just how dangerous if you don't open that door."

"Lacigam Shield," Drahcir said, wiggling his fingers.

"Ow!" Tracy said as she slammed into an invisible wall. Confused, she touched the air. "What in the world…" she muttered as she felt along the barrier. The edges of the wall felt mildly electric, and she could only push through about half an inch before some unseen force stopped her hand completely. *It's like magic,* she thought.

Then it hit her, it *was* magic. Before, when the strange woman had said something about "translate," they'd suddenly been able to understand each other. Tracy hadn't thought much about it at the time, because she figured the woman was just bilingual. The other things she'd seen – the door slamming, the lights coming on – those could all be explained easily enough. Sure, it *looked* like a medieval castle, but it could still be full of modern technology.

But this barrier was either very advanced science, or it was magic. Neither explanation was particularly believable. *So I've either traveled so far into the future that everything looks like the Middle Ages again, or I've traveled to a fantasy world with actual wizards*, Tracy thought. *But hey, at least I'm not going to starve to death in a cave.*

Drahcir and Mada continued to discuss Tracy as if she wasn't there. "Do you think she's some sort of demon?" Mada asked.

The wizard shook his head. "I just sprayed for demons last week," he said. "Besides, she didn't try to eat our faces."

"I'm just a human," Tracy said. "And I don't think I'm from this world. Or time period. Can you send me back home?"

The wizard and his apprentice looked at each other for a moment, then back at Tracy. "Do you know how you happened to come here?"

Tracy told him about the cave, the stone, and the magic words carved into the wall.

"Did the stone look like this?" Drahcir asked, retrieving a yellow stone from a box on a shelf. He held it up for Tracy to see.

"Yes, that's it," she replied. "I touched the stone and read the words on the wall, and suddenly I was here."

"The stones are connected?" Mada asked.

"I believe it's the same stone, simultaneously existing in two different realms," Drahcir replied.

"Can it send me back?" Tracy asked.

"It should be easy enough," Drahcir said. "I imagine it's as simple as touching this stone and saying the words again."

Tracy reached for the stone.

"Wait," Drahcir said, closing his fingers around the stone. "There's no hurry, and we'd love to know more about you and your world. Perhaps we could share an early breakfast first?"

It was a tempting yet terrifying offer. Tracy was anxious about postponing the trip home, but she was also adventurous enough to want to see this new world. And "Do things that scare you" had been her motto as of late. After a moment she lowered her hand and said, "Sure."

The sun was beginning to rise when their food arrived. A white-haired waitress set a plate down in front of Tracy, and the smell was heavenly. They sat around an outdoor table next to a quaint little inn, surrounded by farmers scarfing down their quick breakfasts before heading to the fields.

Tracy tentatively took a bite of the meat, worried that her constitution might not be able to handle the food from this world. But it tasted similar to the steak she was used to, though there was a strange sweetness to it, and she wasn't sure if that was due to the meat itself or the spices. It was cooked to a mouthwatering medium rare, and Tracy found herself moaning out loud.

"Four stars," she said, prompting confused looks from her companions. Rather than explain, she asked, "What kind of animal is this from?"

"Elttac," Mada replied. "It's a beast of burden with hooves and horns. There's one over there." She pointed to a business across the street, where a customer loaded up an ox-like animal with his newly purchased wares. The creature had curved horns like a ram, but otherwise it looked just like its Earth counterpart.

"Ah," Tracy said. "It's quite good. So where are we? The planet, I mean. Is this still Earth?" In the distance she saw some very familiar-looking mountains, the same she saw every morning from her balcony. Except here, the sun was on the wrong side from where it should have been during sunrise.

"You are in the realm of Asu," Drahcir replied. "In the Kingdom Ainrofilac, in the town of Onserf. This is a small farming community, though the great city of Nas Esoj is only two day's journey away. Mada and I are the only magic users in Onserf."

"So wizards are rare?" Tracy asked.

"Very much so, thank goodness," Drahcir said. "Or I'd be out of the job. The farmers pay me to pull the storm clouds in when there's a drought."

"So you only have to work every couple of months, and you spend the rest of the time doing what exactly?" Tracy had shifted into interview mode, and she wished she had a camera handy. She still wasn't convinced this was really happening, but even if it was a dream, she thought she might be able to turn it into a story later.

"Oh, I work more than that," Drahcir said. "Farmers come to me with all sorts of problems. Injuries, diseases, lost children, broken items that need mending. I can't always help but I do what I can. And when I'm not working, I'm studying magic. The more I learn, the more people we'll be able to help."

"So, why are wizards so rare?" Tracy asked.

"Not everyone can perform the hand gestures required for spellcasting," Drahcir said. "Only people born with a specific mutation. See? I have an extra finger." He held up his hands, fingers splayed.

Tracy counted four fingers and a thumb on each hand. "Extra finger?" she asked, sounding confused. Then she looked at the customers at the surrounding tables. Upon further inspection, she realized that the other patrons were missing their pinky fingers.

"We call it the Lacigam finger," Mada said, proudly showing off her hands as well.

Tracy showed them her hands. "On my world, that's the standard amount of fingers."

"Astonishing," Drahcir said, examining Tracy's hands. "Your people must never want for anything."

"If my world had magic, we'd destroy ourselves within a week," Tracy said. She was about to ask another question, but Mada spoke up first.

"There's no magic in your world? At all? What's that like?"

"Oh," Tracy said. She thought a minute before replying. "Well, we have technology that does a lot of the same things as magic."

"What's technology?" Mada asked.

Tracy paused, trying to think of a good example they'd understand. She recalled seeing Drahcir magically light a torch earlier and it gave her an idea. "You know how you can light a torch with a magic word, but you can also light it by using stones to make sparks?" She waited to see if Mada nodded, then continued. "Well, technology would be like using the rocks, but on a bigger scale."

"Like boulders?" Mada asked.

Drahcir snickered. He had an idea of what Tracy was trying to say, but he preferred letting his student work things out for herself.

"No," Tracy said. "But let's say you light a fire. Then you use it to boil water. Then you put a wheel above the water with upside-down buckets on each spoke. The buckets catch the rising steam, which turns the wheel, which you have attached to... I don't know... something that needs turning." It suddenly occurred to Tracy how useless she'd be if she ever got trapped in the past.

"There's a mill down the street that uses a waterfall to grind the grain," Mada offered.

"Yes, like that," Tracy said. "Only with more steps and smaller components. We have carriages that run without horses, big wagons that fly, and little boxes that let you talk to other people from miles away. But none of it is magic."

"How do they get the waterfall inside the carriage?" Mada asked.

"I... I don't know, I'm not a mechanic," Tracy said.

"And the people there," Mada said. "Are they all like you? You know... women with male parts?"

"Oh..." Tracy said. "That's... that's very personal. But no. I'm... I'm special." She sighed, not sure how best to explain it. She didn't even want to explain it. But Mada looked at her with big, questioning eyes, looking very much like her best friend back home. She couldn't just leave it at that.

"It's fine if you don't want to talk about it," Drahcir told her, eliciting a disappointed frown from his apprentice.

"No, it's okay," Tracy said. "Most humans are like you two, I'm guessing. Male or female, and happy to be that way. But some of us... well, not everybody feels it the same way, but in my case I'd say it's like I was the spirit of a woman inhabiting the body of a man."

"We have people like that here, too," Mada said.

"I guess you probably do," Tracy said. "So, I'm in the process of using technology to transition from my original body to my ideal body. I'm taking medicines that are slowly reshaping me, and I'm saving up for a very expensive operation that will, uh, fix the rest."

"Oh," Mada said. "Here we just use magic."

Tracy blinked. "Wait, what?"

"We have a spell that transforms men into women and vice-versa," Drahcir clarified. "I've performed it on several people. They were just like you – their spirits didn't match the form nature had given them. They were so much happier afterward. I've never had such grateful customers."

"Are you okay?" Mada asked. "You look pale."

Tracy's pulse raced. She looked up at the wizard's tower. A couple of magic words and a bit of finger wiggling, and her greatest desire would come to fruition. *Now I know this is a dream*, she thought, but that was no reason to pass up the opportunity. If this was real, she could be a full-fledged cis woman within the hour.

"What's wrong with her?" Mada whispered to her master.

"She's just realized we can help her," Drahcir said. "And she's paralyzed with happiness."

"So you can… you can…" Tracy stammered.

"Yes, and I won't even charge you for it," Drahcir said. "It's the least I can do after you've given us a peek into another world."

But then Tracy got cold feet. What if it wasn't safe? She took a few deep breaths and asked, "Are you sure it will work right on me? Since I'm from another world and all?"

"My translation spell worked just fine on you," Mada said.

"You mean I'm speaking your language right now?" Tracy asked.

"Yes," Mada answered. "Don't worry, it should wear off before we send you back to your home."

Tracy still wasn't convinced. "How exactly does magic work?" she asked. "I don't mean 'how do you cast a spell,' but where does the power actually come from? Does it…

come from gods or something?"

"We were just talking about that yesterday," Mada said, excited to share her newfound knowledge. She glanced at Drahcir, who nodded proudly. "So no one really knows, but we think it works by pulling energy in from parallel worlds."

"Like mine," Tracy said. And then the implications hit her hard. "Like… mine…" She went even paler than before and started breathing faster.

"What's wrong?" Mada asked.

"Oh, no," Tracy said. "I knew it was too good to be true." She put her head in her hands, leaning over the table.

"Is this what happiness looks like on your world?" Drahcir asked, his face full of concern.

"We can't use magic," Tracy said. "Actually, you have to stop using magic altogether." She went on to tell them everything that had been happening on her world. The disappearances, the dwindling animal populations, the decaying plants, and most recently, the death of her friend Asher.

"We can't be sure that's because of our magic," Mada said.

"Actually, I'm afraid we can," Drahcir replied. "I've suspected as much for a long time. I thought the odds were in our favor, but I was wrong. I hoped we were pulling the energy from an unoccupied world. But the existence of that yellow stone proves that our two worlds are linked. Energy lost by one is gained by the other. If we keep casting spells the way we do, eventually we'll turn Tracy's world into a dry husk."

"But people rely on us," Mada said. "How can we live without magic?"

"We'll have to learn new ways," Drahcir said. "If Tracy's

world can do it, so can ours."

"But what about the other wizards?" Mada asked.

"It's not going to be easy to convince them," Drahcir said. "But I'll travel all over the world if I have to, and gather whatever evidence it takes to persuade them. Most of them are reasonable, except of course for Yugdab."

"Yugdab?" Tracy asked.

"A wizard most foul," Drahcir said. "He's a bio-alchemist who spends all his time creating horrible monstrosities, grotesque creatures never intended by nature. It was by his doing that I obtained the stone that links our realms. He'd placed it in the eye socket of one of his creations, in order to bring it to life."

"What if we can't convince him?" Mada asked.

"Oh, you can be certain we won't," Drahcir said. "I'm afraid we may have to kill him."

"Master!" Mada exclaimed. She had never heard him propose anything so violent.

"An entire world will die if he remains alive," Drahcir said. "You can be certain of that as well."

"I'm sorry," Tracy said.

"Why, what have you done?" Drahcir asked.

"This seems like such a perfect world," Tracy said. "This is going to change your whole planet. If I hadn't come here, you could go on living as you have been, none the wiser."

"Knowledge often comes at a price, but it's still preferable to ignorance," Drahcir said. "And who knows? Maybe we'll find a way around it. Perhaps we can reconnect the stone to another parallel world, an uninhabited one this time. If nothing else, the knowledge we'll gain from all this will be immeasurable."

The three stood and walked back to the wizard's tower.

"That's odd," Drahcir said, examining the front door. "When we left this morning, did I forget to cast Aura of Aversion?"

"I saw you cast it," Mada replied. "It shimmered and everything."

Drahcir frowned. "Be on your guard," he said, entering the tower.

It was a total mess inside. Furniture was overturned, storage crates had been opened, and Drahcir's possessions were strewn about every room.

"Someone was looking for something," Tracy said, pushing a pile of robes with her foot.

"The stone," Mada replied. She and Drahcir bolted to the study, with Tracy a few steps behind.

"It's gone," Drahcir said, holding out the empty box for the others to see.

"Who could have done this?" Mada asked.

"The only one who could possibly break the Aura of Aversion is Yugdab," Drahcir said. "He obviously wanted his stone back."

"But… that's my only way home," Tracy said.

"Mada, contact Enaj and Rehsa," Drahcir ordered. "Don't use magic – send a courier."

"How are we going to get the stone back without using magic?" Mada asked.

"I wish I knew," Drahcir said.

"I have a thought," Tracy said.

"Master, the wizard Drahcir is outside." The henchman was an amalgamation of several different beasts, but with a human head so that it could speak eloquently.

Yugdab looked up from the stone and sneered. "I suppose that's not surprising," he grumbled. "Keep the stone safe while I have a talk with him."

"Yes, master," the henchman said, as Yugdab stood and donned his most intimidating black cloak.

"Lacigam Teleport," he said, and suddenly he was outside, standing in front of his tower. Drahcir stood about fifty feet away, his apprentice by his side. "Don't even think about it," Yugdab said, already wiggling his fingers. "I have counters for all of your spells. Any hex that comes my way, I will return tenfold."

"I have not come to fight," Drahcir said. "I need to speak to you about something of utmost importance, something that may affect the fate of our entire world."

"So, you figured out the true nature of the stone, did you?" Yugdab said. "I only just realized it myself, or I wouldn't have risked using it as the aremihc's eye."

"The stone is linked to another world," Drahcir said. "An inhabited one. Every time we cast a spell, something in the other world dies."

"Why should I care about some other world?" Yugdab asked. "I barely care about this one."

"Because the other world is full of powerful wizards!" Drahcir warned. "Every one of them is born with Lacigam fingers. When they find out that we've been harming their world, they will send an army of powerful mages to destroy us!"

"Bring them on," Yugdab said. "None of them will be able to match my power."

"Please," Drahcir said. "You must listen to reason."

"Wait a minute," Yugdab said, spotting a movement to his right. He wiggled his fingers and said, "Lacigam Reveal."

A large stone turned invisible, exposing Enaj's hiding spot. Another rock vanished to Yugdab's left, where Rehsa stood with her bow drawn.

Yugdab's eyes narrowed. "I thought you just wanted to talk," he said. "This looks an awful lot like an execution."

"They're only here for my protection," Drahcir explained. "Please listen to me, Yugdab. We were once friends, we can be that way again. If you will just—"

"Liar!" Yugdab bellowed, and his cloak flared in a crackle of magical energy. "You knew what you were doing when you came here. You knew I'd say no, and you already had a plan to kill me. You accuse me of practicing the black arts, but you're the one who deals in deception. You're the one who intended to murder. You're the one—"

While Yugdab was distracted by the other four, Tracy sneaked up behind him and hit him on the head with a rock.

As Yugdab came to, he realized he was strapped to a table. "Lacigam Freedom," he said, wiggling his fingers. But nothing happened. He tried again and again, but he couldn't tap into the Lacigam energies at all. Straining his neck, he looked down at his hands, and saw that they were covered in bandages.

"Oh, good, you're up," Drahcir said, stepping into view. "I'm afraid we had to sever your Lacigam fingers. I'm very sorry, but it was for the greater good."

Yugdab let out a string of curses and threats, pulling violently at his restraints. Drahcir ignored him and climbed the stairs out of the basement, locking the door behind him.

"What's going to happen to him?" Tracy asked as Drahcir entered the study. Mada, Enaj, and Rehsa were also present, discussing the possibility of losing access to magic.

"He's no longer a threat to the world," Drahcir said. "Later today we'll let the local law enforcement know he's here. He's got quite a few crimes under his belt, but the marshal was always afraid to bring him in. I suspect Yugdab will spend a long time behind bars. But right now we need to discuss your situation."

Tracy nodded. "It was good to meet you. All of you." She nodded to Mada, Rehsa, and Enaj in turn. Now that Rehsa's helmet was off, Tracy was surprised at how much she looked like her late friend Asher. She wondered if there was also a doppelganger of herself somewhere in this world.

Drahcir set the stone on his desk. "You know what to do," he said.

Tracy reached out to touch it, but withdrew her hand. "Wait," she said. "Will using the stone count as casting a spell? Is there a chance it will kill someone from my world?"

"I can't be sure, but I doubt it," Drahcir said. "This isn't the same as casting a spell. The stone exists in both worlds; it's just shifting you to its other location. Even if that does require Lacigam energy, it shouldn't take much. Certainly not enough to kill someone."

"It's a risk I'll have to take," Tracy said. She gave each of them one last look, then touched the stone and said the magic words. She vanished in a flash of light.

There was a long silence, then Drahcir picked up the stone and put it back in the box. "That's it, then," he said. "I'll take this to the mill and have it ground into powder."

"Now?" Mada asked. "I thought you wanted to do more research first."

Drahcir shook his head. "If it's as I fear, every minute I delay causes more death on her world."

"And crushing the stone will break the link between our realms?" Mada asked.

"I believe so," Drahcir said gravely. "It's possible destroying this one stone will end magic as we know it, as we'll no longer be able to draw energy from Tracy's world. But there may be more stones out there, linking us either to her world or to others. I may well spend the rest of my life searching for them."

Enaj drew his sword and studied the blade. His face appeared orange in the weapon's glow. "When the magic ends..." Enaj started.

"*If* I'm right," Drahcir interrupted.

"If you're right," Enaj said, "and destroying the stone causes all magic to cease functioning, what will happen to my sword?"

"I can't say," the wizard said. "It might immediately become a normal sword. It might retain its energy for years before it wears off."

Enaj sighed and sheathed his sword.

"The other wizards are going to be angry with you," Rehsa said.

"I'll deal with that later," Drahcir said. "Now if you'll excuse me, I have errands to run."

The cave reformed back into view. Tracy was in the same chamber she'd left, the one that looked like a church for cavemen. She was naked again, but her clothes lay on the floor behind the lectern. She quickly put them on, gathered her things, and took a few steps toward the outer passage.

Wait, she told herself, and turned around. After a moment of deliberation, she returned to the podium. Using a piton from Asher's pack, she chipped around the glowing stone and pried it out of the larger rock. Then she placed the stone in her pocket.

She wasn't even sure why she wanted it. A souvenir? A reminder that she hadn't dreamed the whole thing? Or maybe she just didn't want anyone else to stumble across it. She wondered if she ought to destroy it, just to avoid any future mishaps.

She decided she'd think about it later, when she got back to the surface. She followed her nylon cord back to the central chamber, then sat down to think.

Her situation hadn't changed. She was still stuck in a cave with no idea how to find her way back to the surface. She was afraid to explore beyond the chamber for fear she might just get more lost.

She thought about all the magic she'd witnessed that day. She wondered if those spells would work in this universe. She had the right number of fingers, and she remembered some of the gestures Dhahcir and Mada had made while casting.

Was getting home simply a matter of saying "Lacigam Home" while wiggling her fingers? Or did that only work in the other world? And if she was successful, would she be killing someone in Dhahcir's world?

She pulled the stone out of her pocket and turned it over a few times. It glowed brightly, and she could feel it vibrate in her hands. The stone obviously had power here, so maybe the spells worked too.

But then the rock shuddered. The light pulsed, then dimmed, then went dark. As Tracy watched in confusion, the stone suddenly crumbled into dust.

So that's that, she thought, shaking the dust off of her hand. *Temptation gone.*

She unclipped the camera from her vest and began watching the footage she'd taken on the way in. If she could spot enough landmarks, she might be able to find her way back out. It was worth a try, anyway.

After half an hour of sifting through video, she thought she heard voices. She turned off the camera and stood up. "Hello?" she shouted.

A light appeared down one of the passages, and it was getting closer.

"Tracy! Asher! Can you hear us?" a voice shouted.

"Over here!" Tracy replied, rushing toward the light.

"We're with Search and Rescue," the voice said. "Stay there, we'll come to you."

"How did you find me?" she shouted back, standing by the passage entrance. She could now see a faint black figure in the dark, squeezing through a tight passage.

"Your viewers contacted us when you didn't post an update," the man said. Tracy could now see two more rescuers behind him, their lights bobbing around the cavern walls.

Oh thank heavens, Tracy thought, leaning by the entrance. Her fans had come through for her. She wasn't sure what she was going to tell them about Asher, but at least the danger was over.

"It is done," Drahcir said as he stepped through the door. Rehsa and Enaj had gone to take Yugdab to the marshal, and Mada sat alone in the study, thumbing through an ancient tome.

"The stone is…" Mada began.

"A fine powder," Drahcir finished. "Which I have scattered to the winds."

"Did it work?" Mada asked.

"I don't know," he replied. "I'm not sure how to test it without causing harm to the other realm."

"We should contact the wizards in Nas Esoj," Mada suggested. "If the magic's gone, I'm sure they'll have noticed by now."

Drahcir nodded. "Good thinking. I need you to ride out to Nas Esoj at once. I'll send couriers to some of the other settlements."

"Yes, master." Mada rose and took a few steps towards the door. Then she stopped and half-turned towards her master. "I do have one question, though," she asked.

"Hmm?"

"When you first saw Tracy, you seemed to recognize her for a moment," Mada said. "Who did you think she was?"

"Oh that," Drahcir said. "It must be my aging eyes. For a moment I mistook her for my sister."

"I didn't know you had a sister," Mada said.

"She died when I was young," the wizard said. "But that was a long time ago, back when I was still called Y'Cart."

"Really? You?" Mada asked, surprised at the revelation. Y'cart was a woman's name, which meant Drahcir…

"Indeed," Drahcir confirmed. "I was much like Tracy. I felt like a stranger in my own skin. The first spells I studied were those that dealt with body transformation. I cast them on myself as soon as I was ready."

"Wow," Mada said. "I didn't know."

"Now go," Drahcir ordered. "I'd like an answer as soon as possible."

Mada left. As her footsteps receded down the hallway, Drahcir sat down at his desk and opened the tome of ancient artifacts.

I suppose my career is over, he thought. He wasn't too worried about money, as he'd saved up quite a nest egg over the years. But he'd also devoted his entire life to the study of something that might no longer exist. If the magic was truly gone, he had no idea what he was going to do with his life.

And if the magic was still thriving, he needed to know how it worked and whether it still drew its power from an inhabited universe. This would require years of travel and a mountain of research.

The only thing he knew for sure was that their lives were about to change forever.

Power Play

"Look, Steph, I don't understand all of this. Sixteen years ago I gave birth to a beautiful baby girl. You always liked girl stuff. Flowers. Kittens. Even when you ran around dressed like a superhero, you insisted I make the costume pink."

"I loved that costume."

"It was hard to get you to take it off. You even put it on under your clothes one time before I drove you to kindergarten. I got a phone call..."

"I remember."

"And now you want to be... what exactly?"

"Mom, it's not that complicated. I don't identify with any particular gender, but I feel more like myself when I present as male, or sometimes gender neutral. Anything but female, really."

"You kids spend too much time on the internet. Everybody wants to make up new identities and redefine biology."

"I've felt like this as long as I can remember. The internet just helped me find the words to define it."

"But you're not thinking about taking drugs or getting surgeries?"

"No, nothing like that. I just want you to accept me for who I am."

"I always do."

"Can you start calling me Ephan?"

"Ephan?"

"Yeah, it's still short for Stephanie, see?"

"Oh, Steph, I don't know if I can get used to this."

"It's not that hard, Mom. Here, pretend this teddy bear is one of your friends from work. Come on, introduce me."

"Oh, um... 'Hello, Mister Bear. This is my daughter, Ephan. She uses they/them pronouns.' Was that good?"

"Uh... we'll work on it."

"Okay, I can deal with that. Just a new nickname. I can deal. As long as you're not thinking of changing your body."

"No, I'm okay there."

"Thank god. Okay, I guess I'll play along for now, if it's that important to you. I'm sure it's just a phase anyway."

Six years later...

Ephan hated Friday night shifts. Working at a fast food restaurant was bad enough, but being on a college campus took it to an all-new level. Half the customers stayed for hours, keeping all the tables full and leaving a real mess for Ephan to clean up later. Some just ordered a soda, then took up a booth all the way until close, getting free refills while studying for class. Sometimes whole groups came in and played their RPG campaigns at the tables.

At least it's not my money, Ephan thought, watching a mousy girl get another refill at the self-serve fountain machine, before sitting back down and burying her face in a Chemistry 101 textbook. The restaurant's manager hated the loiterers and encouraged Ephan to kick them out if they stayed too long. But the manager wasn't there now, and Ephan wasn't invested enough to care. *Stay or leave, I get paid the same*, they thought.

It was eleven PM and all eight tables were currently full, even though there hadn't been a new customer in nearly an hour. *Only two more hours and I can close*, Ephan thought, already working on some of the closing duties.

The door chimed, and a man in his early twenties stumbled in. Ephan knew right off he was going to be an experience. *Drunk or high?* they wondered. The man stepped up to the counter, staring at the menu like it held the answers to life itself. His expression was locked in a look of wonder, as if he were an unfrozen caveman who was experiencing the modern world for the first time.

"Welcome to Sub Servients," Ephan said. "What can I get you?"

The man smiled at them, then frowned. He pulled out his wallet and looked inside. His eyebrows furrowed. Then his expression brightened like he'd just solved a puzzle he'd been working on for years. Ephan could practically see the lightbulb go off above his head.

"I'll take a five-inch club..." he said, then paused. "No... make it a ten-inch. No... make it two ten-inch clubs. With double meat!"

Ah, high, Ephan thought. They doubted this was going to end well, but they couldn't exactly refuse to serve a customer, especially on a hunch.

The customer watched them assemble two perfect subs. Then Ephan wrapped up the sandwiches and rang them up. "That'll be twenty-four thirty-six," Ephan said.

"Okay, here's the thing," the man said. "I... uh... left my

money in the car. Let me take the subs with me, and I'll put them in the car, and come back with the money."

"Sorry," Ephan said. "But I'll hold them here for you while you go get the money."

The man looked crushed. His intricate, flawless plan had come crashing down, thwarted by this cruel food service worker. He stared at them for several seconds, his expression that of betrayed disbelief, as if he'd just watched Ephan chop up a baby and put it in his sandwich. "Okay," he finally said in history's most heartbroken voice. "I'll be right back with the money."

Ephan watched him walk out the door, knowing they wouldn't see him again. They went back to cleaning up the back counter and putting up the bread trays.

The door dinged again. *Did he really come back?* Ephan wondered, turning around. But it wasn't the same guy. This man was older and looked more like a truck driver than a college student.

"Five-inch turkey on white," he said, and Ephan began making his sandwich. When they got to the register, Ephan rang him up, and the customer reached into his jacket pocket. But instead of emerging with a wallet, his hand now held a gun. "Make it a combo," he said. "Chips, drink, and everything in the register."

"Sorry, we don't allow robberies after five PM," Ephan said. "It's store policy. If you like, I'll leave a note for my manager and you can come back in the morning."

"You college kids think you're so smart," the man said. "But I'm not kidding around. I *will* shoot you." To emphasize his point, he thrust the gun forward until it was inches from Ephan's face.

Like a blur, Ephan grabbed the gun and pulled it over the

counter, robber and all. The gun fired, eliciting multiple shrieks from the customers in the lobby. Now on the floor behind the register, the man groaned and tried to pull his hand away. But Ephan's grip was stronger, and they managed to wrestle the weapon out of the robber's fingers.

Ephan held the gun on the would-be criminal while one of the customers called the police. *Guess I'm a hero now*, Ephan thought.

"You're fired," Mr. Tanner said.

"What?" Ephan asked, wondering if they'd misheard.

"Look, I know you thought you were being brave," their boss said. "But we have a policy at Sub Servients. 'The customer is always right, especially if they have a gun.' Do you realize he's talking about suing us now? He says you hurt his back when you dragged him over the counter. And that bullet put a hole in the back wall. You're lucky we don't take that out of your paycheck."

"I see," Ephan said.

"Also, I need you to sign this," Mr. Tanner said, placing a document in front of them. "It says you acknowledge that we fired you for violating policy, and not because you're trans-bionic or whatever you call it."

"I'm non-binary…" Ephan began.

"I don't want to know," he said. "Just sign the damn thing and get out."

"What if I don't sign?" Ephan asked.

"Don't make this difficult," Mr. Tanner said. "We have the incident on camera, and it proves you violated company policy. Sign and I'll hand over your last paycheck right now. Don't sign, and we'll sue you for the damage that bullet did.

Do you have a good lawyer?"

Ephan signed the waiver.

There were only a handful of cars in the parking lot when the sedan pulled up to the curb. Tristan's dad always dropped him off early, since the school was on the way to work. The busses didn't go out to Tristan's house because he lived in a different district. He was supposed to be going to Lakeside High School over near the college, which was so close to his house he could have walked to it. But the bullying had gotten to be too much, and the administration had refused to do anything about it.

West Bedford High School had a more diverse student body, but it still had its share of bullies. Tristan was careful to keep to himself. He kept his head low and wore plain clothing in the hopes of being less of a target. Going to school was like crossing the territory of an angry bull.

So far he'd only had a couple of run-ins, neither of which he'd felt compelled to report to his father. The less he knew, the better. The only thing worse than getting bullied was his father's judgment.

Tristan said goodbye to his father and opened the car door. He felt a hand tap his arm as he picked up his backpack.

"Have a good day at school, son," his father said.

"Thanks, Dad," Tristan replied, shuffling out of the seat and onto the curb.

He was about to close the door when his dad added, "And son? Try not to embarrass me today, okay?"

Tristan nodded and closed the door. *At least he called me son for a change,* Tristan thought as he headed inside.

"They fired you for that?" Corey asked, scowling. They sat in the kitchen of their shared student housing unit. Their textbooks were open, but they'd been too wrapped up in conversation to do any real studying. A small pile of pennies sat to the right of Corey's book.

Tristate Community College was fairly progressive, but they still hadn't known what to do with their gender non-conforming students. Regardless of which dorms they put a trans person in, they always received complaints from someone. In the end they'd taken an unused frat house and converted it into student housing. It currently housed six students, including Ephan and Corey. The residents had unofficially named the building "Pride House," though some of the local bigots had more colorful names for it. The tenants had to clean eggs off their windows once or twice a month, but so far there hadn't been any major vandalism.

"Yep," Ephan replied, chewing on a mechanical pencil. "Policy says that if someone tries to rob the place, I'm supposed to let them do whatever they want. I don't know, I guess I see their point. They don't want to encourage employees to fight back, because they might get hurt and sue the company."

Corey shook his head. "Dude, no. You're a hero, don't you get it? You can't let them get away with this." He idly pushed a couple of the pennies around before picking one up.

"The law's on their side," Ephan said. They turned the page of their textbook, though they hadn't actually looked at it.

"Then we'll start a social media blitz," Corey said, balancing a penny on his knuckles. "Get the court of public opinion involved. They'll rue the day they let you go." He wiggled his fingers, making the penny flip and roll across each knuckle, from his index finger to his pinky and back. He always did that when he talked about something important; it helped him concentrate. Some people had fidget spinners, Corey had his pennies.

"Corey, no," Ephan said, shaking their head. "I appreciate it, really, but I didn't even like that job. I just want to move on."

"Are you sure?" Corey asked. "You know I've got your back if you need it." Now he juggled three pennies on the back of his fingers. The pennies hopped back and forth from finger to finger in a manner that Ephan always found mesmerizing.

"They're not worth it," Ephan said.

"Okay, okay," Corey said, switching hands. "And you really weren't scared?"

"I was more angry than scared," Ephan said. "The second he pulled that gun, I almost told him off, I really did."

"Sounds like you've got a death wish," Corey said. He flipped all three pennies into the air, then flipped his hand over so his palm was up. As the pennies fell back down, all three stopped in mid-air, hovering about two inches above Corey's palm. Then they slowly drifted in a circular pattern, like paper boats in an invisible pool.

Ephan couldn't help but smile. Corey's power, while not particularly useful, never failed to entertain. Ten years ago he could have made a killing as a magician, but probably not now. Not since the meteor. Bedford was less than fifteen miles from the radioactive ruins that had once been Cleveland. An unusually high percentage of Bedford's residents had since developed superpowers, though the majority of these powers were nothing more than parlor tricks.

It was part of the reason Bedford was the largest-growing metropolis in the country. In the six years since the meteor, the city had more than tripled in size. Thousands had moved there in the hopes of hitting the superpower lottery. Not Ephan, though. They were a true local, born in Bedford when it was just a small town. Ephan had yet to develop any sort of powers, though they sometimes showed unusual bursts of strength for someone their size. They weren't sure if that was an actual power or just adrenaline, but it didn't matter. Being able to lift a few extra pounds didn't make someone a superhero any more than being able to levitate pennies.

"I don't have a death wish," Ephan clarified. "I just didn't feel like I was in actual danger. I think... I don't know. I think I just couldn't believe it was actually happening. Like maybe it was a dream or something."

"That's a dangerous way to see the world," Corey said.

Ephan nodded, but didn't say anything. They weren't being honest anyway. Not with Corey, and not with themself. Ephan frowned, then asked, "Corey. How did you figure out you could do the thing with the pennies?"

"It just sort of happened," Corey said. "I'm always playing with something. Pencils, combs, whatever's handy. One time I flipped a penny and it went wide. I willed it to fall back into my hand, and it did, even though it should have missed by a mile. When I saw how it curved in the air, I knew something was up."

"So you never just... *knew* you could do it," Ephan asked. "Like, beforehand."

"What are you trying to say?" Corey asked.

"I don't know," Ephan said. "It's just, when the guy held the gun on me, my brain was like... I don't know. My inner voice told me the gun couldn't hurt me."

"You mean you think you're bulletproof?" Corey asked.

"I don't know, maybe," Ephan said. "I mean, how can I tell? There's no safe way to test that kind of— Ow!" Three pennies hit them in the forehead before bouncing back into Corey's hand.

"Well, you're not penny-proof," Corey said.

"Yeah, but that's different," Ephan said.

Corey shook his head. "Lots of people feel like nothing bad can happen to them, until it does."

"It's not like that," Ephan said.

"When was the last time you bled?" Corey asked, his eyebrows furrowing.

Ephan thought a moment. "A couple of weeks ago, when that stray cat got into our kitchen," they said.

"Then you're not invincible," Corey said. "So please, stop acting like it. I don't want you to get hit by a truck just because you're feeling all full of yourself. Next time somebody pulls a gun on you, just give them the money."

Ephan nodded and changed the subject.

The bell rang, signaling the end of third-period algebra. Tristan gathered up his books, slid them into his backpack, and followed his classmates out the door. It was now lunchtime, but first Tristan needed to hit the restroom. West Bedford High School didn't have any gender neutral bathrooms. Using either restroom made Tristan nervous, so he always held his bladder until lunch. Most of the students rushed to the lunchroom so they could get a good table, so the restrooms were usually empty for a little while.

As an extra precaution, Tristan took the stairs down to the

first floor and headed for the gym. There weren't any gym classes until two, so no one would be using the gym's restrooms. He'd figured this out a couple of months earlier, and so far he hadn't run into anyone. He stopped in front of the two doors, briefly considered his options, and pushed open the door to the boys' room.

He immediately regretted his decision. Brett and Kev turned their heads as Tristan came around the corner. Out of the entire student body, they were the last guys he wanted to see. They were also transfers from Lakeside High, but for the exact opposite reason. Brett even lived on Tristan's street, which was one of the reasons Tristan didn't spend much time outside.

Tristan froze. "Sorry, I'll just—" he said, and started to turn around.

"No, it's cool," Brett said, taking a drag off his cigarette. His shoulders were almost as wide as Tristan was tall, and his bright red freckles matched his hair. And oddly enough, so did his eyes. He could change the color of his irises at will, but he generally kept them red because it looked cool. Some powers were more useful than others, and Brett's was practically useless. But then, who really needed superpowers when they were built like a moving van?

"No really, I'll use the other—" Tristan said.

"Leave and die," Kev said. He was taller than Brett, and a lot thinner. His neck reminded Tristan of an ostrich, and his Adam's apple stuck out nearly as far as his nose. But despite his awkward body, he was every bit as intimidating as Brett. Everyone in school knew about Kev's power, and therefore everyone kept their distance. Everyone except Brett, anyway.

"Now don't be rude, Kev," Brett said, taking a few steps toward Tristan. "Nancy's welcome to join the party. Want a smoke?" He held his cigarette out toward Tristan.

"It's… Tristan," he stammered, ignoring the cigarette.

"It was Nancy last year," Brett said. Tristan jumped as Brett patted him on the shoulder. "You don't expect me to just learn a new name, do you?" As Brett spoke, Kev crept his way around behind Tristan, blocking the exit.

"I guess not," Tristan said. "I, uh, have to get to lunch. Can I just…?"

"Lunchroom's upstairs," Kev mumbled. "You get lost?"

"I just… needed to pee…"

Brett laughed. "Well don't let us stop you. Go pee like a big boy." He took his hand off Tristan's shoulder and gave him a small push.

Tristan headed toward one of the stalls, but a web of smoky black tendrils suddenly crisscrossed in front of them. Tristan turned to see that Kev was making gestures in the air. "Nope," Kev said. Then he gestured toward the urinals with his chin.

"I can't…" Tristan said.

"Are you a boy or aren't you?" Brett asked. He put his hand on Tristan's back and guided him toward one of the urinals.

"Please, I don't want to," Tristan said. Several wispy tendrils roped down from the ceiling, and one wrapped itself loosely around Tristan's neck. He almost screamed but managed to stop himself. It wouldn't have helped. Even the teachers were afraid of Kev.

"You pee or you hang," Kev whispered from somewhere behind him.

Tristan felt sick to his stomach. *This would be a great time for a superpower to kick in,* he thought, but no such luck. Shaking badly, he pulled down his pants and underwear until they were about mid-thigh. His shirt only covered the upper half of his rear, adding to his embarrassment. He straddled himself forward until his chest was touching the porcelain.

"Well, what are you waiting for?" Brett asked.

"I can't go with you watching," Tristan said.

"Get over it," Kev grumbled. The tendril tightened a little around Tristan's neck.

Tristan took a slow, deep breath. He pictured running faucets and waterfalls, and tried to forget about the bullies in the room. After another ten seconds he managed to relax his bladder.

The urinal had a pretty large lip, and most of the urine landed where it should have. Unfortunately, a fair amount splashed onto Tristan's pants as well. When he was done, he flushed, then pulled up his pants and fastened them.

"Can I go now?" he asked.

Brett and Kev looked at each other for a moment, probably considering whether there was more fun to be had. Brett shrugged. "Go on," Kev said, and the tendrils dissipated. Brett grabbed Tristan by the shoulder again and shoved him toward the exit. As Tristan opened the door, Brett kicked him in the rear, knocking him into the hallway. Then the door shut and Tristan was finally alone.

So very alone.

"So I met another Ephan today."

"You did?" Ephan asked, genuinely surprised. They'd never researched the name, and they'd genuinely thought they'd made it up.

"Yes," their mom answered. Ephan couldn't see her face over the phone, but they thought she sounded a bit smug.

"Were they also non-binary?" Ephan asked.

"No," their mom said. "She was just a normal woman. I think she said she was Greek."

"We don't say 'normal,' Mom," Ephan said. "Normal's just a cycle on a washing machine. People come in all varieties. Sizes, colors, genders… There are no 'normal' people, because no two of us are alike."

"Okay, you're right, I apologize."

Ephan didn't think she sounded very sorry, but they weren't going to press it. "It's okay," they said.

"It doesn't bother you?"

"What?" Ephan asked.

"Ephan being a woman's name. Didn't you pick your name to be unisex?"

"Mom," Ephan said. "It doesn't matter what my name means to other people, it only matters what it means to me. I could call myself 'Princess Pinkie Tutu Kittens' and I'd be just as confident of my gender, or lack thereof."

"Fine," their mom said. "So, how's your job going?"

Great, Ephan thought. They briefly considered lying but realized it would be futile. Their mother always found out eventually. "Mom, there's something I have to tell you…"

"I can't believe you made me leave work early. You couldn't just wait another three hours?"

"I'm sorry, Dad," Tristan said, wiping tears from his eyes. "I just couldn't be there anymore." Tristan sat in the backseat of their sedan, even though there was no one in the passenger seat. He'd said it was because he might have to lie down, but the truth was he didn't want his father to see him cry.

But his father craned his neck to look at Tristan anyway.

"They said you were sick. You don't look sick." Sniffing the air, he added, "Did you piss yourself?"

"I think I'm gonna throw up," Tristan said. It wasn't exactly a lie, but it definitely wasn't the whole truth. He couldn't tell his father he'd been bullied. For one thing, Kev and Brett would literally kill him if he told anyone. But more importantly, he was afraid his father would side with the bullies.

Unfortunately, his father was very good at reading between the lines. "Someone's pushing you around, I get it," he said. "It's part of high school. But you can't just run home to your daddy whenever that happens. You have to fight back. Even if you lose, it'll make you stronger. You keep telling me you want to be a boy, but then you cry like a girl whenever you have a problem. That's not how men handle problems. If you want to be a man, you have to start acting like it."

He continued his lecture for the entire ride home.

Shuster Tower was the tallest building on campus. It was a skinny, ten-story tall girls' dorm, made of bright red bricks. Students often called it the "big brick dick" due to its prominence in the campus skyline. Students weren't allowed on the roof, but they often hung out up there anyway.

The roof was empty when Ephan arrived. They stood near the ledge, enjoying the brisk weather and watching the sunset. Of course they didn't have a dorm room in Shuster Tower, but sometimes they came up here to think. It had the best view in town, and it really helped put their problems in perspective.

Their mother hadn't taken the news well. She'd threatened

to sue Sub Servients for discrimination. Ephan managed to talk her out of it, but there was still a chance their mother would go behind their back.

Ephan stared off into the distance. The skies were busy today. A large flock of birds swooped by, then changed direction as one, in a fascinating aerial display. The campus was only a mile from the airport, and planes flew overhead nearly every five minutes. And of course, this being Bedford, the occasional superhero zoomed by on their way to thwart a crime.

Ephan envied the heroes. Most people did, but not for the same reasons. For some it was a power fantasy, others craved the fame, and some just wanted to impress potential romantic partners. Ephan didn't care about any of that. They just genuinely wanted to help people, and not in some vague "part of a larger organization" sort of way. Superheroes got to save lives directly, taking down criminals with their bare hands, pulling citizens from danger when they needed it the most. It probably wasn't as fun as it looked, but it sure beat any of Ephan's post-college career plans.

They leaned over the building's ledge, watching several students stroll across the campus. They imagined swooping down and saving one from a mugger or an out-of-control car. Then they shook their head and dismissed the fantasy. *You can always help people in other ways*, they thought.

Ephan heard the door open and shut behind them. It wasn't surprising. The roof never stayed empty for long. They turned around to make sure it wasn't the buzzkills from campus security ordering them to get back inside.

It wasn't. Ephan recognized the man right off. He wore the same shirt he'd worn the night he'd tried to rob the sandwich shop. It looked like a different gun, though.

"Milton Johnson," Ephan said. They'd learned the man's name from the arresting officers.

"I thought I saw you go up here," the man said.

"You followed me?" Ephan asked, taking a step back.

"Been following you all day," he said, glancing left and right. "Waiting for you to be alone. This'll do."

"Shouldn't you be in prison?"

"Posted bail," Milton said. "You got me fired, you know."

"Likewise," Ephan said.

Milton didn't seem to register Ephan's reply. "My boss told me not to come back," he continued, taking a few more steps forward. "Said he didn't want a criminal on his staff. Why couldn't you just give me the money? Now I've got no job and I'm on the run." He slowly closed the gap between them.

Ephan took another step backward. The back of their thighs pressed against the building's ledge.

"I'm going back to jail either way," Milton said. "So I might as well earn my stay." He raised his gun higher.

There's never a superhero around when you need one, Ephan thought, frantically searching the skies. They considered crying out for help, but what good would that do? Milton would fire as soon as they opened their mouth. *So this is fear,* Ephan thought, remembering Corey's earlier admonition. *But am I afraid of being shot, or afraid of not being afraid?* Ephan braced themself, wondering how far they'd get if they charged straight at Milton and wrestled the gun out of his hand.

"Don't try to be a hero," Milton said, as if reading their mind. "Now, I can shoot you, or you can jump."

Ephan turned their head slightly, thinking about the distance to the ground. Ten stories was more than enough to be fatal, but people had survived worse. People survived bullet wounds, too. How good a shot was Milton? Or did it even matter? Would he fire once and leave Ephan for dead, or would he empty the clip into Ephan's body? And if Ephan jumped, would it be better to go feet first or —

"Trick question!" Milton shouted, then squeezed the trigger.

The muzzle flashed, and the bullet instantly appeared about a foot away from Ephan. It visibly slowed in mid-air and struck their chest at about the speed of a softball. They still felt the impact, but it wasn't much worse than being hit by one of Corey's pennies. Ephan had often heard of time seeming to slow down during life-threatening situations, but that didn't seem to be the case here. The rest of the world beat on just fine. The wind still blew, the birds continued to flock by, and Milton's expression changed from furious to confused. Only the speed of the bullet had been affected.

Not believing what he'd just seen, Milton fired five more times. Each bullet left the barrel at a normal speed, then slowed to a crawl when it got within a few feet of Ephan. The bullets softly bounced off their face and chest, then clattered harmlessly around their feet.

"You're... one of *them*," Milton said, still confused. Then his face twisted in anger. He rushed forward and tackled Ephan, sending both tumbling over the ledge.

As they plummeted toward the ground, Ephan wasn't frightened so much as curious. Would the same power that had saved them from the bullets protect them from the impact? Then they thought about Milton. He was a bad guy, but it was still Ephan's duty to save his life.

Ephan had seen this scenario in dozens of comics and movies, and most of those stories broke the laws of physics. The citizens fell from buildings, the heroes caught them, and they went home without injury. But wouldn't slamming into a superhero at that speed be just as deadly as hitting the ground?

But maybe Ephan's protective power could save them both. Milton had lost his grip after the initial impact, but he was still just inches away. Ephan grabbed him and pulled him into a hug.

The fall seemed to take forever. The power kicked in when they were about ten feet from the ground. It felt like a warm cushion of air enveloped them, slowing them until they landed relatively softly on the concrete. It was still enough to knock the wind out of Ephan's lungs, but it wouldn't leave a bruise.

Milton recovered before Ephan did. He clambered to his feet and ran. Ephan rolled over into a crawling position, then carefully stood up. The world was spinning, and it took a few seconds for everything to come into focus. Several college students approached, eyeing Ephan with concern and curiosity. Milton was already halfway across the parking lot, too far gone to catch up to now.

Guess I have my first arch-enemy, Ephan thought, dusting themself off. *Wish he had a cooler name than Milton.*

The sun had now fully set. Ephan waved off the well-meaning students, pondering their new power. It wasn't much, but it had already saved their life twice. *I can make this work,* they thought. Then they began the short trek back to Pride House, thinking of superhero names as they walked.

Tristan sat in his room, staring out the window. His father's voice still echoed through his head. "No phone. No video games. If you're too sick to stay in class, you're too sick to have fun. And no dinner tonight, since you're *so nauseous*." He'd said those last two words with an extra serving of sarcasm, as if challenging Tristan to come clean and admit he wasn't really sick.

It didn't matter. None of it mattered. Tristan wasn't hungry, and he didn't feel like playing any games. In a couple of years – if he lived that long - he'd be off at Tristate Community College, where he had to believe people would be more enlightened. Maybe he'd still run into bullies now and then, but at least he wouldn't have to listen to his father's tirades every day. The college was only a couple of blocks away, but living in a dorm meant that he'd be out of his father's grasp.

He missed his mom. She'd been more understanding. Tristan would have felt comfortable telling her what had actually happened at lunchtime today. But she was long gone, living on the other side of the country, having had her fill of her ex-husband's verbal abuse. Tristan wished he could have gone with her, but it just hadn't been possible. Maybe after college he'd...

There was movement outside the window. Tristan stood up and looked down at the street below. A delivery driver had pulled up. It was Tristan's favorite, Zippy's Pizza. *Dad doesn't even like Zippy's*, Tristan thought. For a moment, Tristan wondered if this was his dad's way of apologizing. But then he pushed that thought aside. He'd never seen his father apologize for anything.

It's a trick, Tristan thought. *Psychological warfare. Either he's trying to make me feel extra guilty for leaving school early, or he's hoping I'll be so hungry that I'll admit I wasn't sick.*

Tristan fumed as the delivery car drove off. He could hear his father moving around downstairs, deliberately making as much noise as possible. The pizza smell wafted upstairs, through Tristan's open door – he wasn't allowed to close it tonight because, as his father put it, "in case you get so sick you need to go to the hospital." Once again, the sarcasm had been blatantly obvious.

He detected the distinct aroma of mushrooms. His father hated mushrooms. If he hadn't known it was a game before, he knew it now. He wouldn't be surprised if he looked downstairs and saw his father holding the pizza up to a fan, blowing the smell upstairs. Tristan's stomach growled, and he involuntarily took a step toward the door.

No, Tristan thought, sitting back down. *I told him I was sick, and I'm sticking to my story.*

It was infuriating. His dad was always pulling tricks like this. Supposedly they were intended to make Tristan a better person, but these little mind games always seemed to occur after his dad had been inconvenienced in some way. *He's not mad because I left school*, Tristan thought. *He's mad because he had to come get me. That's the difference.*

"Tristan!" his dad yelled from the bottom of the stairs. "If you're feeling any better, dinner's ready! It's your favorite!"

He really didn't sound mad. If anything, he sounded like he really cared for Tristan's well-being. *But I've fallen for that before*, Tristan thought. His dad wasn't a total monster. He'd never hit Tristan, not even once, and he even called him by his preferred name most of the time. And yet, when Tristan thought of all the bullies he'd faced in the past, his dad's face was always first and foremost.

Maybe his dad didn't use his fists, but he was still of the mindset that the strong should dominate the weak. Tristan thought back to the bathroom incident and wondered what his dad was like back in high school. Had he been one of the bullies or one of the victims?

Brett's taunts echoed in Tristan's mind. He could almost still feel Kev's tendrils wrapping around his neck. He'd been petrified at the time, but now he was just angry. Brett, Kev, his father – he hated them all and wanted them to suffer. His fury grew until he could feel it all over his body, a tangible thing that rippled over every inch of skin. He looked down at his hands and saw them undulating under waves of orange light. *What is this?* he wondered, but his curiosity melted away in favor of greedy anticipation.

It's finally happening, he thought. *I finally have the power to fight back.*

The pizza sat untouched on the kitchen table. Tristan's father brooded in a wooden chair, eating a peanut butter and jelly sandwich and muttering something about how ungrateful kids were these days. Then there was a crashing sound from somewhere up above, and the entire house shook. He dropped his sandwich and rushed to the stairway.

"What the hell is going on up there?" he shouted as he climbed the stairs. The more seconds that passed without an answer, the angrier he got. But when he reached Tristan's room, his rage was replaced with shock. Where there had once been a window, there was now a hole in the wall the size of a wrecking ball. Tristan was nowhere to be seen.

Ephan waltzed down the sidewalk, still on cloud nine. They looked forward to getting back to Pride House so they could show Corey their new powers. And yet, they just couldn't bring themself to head that way yet.

Am I looking for trouble? Ephan wondered, as they realized they were in a sketchy part of town. Their newfound power had them feeling invincible, which wasn't the wisest frame of mind considering they didn't know the extent of their abilities.

They heard a clattering sound in the distance and turned to see a flash of orange light, maybe two blocks away. Ephan froze for a second, their fight-or-flight response doing the hokey pokey in their head. It had to be a supervillain up to no good. Maybe someone was hurt. *If I go over there, will I be able to help, or will I just get in the way?* Ephan wondered. They didn't hear any emergency sirens yet, nor had any superheroes flown overhead. Ephan took a few steps in the direction of the strange light, then stopped again, undecided.

It can't hurt to look, Ephan thought, then broke into a run.

"Somebody help!" Brett shouted, running through empty parking lots to get away from… whatever it was. Kev was at his side, somehow keeping pace despite not being nearly as athletic. As Brett ducked around the corner behind a long-closed bank, he risked a look at their relentless pursuer. The energy cloud was the size of a school bus and floated about ten feet above the ground. Bits of orange energy sparked off its perimeter like tiny bolts of lightning. At the cloud's center, Brett could just make out the silhouette of a human figure.

"You run, I'll hold it off," Kev said, and Brett didn't think twice. As Brett disappeared down the street, Kev turned and threw a weblike mass of dark tendrils at the center of the cloud. As soon as the tendrils got near, however, they were shredded into nothingness, torn apart by the strange orange energy.

Realizing his powers were useless against this thing, Kev

tossed a couple of wispy lines toward the third level of a parking garage. The dark vines wrapped around a concrete column and pulled Kev to safety. The orange mass paused for just a moment, deciding which target to pursue. It rose a bit higher in the air until it spotted Brett running down Emery Road. Then it shot forward with the power of a tornado, ready to rip its prey to pieces.

Ephan didn't want to make snap judgments, but sometimes it was immediately obvious who the bad guys were. A young man, probably a West Bedford High School student judging by his red-and-white jacket, cowered behind a bench in front of a café. He was built like a quarterback, but he was powerless against his attacker, a menacing orange cloud of ominous energy. A being inside the cloud pointed angrily at the student, and orange bolts of lightning blasted the bench into smithereens. Now out in the open, the student backed away slowly, whimpering.

The cloud fired another blast, but now Ephan was there, standing between the monster and its victim. The orange lightning came within inches of Ephan's face before getting absorbed by their dampening power. This infuriated the cloud creature even further, and now a barrage of electric bolts jolted toward Ephan. Once again they were nullified.

Ephan stood in a confident pose, but they weren't quite sure what to do next. Sure, they could survive the enemy's attacks and keep them from harming the student, but then what? Ephan had no way to fight back, so they were at an impasse, destined to act as a protective wall until the creature got bored and left.

Guess I'll try talking to it, they thought. "Stand down!"

Ephan ordered, shouting as loud as they could manage.

The orange thing turned an even brighter shade, then bombarded Ephan with more blasts. Each and every one dissipated before they could cause any harm. Confused, the cloud diminished a bit and floated towards the ground. Soon it was just another teenage boy, half the size of the other student, surrounded by a small corona of energy. The boy stomped forward and glared at Ephan with eyes that glowed bright orange.

"Don't you dare protect him!" the boy shouted. "You don't know what he did! He's a bully!"

"I only see one bully at the moment," Ephan said. "And it's not the guy cowering over there."

"He started it!" the boy said. "He's always pushing people around! He forced me to... to..." He started beating on Ephan's chest with his fists, but he couldn't seem to get any more words out.

Ephan noticed that even the boy's blows were softened by their power. They slowly exhaled. "What's your name, kid?"

"Tristan," the boy said, sniffling.

"Look, Tristan, I could give you some clichéd speech about powers and responsibility, but I'd probably get hit with a lawsuit for copyright violation. So instead, I'll just say this. We have to be better than them. If all we do is bully each other back and forth, the conflict never ends, it just escalates."

"Not if I kill him," the boy said, his face as hard as stone. He dropped his hands to his sides, still clenched in tight fists.

Ephan blinked in surprise but kept talking. "If you kill him, then his family will come after you. And then the cops. And then the army. Soon the whole world will be after you. And maybe you're still more powerful, maybe you can still fight off whatever they send after you. But that's your life now, a never-ending series of threats and counter-attacks, until you're all by yourself, alone in the world. Is that really what you want?"

Tristan took several deep breaths, then finally shook his head no. "I don't want to be alone," he whispered.

"It's nice to have power," Ephan said. "I highly recommend it. But when you use it, you're telling the world who you are. Someday they'll write comic books about you, Tristan. I guarantee it. But do you want to be written as a hero or a villain? Because that's the choice you're making tonight."

Brett carefully stepped forward, looking like he might bolt at any moment. He looked at Tristan with sudden recognition. "Nan... Tristan?" he asked. "Oh god, man, I'm sorry. I'm so so sorry. We won't bother you anymore. Never again." He started to back away.

Tristan turned toward Brett, and his eyes glowed again. "Not good enough," he said.

"Tristan..." Ephan warned, but the boy held up a hand.

"Whatever you want, anything," Brett gushed.

"Leave them *all* alone," Tristan said. "Tell Kev, too. If you bully anyone else, you'll answer to me."

"Okay man," Brett said, then turned and ran.

The orange corona faded away, and Tristan sank to his knees. As he sobbed into his hands, Ephan crouched and hugged him. "You're going to be okay, kid," they said.

"Hey, Mom."

"Ephan? *You* called *me*? This is a nice surprise."

"Sorry, Mom. You know, college life. There's always

something keeping me busy."

"Let me guess, you need money."

"No! No, things are good, I mean it. I just wanted to let you know what's been going on in my life."

"So, what's been going on?"

"Well, I saved a life last night, maybe two. It all started when…"

Bubbles

Nisha knew it was going to be a difficult day from the moment her house exploded. Now it was just before lunchtime and she was barefoot, in the cold, trying to keep hold of a squirming tabby cat. *Mom and Dad are going to freak when they get home,* she thought.

She watched from an alley across the street, peeking out from behind a trash receptacle. The fire drones sprayed bright blue extinguishing foam at the dwindling flames. But Nisha wasn't watching the drones. She was looking for… kidnappers? Terrorists? Gang members? She wasn't sure who they were, to be honest. They were after her, and that was all that mattered. She'd first seen them the day before, right after her meeting with Professor Alex. She'd seen them again this morning, shortly before the grenade crashed through her window.

But she didn't see any of them now. They'd fled the scene of the crime before the drones showed up. Still, Nisha wasn't quite ready to show herself. They could still be out there, watching and waiting, ready to grab her as soon as she exposed herself.

Kerwin suddenly growled and hissed, and Nisha nearly dropped him. "Shush," she said, rearranging her grip on the angry cat. "If someone hears us, they might—"

"Might what?" came a voice behind her.

Nisha turned around. She recognized the man right off. He'd been driving the van she'd seen following her yesterday. He was dressed like a street punk, with ripped jeans and a studded leather jacket, but it looked all wrong on him. His face was too clean, his hair too neatly combed. Also, his shockgun, which he pointed at Nisha's face, looked more expensive than the kind of weapon gang members typically brandished. Not that Nisha was an expert.

"Arjun Bhakta?" the man asked.

"It's Nisha now," she answered.

"Well, your birth certificate says Arjun," the man said.

"It also says I'm six pounds, three ounces," Nisha said. "Things change."

"You're fifteen," the man said. "You shouldn't be thinking about all that gender crap."

"Did I ask for your opinion?" Nisha asked. "My house just blew up, and you want to debate gender identity at gunpoint?"

"We don't want to hurt you," the man said. "We just want the schematics for your science project."

"They were in the house," Nisha replied. "Not a great plan on your part." She tried to sound calm, but her voice threatened to crack. She'd never been good at lying.

"The explosion was an accident," the man said. "It was a pyroteck grenade. It was supposed to scare you. How were we supposed to know you keep explosive chemicals in your house?"

"My dad's a scientist," Nisha said, wondering why she felt

the need to explain herself to this guy. Kerwin was getting extremely agitated, and she was having a hard time keeping him from escaping.

"We're not idiots," the man said. "I know you keep your notes backed up in the cloud somewhere. Give me your password, and I'll let you go."

"Sorry, it's all up here," Nisha said. She tried pointing to her head, but it wasn't easy while holding the cat.

The man cursed under his breath. "Then I'm afraid you'll have to come with me." Behind him, two more men entered the alley. They were also unconvincingly dressed as gang members. One of them looked strangely familiar.

"Or you'll shoot me?" Nisha asked. "You won't get anything that way." Part of her was tempted to give in, but she'd been working on this project for months, and her family seriously needed the money. Losing their house wasn't going to help their financial situation.

"It's on sedation mode," the man replied, nodding toward his pistol. "Conscious or unconscious, you're coming either way. But if I have to knock you out, your cat'll get away."

Nisha was scared out of her mind, not to mention freezing and covered in cat scratches, but she couldn't let these people take her away. She just couldn't. She thought about screaming, but she was afraid they'd fire. She thought about running, but again, they'd fire. Emergency drones scanned the street behind her, searching her property for survivors. If she screamed or ran, would the drones investigate? Would they stop the kidnappers before they carried her unconscious body away? And would she be able to find Kerwin again when this was all over?

"Well?" the man asked. "Which is it going to be?" All three men held their guns on her, looking like they might fire at any moment.

Nisha exhaled. "Fine," she said. "The device is in my pocket. Take it, reverse engineer it, just let me go. Please?"

"You actually finished it?" the man asked, his eyes wide. "Let me see."

Tucking the cat under one arm, Nisha reached into her pocket and pulled out a rectangular metal box, roughly the size of a hot dog. One side had a touchscreen that displayed several buttons and numerical readouts. "It still needs some work, but—" Nisha began.

The man reached for the device, but Nisha quickly tapped the controls. A transparent blue bubble appeared around her, creating a barrier between Nisha and her potential kidnappers. The head thug took a step back, then tapped on the bubble experimentally. He felt a mild shock and withdrew his hand. "Amazing," he said, blowing on his finger.

"It can do more than that," Nisha said. "So you better back off."

The man chuckled. "Shoot her," he said, turning his head slightly to the left. His partners fired, but their blasts were absorbed by the bubble.

Nisha put on a confident smile, but it was all an act. She really wasn't sure how much firepower the bubble could withstand. True, not half an hour ago, it had saved her from a raging fire. But she hadn't tested it against all types of energy, and there was no telling how long the bubble would last before it gave out.

"Fine, we'll do this the hard way," the head thug said. He turned a dial on his weapon. "At the highest setting, this gun can vaporize a brick wall. I'm sure it'll go through your bubble like it was paper. This is your last chance. Hand over the device or else." Once again he pointed the gun at her face.

Nisha tapped the controls again. The bubble burst, releasing a wave of energy that knocked all three thugs a few meters backward and blew the trash receptacle out into the street. Nisha stared at her device in awe. The display screen currently indicated that its power levels were low. It would recharge over time, but that was something Nisha didn't have at the moment. At the other end of the alley, the thugs groaned and tried to get to their feet. Slipping the device back into her pocket, Nisha turned and ran.

"Can-you-please-watch-Kerwin-for-a-couple-of-hours-thanks-bye!" Nisha blurted, practically throwing the cat at her best friend.

"Nisha?" Manju asked, staring at her with confusion. "I saw your house on the news—"

But Nisha was already gone, running down the sidewalk at top speed. Manju stood in her doorway, holding the cat, watching her friend fade in the distance.

Why didn't I just call the police from Manju's house? Nisha wondered, running down the sidewalk in her bare feet. But she knew why. She was being tracked. She'd seen the drones overhead, and these weren't from Emergency Services. If she stayed in one place too long, another van would show up to take her away. She had to find someplace the drones couldn't follow.

Maybe I should head for the police station, she thought. Except she couldn't remember how to get there from here, and she'd lost her phone when the house blew up. She supposed she could stop someone and ask to use their phone, but they might ask too many questions, and the thugs would catch up to her. Besides, something in the back of her mind told her not to trust the police.

And then it hit her, where she'd seen that one kidnapper before. The guy in the back, on the left... she was sure he was one of the cops who'd come to her school to speak on Career Day. Officer Mike. She remembered his name because he'd said Michaels was his surname, but everyone still called him Mike. Just what was going on here?

I just need a place to think. She was running out of breath, her feet were getting numb, and her Bubble Box - she was still workshopping the name - was only up to thirty percent. *Where can I go that the drones can't find me?*

She passed a manhole cover and did a double-take. *Not a chance,* she thought, and kept running. Real-life sewers were nothing like the movies, and the gasses alone would probably kill her. Besides, the thought of running around a sewer barefoot made her stomach churn.

She ducked into a fast food restaurant as another drone flew overhead. She couldn't be sure if it had spotted her or not. "Hey!" an employee shouted. "No shoes, no service!"

Nisha ran back outside, then took a random, zig-zag route through town. San Lavergne wasn't huge, and had rather eclectic zoning laws. Rows of brick townhouses stood across the street from vehicle recharge stations and mom-and-pop grocery stores, while the factories were always visible in the distance, no matter which direction you looked. There was no real downtown, just a row of touristy businesses across the street from Nisha's school.

School. It was Saturday, but Professor Alex had said he was planning to work all weekend, setting up for the science fair next week. Maybe he could help her. If nothing else, he could find her a good place to hide while he figured out who to call. Carefully watching the skies, Nisha made her way towards the school.

The sun was setting when Nisha reached the school. She hadn't seen any drones for a while. Occasionally a police cruiser would speed by, lights flashing, but Nisha always hid until they passed. She still wasn't sure who to trust.

Her parents would be home from work soon, though they'd probably already been called when the house burned down. Then she realized her parents might think she was dead. Instinctively she reached for her phone, then remembered she'd lost it in the fire. *No, wait*, she thought. Manju had seen her since then. She'd be able to tell Nisha's parents that she'd survived. But they'd still be worried. Those police cruisers she kept seeing – they were probably looking for her.

Sticking to the shadows, Nisha gave the parking lot a wide berth and approached the school from the playground out back. From her vantage point, she could see a police car parked out front. Rather than enter the school, she crept behind it, walking around until she reached the gym. She knew that's where the science fair would be held, and therefore, where Professor Alex would be. The gym only had a couple of small windows, and she had to stand on tiptoe to peek into one.

The professor was in there, talking to a cop. Only it wasn't just any cop. Officer Mike was now dressed in his police uniform, a huge change from the punk outfit he'd worn a few hours earlier. Was Professor Alex working with him?

Nisha turned from the window and sat on the cold ground. She had to think. Other than her parents and a couple of friends, Professor Alex was the only one who knew about Nisha's invention. Was this some side business of his? Waiting for students to have a breakthrough, so he could steal the idea and profit?

But that didn't make any sense. The professor had always been so nice, was that all a lie? He was one of those "cool" teachers who let kids call him by his first name, and tried to keep up with current trends so he could use them as analogies in his lessons. Some of Nisha's classmates thought he was a dork, but he'd always been her favorite teacher.

I guess it was all part of the con, Nisha thought. Multiple revenge plots played out in her head. But she'd have to save that for later. Right now she needed someone safe to talk to, and apparently Professor Alex wasn't it.

She was cold and hungry and worried about her parents. She'd wasted half her day running toward the man who'd betrayed her. To say she was angry was an understatement. She wanted to hurt Professor Alex. She wanted to go in there and use her invention to… to…

Nisha sighed, slowly exhaling her anger. No, she really didn't. She didn't want to hurt anyone. She was disappointed in her teacher, disgusted even, but violence wasn't the answer. At most, she hoped he'd face jail time. But given that the cops were in on it, that seemed doubtful.

She saw movement near the parking lot. The officer was leaving the gym. Nisha stayed perfectly still as he got into his patrol car and sped off.

Where to now? Nisha wondered. She supposed she needed to track down her parents and tell them everything that had happened. *Ugh,* she thought. *I'm not walking all the way back home tonight. I'll have to find a way to call them.* She considered sneaking into the school to find a phone.

"Nisha?"

She jumped to her feet and backed up against the wall. Professor Alex stood just a few meters away. "Don't come any closer," Nisha said, reaching into her pocket.

"It's okay, Nisha," the professor said. "The cops are gone. You want to tell me what's really going on?"

"Y-you sent the cops to steal my invention," Nisha said shakily.

Professor Alex took a step back. "Nisha. I wouldn't dream of it. The greatest joy in my life is to see my students flourish. When you came to me with your device, it was one of the greatest days of my career. When I retire, I can look back at students like you and say, 'I did that. I changed the world.' Why would I ever want to give that up?"

"Money?" Nisha offered.

The professor chuckled, shaking his head. "Oh, Nisha. I don't care about money."

"Everyone cares about money," Nisha said. "Even if you're not greedy, you still need it to live."

Professor Alex laughed. "True, but you don't understand. I don't care about money because I already have it. I've made a fortune investing in some of my former students' inventions. Just as I plan to invest in yours. I don't have to work. I just do it because I want to help your generation craft a better future."

"Oh," Nisha said. "You really think I'm going to change the world?"

"I have no doubt," Professor Alex said. "Now come inside, and we'll give your parents a call."

They were about to enter the building when a shimmer

appeared in the air, revealing a police car. Officer Mike stepped out and raised his weapon. "I knew you were hiding her," he said. Keeping his shockgun trained on the pair, he tapped his earpiece. "Found her," he said. "Yes, at the school. I figured her teacher was lying, so I cloaked the car and stayed nearby. Will do. Yes, I'll make sure there's no witnesses. See you soon."

"Get behind me, Nisha," Professor Alex said.

"Won't help," Officer Mike said, and fired.

But Nisha acted quickly, and the jolt of energy dissipated against the bubble that suddenly appeared around Nisha and the professor. Before the officer had a chance to get off another shot, Nisha expanded the bubble, slamming it into the cop and throwing him onto the hood of his car. He dropped his weapon and just lay there for a minute, stunned.

Professor Alex grabbed the gun and held it on the officer.

"It's not like you're going to use that thing," Officer Mike said as he came back to his senses.

The professor lowered the gun's setting to sedation mode and fired. Then he and Nisha dragged the unconscious officer into the building. "We're going to get arrested, aren't we?" Nisha asked.

"I can get us out of this, but we're going to have to hurry," Professor Alex said. "How much charge does your device have?"

"Well, it was almost full, but now it's back down to twenty-one percent," she answered. "Next upgrade, I've got to work on its power usage."

"Can you plug it into the wall or something?" the professor asked.

Nisha frowned. "No, it had a charging base back at the house, but that's gone now. It also self-charges from my body heat, but it's pretty slow."

"We'll just have to hope it's enough," Professor Alex said.

Ten minutes later, another police cruiser pulled up in front of the school. Watching through the window, Nisha immediately recognized the three men who stepped out. The two officers were the other gang members she'd encountered that morning. The third man wore a business suit and looked very annoyed. Nisha's eyes widened. "That's Mr. Karnik," she whispered. "Manju's dad."

Professor Alex recognized him as well, having met him at previous science fairs. "He must be the one who hired the officers," the professor said. "Manju must have told him about your invention, and now he wants to steal the patent."

"He'd never get away with that," Nisha said softly. "I backed up every step of the process. He had to know I'd be able to prove it. The only way he'd be able to take credit is if he…" she trailed off, and her face looked grim.

Professor Alex nodded. "Welcome to the business world," he said.

Outside, the two officers examined the abandoned police car while Mr. Karnik tapped his foot impatiently. Finally they turned toward the building. A few seconds later the gymnasium door opened.

The two officers entered first, followed by Mr. Karnik. The first thing they saw was the unconscious body of Officer Mike tied to a chair. Professor Alex stood behind him, holding Nisha's bubble device. Nisha stood halfway behind her teacher, peeking out from just over his left shoulder.

Both officers trained their weapons on the professor. "You know why we're here," Mr. Karnik said.

"You want to steal my invention!" Nisha shouted.

"Tut tut," Mr. Karnik said. "You're just a confused boy. No one will believe a mentally deranged child was capable of designing such a device."

"What?" Nisha asked. "Of course I did! I—"

"This is what I'm thinking," Mr. Karnik said. "You and my daughter invented it together. It was her idea, and she did most of the work, but you helped. Your name will still appear on the patent as a contributor, but Manju will be credited as the inventor. You will still get a portion of the profits. This is my final offer. I suggest you take it."

"Not a chance," Nisha said. "I'm not going to lie for you!"

"Your funeral," Mr. Karnik said, and the officers took aim.

"Wait," Professor Alex said, and the officers lowered their shockguns a little. "Let's not be hasty. I want you to know your actions are being recorded." He pointed to Officer Mike's body cam, which was now turned on and pointed at Mr. Karnik and his cohorts.

"That's easy enough to erase after we kill you two," Mr. Karnik said. "This is your last chance. Hand over the device or we'll take it off your corpses."

Professor Alex glanced to his left. Nisha silently nodded, though her expression was pained. "Fine," the professor said. He tossed the device to Mr. Karnik, who examined it eagerly.

"It seems a little light," Mr. Karnik said, shaking the device.

"Compact circuitry," Nisha said, but Mr. Karnik didn't look convinced.

"You've got what you wanted, now leave us alone," Professor Alex said.

"Very well," Mr. Karnik said. Then, to the officers, he ordered, "Kill them."

The officers fired, but a translucent blue bubble appeared

and enveloped Nisha, the professor, and Officer Mike. Mike suddenly woke up to see his fellow officers firing at him. "Hey!" he shouted, but they continued to fire.

Mr. Karnik examined the device in his hand, then opened up the back to find it was just an empty casing. Cursing, he threw the hollow device to the floor. Nisha held up the device's internal circuitry, staring at the battery indicator. "It's not going to hold much longer," she said.

"It'll be okay," Professor Alex said. "Help is almost here."

"Drop your weapons now!" a voice boomed from behind the officers. They turned to find the police chief and six additional officers had entered the gym. The rogue officers complied, setting their weapons on the floor and putting their hands behind their heads. Mr. Karnik surrendered as well.

"I called them," Professor Alex said to a confused-looking Nisha. The bubble dropped as the device's power finally hit zero. "I know, you were afraid we couldn't trust them. But the chief and I go back a ways. His son was in my class last year."

Mr. Karnik and the officers he'd hired were arrested and taken away.

The following week, Nisha's invention won the top prize at the science fair. She was approached by several big tech companies, and she made a deal that would more than make up for her family's lost house. In fact, her family would probably never have to work again. A few months later, the government presented her with a special award for her scientific achievement.

And a few decades later, she ran for president.

Consequences

The frigid winds bit at Cazandra's face as she pushed through the snow. She pulled her cloak tighter, but the tattered cloth offered little protection against the cold. She was tired and bleeding, and she was pretty sure she'd sprained an ankle while fleeing the angry mob. *I don't know where to go,* she thought. Her friends had turned against her. Her fans no longer respected her, and without their support, her magic had grown weak.

"Warmth," she whispered, using her Author voice. Her hands glowed slightly, and her body temperature rose by about two degrees. *Someone out there still believes in me,* she thought, and if not for that tiny ray of hope, she might have collapsed in the snow right there. But she trudged on, putting as much distance as she could between her and the burning tower on the north side of the city.

All her books, gone. Early drafts. Works in progress. Not to mention her clothes, furniture, and all her other possessions. The clothes she currently wore – ripped and soiled as they were – represented all she owned in the world now. And even that would be gone if the mob spotted her. *I don't deserve this,* she thought, but she wasn't sure if she believed it.

She'd nearly crossed the entire city, and the south gate was barely visible through the thick snowstorm. But she couldn't leave town that way. The guards stopped everyone, kings and peasants alike. She would be recognized and brought before the courts, and she was afraid to speculate what would happen to her after that.

Instead, she veered to the right, to the black tower that stood in the southwest corner of the city. It was a long shot – no, even that was optimistic. She would be at the mercy of her greatest enemy. She could only hope that Zen still held onto some shred of the love they'd once had for each other. It was a minuscule hope, but it was all she had.

Twenty minutes later, the tower loomed over her. Still dragging her useless ankle, she climbed the stairs one painful step at a time, stopping frequently to take a few labored breaths. When she finally reached the wooden door at the top, she grabbed the large iron knocker and clanged it four times. Then she collapsed onto the top step and waited.

Thirty seconds passed. A minute. Two. She was about to reach for the knocker again when the door opened. Zenitha Willowbrook stood in the doorway, an imposing silhouette that seemed both terrifying and beautiful.

"I knew it would be you," Zenitha said.

"I don't know where else to go," Cazandra replied.

"You're not welcome here," Zenitha said, and began to close the door.

"Please," Cazandra wailed. "You're my last hope. There has to be some part of you that still feels for me. If not love or respect, then at least concern. Do you really want to see me die?"

The door was nearly shut, but Zenitha held it open a few

inches. "Tell me," she said. "If our situations were reversed, and it was me begging at your doorstep, would you let me in?"

"Of c—" Cazandra started to say, but the second word caught in her throat. "Y—" she tried again, but the word wouldn't come. She looked up and saw a rune of truth carved into the stone above the door. *I should have known*, Cazandra thought. She'd always wanted to get one for her own front door, as a protection from dishonest door-to-door vendors. Unfortunately they were extremely rare, and Cazandra wondered how Zenitha had acquired one.

Would I really have turned her away, though? Cazandra wondered. She liked to think she was the forgiving sort. *Who am I kidding*, she told herself. She'd become bitter in these past few years, and she knew it. The truth rune could not be fooled by conflicted emotions and inner turmoil. If it silenced her attempts to answer Zenitha's question, then that meant that deep down, Cazandra knew her answer was a lie. If Zenitha had come to Cazandra for help in her darkest hour, Cazandra would have turned her out into the cold. Whether Cazandra wanted to believe it or not, that was the truth of it.

"Your silence is deafening," Zenitha said. The door closed another inch.

"I... I..." Cazandra stuttered, struggling to find an honest set of words that would save her skin. "I... want to change," she managed finally.

Zenitha considered her words for a moment. She studied her rival, the once-incomparable Author now broken and freezing on her front steps. She knew, as did Cazandra, that closing the door would be an act both literal and metaphorical. It would mean cutting her adversary out of her life forever. It would also spell doom for this woman, this now-helpless wretch who had once been the most respected

Author in Forzeen.

Closing the door would be like murder. The question was, was the murder justified? Were Cazandra's crimes deserving of such a fate? And would Cazandra's downfall actually make the world a better place, or would she become a martyr to the few supporters she had left?

"You earned what's coming," Zenitha finally said, and slammed the door.

The world of Tarthandia was filled with magic for those who knew how to earn it. Almost everyone knew a few spells, and they practiced them daily at home and as part of their careers. Farmers used growth charms to ensure a bountiful harvest. Carpenters infused their wood with spells that repelled termites and resisted rotting. Candlemakers produced candles with magical flames that burned for days without melting.

For reasons no one understood, a caster's magical ability was based on how much they were loved. The tradesmen with the most satisfied customers were rewarded not only with repeat business, but also with the power to cast stronger spells and to cast them more often.

This system bred competition and innovation. Bakers designed the most delicious pastries to win their customers' love. Bartenders never watered down their drinks. Cobblers crafted shoes that lasted for years instead of months. Law enforcement officers stayed honest, lest their powers fade along with the public trust.

But the most powerful of all wizards were the Authors. Because their works were copied and distributed throughout the kingdom and beyond, they became the most famous and most beloved of all of Tarthandia's citizens. Other creators and performers were just as beloved, such as actors and singers. But a performer could only ply their trade in one city at a time, while a good book could entertain people the world over.

The kingdom of Forzeen consisted of dozens of cities and townships, with miles of farmland in between. Most cities were only home to one Author, if that. In many cases the Author's tower had come first, and the city had grown up around it as devoted fans wanted to be the first to read the Author's next work. The city of Warrikstan was one of the largest in the kingdom, mostly due to the popularity of Author Cazandra Warrik.

But it was also one of the few cities to host two authors. Zenitha Willowbrook wasn't particularly well-known, but she had her fans. Her stories were written for a niche audience, and while her books were also distributed throughout the kingdom, only a handful of people in each town had read them. But Zenitha never envied Cazandra's fame. As long as she had a roof over her head and a quill in her hand, Zenitha had all she needed out of life.

Well, that and a safe town in which to live. Warrikstan had become increasingly dangerous to Zenitha in the last couple of years, due to a political uprising that was more than a little Cazandra's fault.

It all started fifteen years earlier.

Cazandra was as nervous as a thorkbeast in a butchertorium. She'd breezed through school and graduated with honors, so she had every reason to be confident in her abilities. But today was the first day of her new job in a new city where didn't know a soul. She wasn't worried that she'd get fired and end up on the streets. No one went hungry in Forzeen. If Cazandra failed she'd be transferred to another job, something less demanding but much less interesting. And if no job suited her, the government would still provide. She might lose her access to magic – the unemployed weren't loved by many - but she wouldn't wind up homeless.

But failure wasn't an option. This was where she wanted to be. As an editor for the Midlake Crier, her words would be read by citizens across the kingdom. She would be responsible for ensuring Midlake's citizens knew the honest truth on a daily basis. It would be her duty to screen the articles submitted by her subordinate reporters, and strip out any bias or unverified facts.

By the end of the first day, she knew she belonged. The other employees loved her right away, and she could already feel her magic growing. She'd never craved power, but she knew she could put it to good use. She made the most of her enhanced abilities, catching even more mistakes and uncovering more lies. After a couple of months, the local law enforcement came to her when they needed tips. They even offered her a job, but she turned them down. Writing was her calling.

She even started writing fiction in her spare time. She had an idea for a story about a school for children who couldn't use magic. Over the school year, they learned how to engineer whimsical devices that used springs and cogs instead of charms and spells. They also solved mysteries and fought strange monsters. The first book received rave reviews and was praised throughout the kingdom. Knowing she had a hit on her hands, she had her hours reduced at the Crier so she would have more time to work on the series.

And then she met Zen. He was a newly transferred

reporter who mostly covered fluff pieces, such as reviews of plays or heartwarming local interest stories. The two hit it off right away, mostly due to their shared interest in literature and the arts. Their friendship quickly turned into a whirlwind romance, and within a few months they were already discussing moving in together.

"You spend most of your time here anyway," Cazandra said, soaking in a tub of warm water. Several tiny, magic-infused spigots sent jets of air into the water, creating a swirl of bubbles that circled Cazandra's body.

Zen frowned. He studied the hairbrush in his hand, turning it over and over as if it held a hidden message. "There's... things I haven't told you about myself," he finally said. "Things you need to know before we take such a big step."

"So say them," Cazandra said. "What could you possibly have done that would make me hate you?"

"I've been seeing..." Zen started, but trailed off. He just couldn't bring himself to finish the sentence.

Cazandra's face went red. "Who is she?" she demanded. She put her hands on the sides of the tub, ready to climb out and tear Zen to pieces.

"No!" Zen said. "No, I'm not... I'm not courting anyone else. I promise."

Cazandra relaxed a little, but she still looked suspicious. "Then what were you going to say?" she asked, sinking back into the tub.

Zen took a deep breath. "I've been seeing a therapist. You know, a mind doctor. We—"

"I know what a therapist is," Cazandra said, her temper rising again. "And they're all charlatans. They pretend to listen to your problems and tell you what you want to hear.

Then they live off that unearned prestige. Easiest job in the kingdom. Tell me, what lies has this therapist been telling you?"

"Oh, wow," Zen said. "You're really not going to like this. Maybe I should just leave."

Cazandra glowered. "You will tell me this instant or I'll... I'll..." She couldn't think of a way to finish the threat, and she started looking around the tub for something to throw.

"Okay, okay," Zen said. "Well... There's these feelings... Feelings I've had for a while now. All my life, really. Something I've known, but I just couldn't put it into words. Something that changes everything. Something..."

"Get. To. The. Point," Cazandra said, fuming. The tub water should have been cooling off by now, but fresh steam was starting to rise from it.

"I'm a woman," Zen blurted. Seeing Cazandra's shocked face, he continued. "At least, I believe I was meant to be one. The therapist has been giving me lots of tests, but I still have more to take." The more words that came out, the faster he spoke. "Once we're both sure it's for the best, I'm going to travel to Greater Mountainside. There's a doctor there – a powerful genderthurgist – who can transform my body until it matches what I see in my mind. And then I'll finally be happy."

Cazandra was silent for a moment, then she shook her head. With a sarcastic half-smile, she said, "This so-called 'therapist' is filling your head with lies. The genderthurgist is probably a friend of his, and they like to throw work each other's way."

"No, it's not—" Zen said.

"You're just having an identity crisis," Cazandra said. "Your life isn't turning out like you planned, and you're trying to find yourself. Everybody feels that way sometimes. But you're not a woman. Believe me."

"It's the only thing that fits," Zen said. "When the doctor told me what it meant to be transgender, it was like all these random puzzle pieces suddenly fit together. So many childhood memories made sense. So many—"

"All kids experiment with gender," Cazandra said. "You're not a woman just because you tried on your mother's dress one day."

"It wasn't one day," Zen said. "It was every day. All the time, being jealous of my female friends, identifying with the female characters in books and plays. You yourself have called me feminine. You said it was one of the things you liked most about me."

"It's not real, Zen," Cazandra said. "People are who they are. You can be a man with feminine interests and mannerisms. You can even wear dresses if it makes you happy. But you can't be a woman."

"It *is* real," Zen said. "It—"

"No, *this* is real," Cazandra blurted, standing up. She touched her pubic area and even spread her labia in a vulgar attempt to drive her point home. "This is what makes me a woman. It doesn't matter what I wear or what hobbies I have. I was born this way and I will die this way."

"And that's what I'll look like after my visit to the genderthurgist," Zen said.

"No," Cazandra said. "You'll be a man suffering from a transformation spell, just as if they'd turned you into a frog. You were born male and you will die male. I don't care what parts you have."

"But you just said—" Zen started.

"Just get out," Cazandra said. "Get out and don't come

back. And while you're at it, find somewhere else to work."

They went their separate ways. Zenitha went ahead with the procedure, and afterward she was the happiest she had ever felt. Then she wrote stories about her life experiences, both autobiographical and fictionalized, and found modest success as an Author. Most of her fans were transgender as well, and while it wasn't a huge audience, they were very devoted.

Cazandra, meanwhile, found much greater success with her books. So much so, that they renamed the city after her. But she didn't just write fictional novels. She kept her job at the Midlake Crier - now the Warrikstan Crier - where she received several promotions. She now controlled the press, and she used her power to make her opinions known. Her anti-trans essays divided the city, and a growing portion of the populace made trans people feel unsafe.

Zenitha had never been the type who needed an ostentatious living space, but she had an Author tower built anyway. It just felt more secure than a standard home.

As the years went on, Cazandra began printing more and more outlandish accusations, and her followers began to trickle off. Things came to a head when she began openly criticizing Forzeen's king. Cazandra felt he hadn't done enough to keep women safe from what she called the "trans menace." While no actual cases of trans-on-cis violence had ever been reported, Cazandra was certain that these crimes occurred on a daily basis, and she wrote essay after essay claiming these events as fact.

It's debatable whether she knew how devoted her fanbase had become. Many of her former fans had gone on to follow other Authors, as reading Cazandra's books now felt like a political act. But those who remained loved her to an unhealthy degree. And so, when she was asked to deliver a speech in Lawthorn, the capital of Forzeen and the home of King Fairthane, even Cazandra was surprised at the exuberance of the crowd gathered before her.

A more sensible Author might have recognized her audience's fervor and realized she wielded too much power over them. A more rational mind would have understood that she was addressing a lit powder keg, and might have chosen words designed to quiet them. But Cazandra could feel their love for her. Their obsession invigorated her to the bone, and it made her feel absolutely invincible. Rather than give them a soothing speech of reassurance, she made the choice to see just how far she could rile them up.

She covered every topic from her essays, repeated every talking point, and quoted every made-up statistic. Her fans ate every word and asked for more. Her speech built up such a momentum that even Cazandra didn't know what she was saying anymore. As the crowd's collective mood reached an apex of blind, rabid fealty, Cazandra suggested they take the power back into their own hands.

And suddenly the crowd was gone. Cazandra stood, blinking in confusion, as her followers marched away from the stage, making a beeline for the castle. "Wait," she said, but no one was listening. All they could hear were the echoes of her magic-infused speech. "It was just a metaphor..." she said weakly. She leaned on the podium, suddenly very tired.

"We have to get you out of here," a man said, grabbing her by the arm. It was Jerald, her personal assistant and bodyguard.

"Shouldn't I try to... stop them or something?" Cazandra asked.

"That ship has sailed," Jerald said, leading her to her carriage. "This city is about to become a warzone. If you want to live, you have to go home."

"I can't just…" Cazandra said, but she was too tired to argue. Jerald helped her into the carriage and they fled the scene. It was just starting to snow as their carriage passed through the south gate. No guards were on duty to record their exit, as the town's law enforcement officers now had their hands full.

Cazandra didn't remember the ride home. The six-hour journey was a blur, as the magic-powered carriage took them over dozens of bumpy gravel roads. By the time they reached Warrikstan it was well after dark, and what had started as a light snow had become a near-blizzard.

I'll get a good night's sleep and make a public apology in the morning, Cazandra thought. But as they neared her tower, she saw that it was in flames and surrounded by a crowd of angry townsfolk.

"Go!" Jerald ordered, slowing the cart. "Now, before they see you!" But several in the mob had already turned their heads and recognized Cazandra's ornate carriage.

Cazandra jumped out of the cart, severely hurting her ankle as she landed. Three of the closest townsfolk converged on her, grabbing her by the shoulder and pulling her off her feet. Then all three of them screamed and backed off, their faces on fire. Jerald now stood between Cazandra and her attackers, brandishing his favorite weapon, a pistol that fired magical balls of flame.

"Go!" Jerald ordered, as he fired more shots at approaching townsfolk.

Cazandra stumbled through the snow, moving as fast as she could physically manage. She frequently looked behind her to see if she was being followed, but she could only see so far through the dark and the snow. Her heart froze as she heard Jerald's blood-curdling scream in the distance. *Mourn later*, she thought. *I've got to keep moving*.

She was now in the business district. A pair of torches bobbed towards her, so she hid between two shops. She pressed her back against a wall as a pair of guards passed, headed in the direction of Cazandra's tower. They discussed the situation as they marched. Cazandra couldn't pick up every word, but she got the gist.

The king was dead. Fairthane castle was in ruins. Half the king's guard had perished. Many of the rioters had been arrested, and some had already been executed. The queen was furious, and there was a huge bounty on Cazandra's head.

How did it come to this? Cazandra wondered. *I just wanted to make the world safer for women.* She sat down in the snow, catching her breath for a moment. *I have to get out of town*, she thought.

But to where? she thought. No place in the kingdom was safe for her, and she wasn't going to get far with her twisted ankle. *A friend*, she thought frantically. *I have to find a friend. Surely not all my fans have turned against me.*

But she knew better. She didn't have friends these days, not real ones. None of her acquaintances would care about her fate; every last one of them would betray her in a heartbeat. The best she could hope for was a soft-hearted humanitarian, someone who would care less about Cazandra's indiscretions and more about protecting the life of a hopeless fugitive. But where could she find such a person?

"You earned what's coming," Zenitha said, and slammed the door.

So that was it, then. Her last hope was gone. Cazandra sat on the top step in front of Zenitha's door, her back pressed against the wall with her knees pulled up to her chest. It was only a matter of time before some passing guard or villager spotted her and dragged her away. Would she even have a day in court, or would her captor go the literal route and only deliver the head?

"All I wanted was to help people," she said out loud. She blinked, a bit surprised that the rune had allowed her to finish the sentence. Staring up at the rune, she said, "I wanted to make the world safer." Again there was no pushback, no magical resistance.

"Trans people are d—" she said. "Trans people are d—" she repeated, but the rune wouldn't let her say "dangerous." She decided she'd try something else. "Trans women are m —" she tried to say, but it wouldn't let her say "men" either. Finally, just as an experiment, she said, "Trans women are women." She paused, then added, "Trans men are men."

She gasped. The revelation hit her in the gut, taking the air from her lungs. When she could speak again, she said, "I've been fighting the wrong people." And she knew it had to be true, because otherwise she couldn't have said it. "I deserve what's coming to me," she said, and was utterly devastated that she'd been able to say it. She buried her face in her hands and wailed.

She looked up and saw a torch bobbing in the distance. It wouldn't be long now. She thought about standing up and making herself known, but she just didn't have the energy.

She knew the courts would go easier on her if she turned herself in, but she no longer cared about her fate. "I wish I could repay all the lives I've ruined," she said, and she meant it with all her heart.

Just then the door opened again. Cazandra's greatest rival once again stood over her, but this time she made a "come in" motion with her chin. "Hurry, before I change my mind," Zenitha said.

"I promise I'll do better," Cazandra said, making sure she was still under the runestone as she said it. Then she shuffled inside, and Zenitha closed the door behind them.

It was a beautiful spring day, the last of the snow having melted weeks before. Cazandra whistled as she performed her chores, changing all the sheets in the bunkhouse before pulling the overstuffed laundry cart outside to the washing well.

Zenitha had really come through for her. Cazandra still didn't know how she'd done it. Zenitha had somehow been granted an audience with the queen, and she'd convinced the angry widow to show mercy.

And now Cazandra worked at the city's poorhouses, taking care of orphans and helping reformed criminals get back on their feet. Cazandra didn't feel she'd earned this second chance, but she was determined to make the most of it. She would earn back the public's trust if it took years.

She still wrote in her spare time. Not the inflammatory diatribes that had led to her ruin, but well-researched articles that kept the public informed. Maybe someday she'd be able to go back to writing full-time, but she wasn't going to rush it. She was prepared to work at the poorhouses for the rest of her life if that's what it took to repay her debt.

Once the laundry was clean and hung up to dry, she went back inside to do some sweeping. She entered a bunkhouse and saw a girl sitting on one of the beds. She was in her early teens, and she looked distraught.

"Is something wrong?" Cazandra asked, sitting down next to her.

"I don't want to talk about it," the girl said, staring at her knees.

"That's up to you," Cazandra said. "But here's the thing. Whatever's bothering you, it's going to keep bothering you until you tell someone. Your bunkmates are prone to gossip, but those days are long behind me. If you confide in me, I can personally guarantee I won't tell a soul without your permission. So you might as well take advantage of me while I'm here."

The girl appeared to think it over, and she took a deep breath. "I just feel… I mean… sometimes I think I was meant to be a boy." Then she looked away from Cazandra in embarrassment.

"I understand," Cazandra said. "How long have you felt this way?"

"As long as I can remember," the girl said.

"Well, now," Cazandra said. "That's not so bad."

The girl turned to look her in the eyes. "Really?"

"Really," Cazandra said. "Look, I'm no expert. Maybe you're just a tomboy, or maybe it's as you say - you were meant to be a boy. But either way it's nothing to be embarrassed about. I know someone you can talk to, someone who can help you. Would you like to come with me?"

The girl nodded. Then they stood and left the bunkhouse

together.

Jealousy

"God, you men are so silly," Jenna said.

"What?" Jason asked, holding a small stack of dresses for Jenna to try on.

"You get so irritable when we go clothes shopping," Jenna said. "First impressions are everything. Our clothing is how we present ourselves to the world. It's how we tell the world who we are. Don't you care how the world sees me?"

Jason wasn't sure how to answer that question. On the one hand, no, he didn't really care. He knew Jenna was an amazing woman with an adventurous spirit. She was often brash but never boring. If the rest of the world couldn't see her virtues, then that was their failing, not Jenna's. On the other hand, Jenna's appearance was important to her, so it should have been important to him as well.

"I'm sorry if I seem irritable," Jason said.

"Oh, just come on," Jenna said, leading him to the dressing rooms.

A woman at the counter smiled at them. Her nametag read "Charlotte," and she had red hair and looked like she was in her twenties. "Three items at a time," Charlotte said.

Jenna huffed, then selected three dresses from Jason's stack before going into the dressing room. Jason stood around awkwardly, trying not to stare at Charlotte.

Jason didn't usually have a wandering eye. Jenna was everything he'd ever wanted in a partner, and more. The thought of being with someone else never even crossed his mind. But sometimes he ran into women who were just... *distracting*. It wasn't attraction, not really. Even if Jason had been single, he'd have had no desire to ask Charlotte for her number. The woman was certainly beautiful, and Jason felt an almost magnetic pull from her. But the pull wasn't sexual. If anything, it was closer to familial. But that wasn't quite right either.

So if this strange pull wasn't attraction, what exactly was it? As near as he could determine, it felt like jealousy. *But jealous of what*? Jason wondered. He didn't know anything about this woman, other than the fact that she worked retail and had a cute smile. He could almost guarantee that she made less money than Jason did, and while money wasn't the end-all-be-all of happiness, it sure had a way of making happiness more accessible.

He turned away from Charlotte and looked at the dresses he was holding. Again he felt a twinge of green-eyed longing when he beheld the garments. *These will look beautiful on Jenna,* he thought. He pictured the two of them standing together, both dressed in their best outfits. He always felt like a chimpanzee standing next to her.

Jenna always assured him that he was good-looking. And whenever Jason looked in the mirror, he had to admit that he looked, well, fine. Maybe he wasn't some hunky dreamboat, but he had the kind of clean-cut, handsome male face that was all the rage these days. But when he looked at that face, he just didn't connect with the guy staring back at him.

He took another glance at Charlotte. She wasn't looking in his direction, but was writing something in an inventory book. She had a nice face. Not like Jenna's, but still attractive. Jenna had the kind of face Jason looked for in a partner. She had movie-star cheekbones and eyes that could make a monk break his vows. It was the kind of face that nearly every straight man dreamed of taking to bed, and Jason couldn't believe how lucky he was to have ended up with such a goddess.

Charlotte was a bit more plain, more "girl next door," but no one was going to kick her out of bed. There was nothing about her face that made her more remarkable than half the women in the store. Jason couldn't figure out why he couldn't stop looking at her. *I'm being creepy*, he thought.

Just then, Jenna emerged from the changing room in a sexy red dress. If she noticed Jason staring at Charlotte, she didn't react to it. "Thumbs up or down?" she asked, and Jason gave her an enthusiastic thumbs up. She smiled and went back into the dressing room.

Once again, Jason looked down at the dresses he was holding. Just looking at them put him on edge, but he wasn't sure why. He didn't mind waiting for Jenna. He didn't mind giving her his opinion on each dress. The clothes were a bit on the pricey side, but he'd budgeted for this. There was no reason clothes shopping should put him in a bad mood, but it did, every time. He felt that odd twinge of envy every time Jenna came out of the dressing room, rocking a hot new ensemble. Later she would do the same for him, helping him pick out some clothes and offering her opinion whenever he tried something on. But he knew he'd feel jealous then too. He always did.

He held out one of the dresses he was holding, looking it up and down. He pictured how Jenna would look in it. Then for some odd reason, he imagined what Charlotte would look like in it.

There. Right there. The realization slammed into him like a moving van, and the image stunned him for several seconds.

That was the person he expected to see in the mirror. That was the face, that was the dress, that was the body. He wasn't agitated because he hated clothes shopping. He was resentful because Jenna got to wear all the good clothes. She got to look in the mirror and see a face she expected to see. She got to wake up every morning in a body that felt like her own.

There was a mirror outside the dressing room. Jason looked around to see if anyone was watching, and then he held one of the dresses up to his chest. He pictured himself with more feminine facial features, with longer hair and makeup.

"What are you doing, goofball?" Jenna asked, laughing as she stepped out of the dressing room.

"Just curious," Jason said, and gave her current outfit another thumbs up. She smiled and went back in to try on the next dress.

In their four years together, Jason had never given her a thumbs down. There was no dress on Earth ugly enough to diminish her beauty. Jason was jealous again, and now he knew why. And with that realization, his life would never be the same again.

A bright flash of blue lightning flared and crackled through the store, but Jason didn't see it. No one ever saw these flashes, because they happened in the seconds between seconds, in moments out of time. A juncture point had been created, the kind that separates reality into two paths.

Two Jasons left the department store that day. Both drove home with three bags full of new clothes. Both had dinner at a fancy restaurant with Jenna, who kept asking them why they seemed so distracted tonight. Both had trouble sleeping that night, tossing and turning until they finally got up around three AM and did some research on the internet. And that's when their two lives began to diverge.

The first Jason decided to live a lie. He pretended nothing was wrong, and that nothing had changed. He'd played this part for twenty-seven years, and this little revelation didn't mean things suddenly needed to change.

But things changed anyway. Life became a chore. Everything felt harder than it should have - heavier, slower, more annoying. He had trouble controlling his temper. He smiled less, he lost sleep, and he never felt like doing anything fun. He no longer saw Jenna as a goddess, and her flaws began to grate on him.

He'd decided to ignore the problem because he didn't want to drive Jenna away, but she ended up leaving him anyway. She never knew what had changed, but she knew he wasn't the man she'd married. After Jenna left, Jason never felt the urge to date again. It just took too much energy to look nice and talk to people. Even his friends stopped calling him, because he just wasn't fun to be around anymore. Jason always wondered what might have been, but he never took steps to find out.

The second Jason took the hard path. Jenna walked out the day he came out to her. He lost his job and his family stopped talking to him. But he found out who he really was, and he made new friends who accepted him. He became a target for bigots and had trouble finding a new career. It was a life that took a lot of work and required a mountain of sacrifices.

But in the long run, she was much happier.

Meanwhile

ED.02499.12.31

Got to keep running, Tava thought. She didn't risk looking back. She wasn't even sure how many of them there were. It sounded like three, but it might have been more. All human, from the glimpses she'd seen. But she didn't dare take the time for a longer look. If they caught up to her, she'd never make it home alive.

"Get back here, puss," one guy shouted.

"We just want to have a little fun," another yelled.

"Here kitty, kitty, kitty," a third voice taunted.

Tava turned a corner and ducked into a dark alley. With any luck they'd run right past it. But they didn't. She still heard them behind her, a cacophony of pounding feet and puerile threats. The beams from their flashlights bobbed up and down across the walls. Tava didn't have a flashlight, but her night vision was much better than theirs.

The alley turned to the right, and Tava risked a quick glance as she skidded around the corner. Four teens. Two held baseball bats, another had a chain, and the last held a crowbar. What were these guys doing in Little Glaring in the

106

first place? Why couldn't they just stay in their own neighborhood?

She looked straight ahead only to realize the alley was a dead end. *Crap*, she thought. She should have known better than to take a route she'd never used before. Without slowing down, she bounded onto a pile of crates, then leaped up to the roof of a grocery store. The humans weren't nearly as agile, and they lost a good twenty seconds climbing up after her. By then she'd already run to the opposite side of the roof. She stood still for a moment and contemplated jumping over an alley to the next store's roof.

It looked too far, but she was more afraid of her pursuers than she was of falling. She took a few steps back and jumped. She almost made it, slamming her stomach into the ledge of the shop before scrabbling to find purchase. Her claws couldn't quite find a grip on the store's tin-shingled roof, and she slid off into the alley below. Landing on her feet as usual, she ran for cover, looking for anywhere she might hide.

The four teens reached the edge of the roof and looked down at the alley below.

"Where'd she go?" one said. The moon was full, but it was still dark in the alley. The dim streetlights didn't help much.

"She can't have left the alley," said another. There just hadn't been time. One side was another dead end, and the other end emptied into the street. No one was in the streets, so she had to be hiding somewhere.

"She's gotta be in there," a third punk said, pointing his flashlight at a large, wheeled trash bin at the end of the alley.

They climbed over the edge of the roof and dropped down to the ground. Surrounding the bin on three sides, they opened the lid and peered in. Nothing but putrid odors and trash bags. One of the teens boosted another into the bin, and he rooted around with his baseball bat, looking to see if their target was hiding under the garbage. "Come on, guys, I'm gonna need a shower now." He climbed back out and the four reluctantly walked back out of the alley.

Tava watched them leave from her hiding spot underneath the bin. Once they were gone, she waited another twenty minutes before venturing out from safety. Then she took a circuitous route back home, trying to stay out of the moonlight.

Little Glaring was a slum, no question. The government preferred to label it as "a safe haven where immigrants can express their culture without pushing their values on Earth's native citizens." But it wasn't safe, it was hardly a haven, and the inhabitants didn't all come from one culture. While more than half of Little Glaring's population consisted of Galeans, it also hosted its share of Vhelrans, Kalarans, and even a few impoverished humans.

But even those from the same planet didn't necessarily share a culture. Galea was home to both the catlike Meu and the doglike Caniks, and the two couldn't be more different culturally. Little Glaring was a hodge-podge of customs, a melting pot of social dynamics that weren't even remotely reminiscent of its denizens' former planets.

Home was in sight, but Tava had one more stop to make first. She climbed up to another roof, then tiptoed across the eaves until she spotted the balcony she needed. Before dropping down, she paused to look at the sky. The moon was full, but it wasn't alone. A second white orb shone just to the moon's left. It was smaller and not nearly as bright, but it was still an impressive celestial body in its own right.

The IGP's "Earthstation 1" was an absolutely massive piece of tech. The space station housed more than fourteen thousand police officers, and it could deploy them all over the world at a moment's notice. To most of Earth's population, the station was a symbol of peace, protection, and unity. Tava wasn't so sure. Like most of those who lived in Little Glaring, she'd had her share of run-ins with the police. She was no criminal, though sometimes it was hard to stay on the right side of the law and still eat. But in the slums, it barely mattered whether you were guilty. The local cops tended to harass immigrants simply for the crime of not being human.

Supposedly IGP officers weren't like the local police. The IGP served the entire planet, as well as several other planets in the Galactic Nations, so they were trained to accept diversity. Tava had never met an IGP officer, but she imagined that she'd be just as skittish around them as she was around the local cops. Some things were just universal.

Nevertheless, the station was an inspiring sight in the night sky, a monument to modern technology. Tava made a point of looking for it every time it passed overhead.

She dropped down from the roof and tapped on the balcony door. The glass door slid aside, and Tava stepped into the apartment. The room was sparsely furnished, with a bare mattress on the floor and a few folding chairs surrounding a card table. An old television sat on top of a cardboard box in the corner. A Canik closed the door behind her, then followed her to the table. They sat down and got straight to business.

"Twelve credits," the Canik said. He was about human height, but he had gray fur and the face of a bulldog.

"Last week it was ten," Tava said, digging into her pockets.

"Sorry, kitten," he replied. "It's not me, I swear, my supplier raised his rates."

"You're killing me, Crunch," Tava said. She handed over a handful of square silver coins. It was everything she'd made that day, and she'd even skipped dinner.

"I'm not even making a profit," Crunch said. "You're lucky I like you." He palmed the coins and started rooting through a satchel attached to his belt. When his hand finally emerged, he held a small box made of thin cardboard. He handed it to Tava and she tore open the top, revealing the seven vials inside.

"Yeah, well, maybe I should shop around," Tava said. She unzipped her hip pouch and removed a single-use syringe, still in its shrink-wrap. Crunch also kept syringes on hand, but Tava always brought her own. Given the perpetual state of filth in Crunch's apartment, Tava didn't trust that his syringes would be exactly sterile.

"Kitten, you know you're not going to do better than me," Crunch said with a wide, toothy grin.

Tava found Crunch's smile absolutely terrifying. He looked like a cross between a carnivorous frog and a killer potato. She wondered if other Caniks found him attractive. It didn't matter; she didn't visit Crunch for his looks. She filled the syringe from one of the vials, then injected it into her arm.

"Feel better?" Crunch asked.

It should have been a silly question. Meu estrogen wasn't a recreational drug, and it didn't have any immediate effects. It had to build up in the user's system over time, to promote the changes that would eventually grant Tava the body she'd always wished for. And yet, she did feel much better after taking it. It was just a placebo effect, but knowing it was flowing through her veins made her feel better all over. It was like liquid femininity. *Eww*, she admonished herself. *Let's never call it that again.*

"I'll see you next week," Tava said, getting up.

"Hold on, hold on," Crunch said. "It's almost midnight. You sure you don't want to just stay over?" He gestured to his mattress.

"I like you, Crunch," Tava said. "But not that way."

He laughed out loud, a barking guffaw that probably woke the neighbors. "Naw, even if I was into cats, it wouldn't be you. No offense. I just thought we could stay up and play poker or something."

"Sorry, I've got nothing left to bet," Tava said. "Besides, with your prices I'm going to have to work overtime tomorrow."

Crunch gave her an understanding nod. "At least stick around for a bite to eat," he said.

"Now that I'll do," Tava replied, her stomach rumbling.

The Canik disappeared into the kitchen. After a moment he came back with a box of leftover pizza and two beers. "It's not much, but it's what I've got," he said.

"It'll do," Tava said, biting into a cold slice of pizza. She wasn't a fan of pepperoni, but right now it was delicious. Tava and Crunch didn't hang out often, but he was good enough company. It was kind of funny. Back on Galea, they might have been bitter enemies. The Meu and the Caniks had a history of unstable relations. Things were getting better, but violence between the two species was still distressingly common. Both were often targets of discrimination, depending on which Galean continent one happened to be on.

But here on Earth they were equals, or at least, equally spat upon. Humans had a long history of racial injustice, but the moment they met life from other planets, they stopped seeing skin color. Human-on-human prejudice was extremely rare now that the bigots had new targets to focus on. To be fair, the majority of humans embraced alien immigrants, or at least tolerated them. But even the most enlightened humans seemed to turn a blind eye to the inherently racist power structures that defined their laws and government.

Crunch turned on the television while they ate. The reception was poor, but the audio worked just fine. An emergency news report had interrupted regular programming, so Crunch changed the channel. The same report was on every station. "Ugh," Crunch said, and started to turn the television off.

"Hold on," Tava said. She didn't have a television at her place, and something the reporter said had piqued her interest.

Earthstation 1 was in peril. A terrorist threatened to detonate the entire station unless her demands were met. A high-ranking official denied her requests. And then, a few seconds later, the screen went blank. When the feed came back on, a distressed anchorwoman announced that the space station had exploded.

Tava ran to the window and opened it. To the left of the moon she saw a bright ball of light, much brighter than it had been earlier. It only lasted a moment before it faded away and was gone.

"Whoa," Tava said, sitting back down. *All those lives…*

Crunch took a sip of beer, not looking very impressed. "Why the frown, kitten?" he asked. "It's just cops."

Tava slouched her shoulders. Maybe she wasn't a big fan of police, but this was just too much.

ED.02500.01.08

Got to keep running, Tava thought. A week had passed since the disaster, and Little Glaring was in flames. Fleeing residents filled the streets. Tava stumbled as a frightened Vhelran woman bumped into her on the way by. As she passed Crunch's place, she saw a shadow pass by his window.

Surely he's not still in there, Tava thought. But she had to be sure. She climbed up onto the balcony and forced the door open. The room was filled with fire and the floor had partially collapsed. Crunch lay by the door. At first Tava thought one of his legs had been severed, but it had actually gotten stuck in a hole in the floor.

"Little help here?" Crunch asked.

Tava took his hands in hers and pulled. It took a few tries, but she managed to extract him from the hole, and they escaped over the balcony. Tava once again joined the crowd of panicked citizens. Crunch walked with a limp, but Tava stayed with him, letting him hold onto her arm for support.

A blast knocked them to the ground as the windows blew out of a nearby shop. Across the street, another building collapsed. As far as Tava could see, there wasn't a single building in the neighborhood that wasn't on fire. Just a few meters away a manhole cover flew into the air, propelled by an explosion in the sewer.

Tava helped Crunch to his feet and they continued to hobble their way to the edge of town. *Goodbye, Little Glaring*, she thought. She couldn't believe things had gotten so bad, so fast. The riots had started within hours of the space station explosion. There simply weren't enough police to go around. Criminals acted as if they were invincible.

In the distance, Tava could just make out the magnarail

tracks that marked the edge of Little Glaring. Beyond that, downtown Atlanta looked untouched. The lights of police cars flashed in the distance, but they didn't look like they were getting any closer.

Several humans stood in the street, just beyond the rail. They were young, dressed in gang colors, and heavily armed. *Where did they get that hardware?* Tava wondered, eyeing the rapid-fire energy rifles and lava-throwers they wielded. One even had… *Is that a rocket launcher?*

The question was answered as soon as Tava thought it. The young terrorist dropped to one knee and fired into the crowd of fleeing residents. The rocket hit about twenty meters to Tava's left, killing at least fifteen people. Another of the humans fired his rifle into the crowd, and several victims went down. Now the mass of panicked citizens scattered, some going back the way they'd come, even though the fires had spread everywhere.

There was nowhere to run. Buildings crumbled all around them, and flaming ruins blocked every route. These terrorists stood between the survivors and safety, and they threatened to kill anyone who came close.

Tava held Crunch close and looked around for any path to safety. Some of the other survivors tried to rush the armed humans, hoping to overwhelm them with numbers. None of them even got close, as most were burned alive by bursts of artificial lava. Their screams broke Tava's heart.

And then the skies filled with light. Ten or twelve ships appeared overhead. Some went to work spraying the closest buildings with blasts of water. Others dropped down into the crowd, their hatches opening, the occupants beckoning the citizens to safety. Two of the ships shone their spotlights on the assailants. "Drop your weapons immediately!" an amplified voice commanded. The terrorists fled towards downtown, but the ships followed them from above, dropping canisters of gas in front of them.

A shuttle landed in front of Tava, and a Vhelran woman in an IGP uniform helped her and Crunch climb aboard. As the officers ushered more survivors onto the ship, a pair of EMTs strapped Crunch to a gurney and began examining his wounds. "Took ya long enough," Crunch grumbled.

"We're stretched pretty thin," one of the EMTs told him. He was a Meu, like Tava. "I'll be happy to get you an application if you want to help." It was probably meant as sarcasm, but Tava took the words to heart.

Once the ship was filled to capacity, it took off and rushed them to the nearest hospital. Tava stayed by Crunch's side for the entire trip, holding his hand tight.

ED.02500.03.23

Got to keep running, Tava thought. Her feet pounded rhythmically on the concrete as she pushed herself to the limit. She could hear other footsteps gaining on her, but she didn't risk taking a look. Nothing was going to slow her down.

"Ninety-seven seconds," the instructor announced as she crossed the finish line. Three more trainees finished within the next ten seconds, including Crunch. "Good job, Tava," the instructor said. "Fastest in your squad."

Tava hit the showers then returned to her quarters. She lay on the bed for a while, staring at the ceiling, reveling in her good fortune. The IGP training facility had everything Tava could ever need. Free room and board, adequate food, and access to high-quality health care. Sure, she'd get shot at once in a while, but her former life hadn't exactly been safe either. The IGP was even going to help her transition.

The IGP life wasn't for everyone, but as far as Tava was concerned, she'd finally found a real home.

Midnight Snack

A chill wind blew through the cemetery. White petals, fallen from a day's worth of funereal bouquets and wreaths, spiraled on the updrafts like souls ascending to heaven. Heavy footsteps pounded on the dirt as a frightened man ran between the headstones.

I could have turned left, Eric thought. *I could have run across the street and hid in that all-night mini-mart. I could be sipping an iced coffee right now instead of running through a graveyard.*

But he'd never been good at split-second decisions. When he'd seen the shape, there hadn't been time for internal debate. He'd turned into the first open gate he'd seen, a gate that happened to mark the entrance of the Westin Pierce Memorial Cemetery. And that shape – whatever it was – was hot on his heels.

I'm going to feel really stupid if it's just some big, friendly dog, he thought. But it was too big to be a dog. It was closer to Eric's size, maybe larger. And from the glimpses he'd seen, it looked like it had wings.

He wasn't sure how close the thing was, but he was running out of breath and needed somewhere to hide. The graveyard was mostly headstones with a few mausoleums. He considered ducking into a mausoleum, but that thought scared him almost as much as his pursuer.

He kept catching glimpses of the creature. Sometimes to his left, and sometimes on the right. It seemed awfully fast; how had it not caught up to him yet? Was it toying with him?

He crested a hill and caught sight of a tiny chapel down below. It would have to do. Hopefully the doors would be unlocked, but he'd break one of those stained-glass windows if he had to. Now that he had a clear destination, he found the energy for one last burst of speed. He reached the building and pushed on the wooden double doors. They opened easily, and he slammed them shut behind him. Then he locked the doors and looked for a light switch. He couldn't find one – in fact, he couldn't see any light fixtures at all - but the building had a large skylight and the full moon was bright enough to see by.

The chapel was larger than it had looked from the outside, but not by much. It had four rows of pews with an aisle in the middle. Each pew was only wide enough for maybe four people. That meant about eight people per row, which meant the chapel could seat about thirty-two people... *This is important right now*? Eric thought. But that was where his mind always went during a crisis. Somehow math calmed him down.

There were three stained-glass windows on each side of the chapel, depicting the usual religious scenes. The aisle was covered by a red carpet that ended in front of a lectern. There was a coffin-sized shelf on the back wall, though it currently held no coffin. A large cross adorned the wall above the shelf, and smaller crosses decorated the other walls of the chapel.

As far as Eric could see, there were no other exits.

Something pounded on the door. Once, twice, three times, each thump louder than the last. Then it was quiet for a moment. Eric jumped when he heard rapping on the windows. Three taps on one, then another three on the next. *Sixteen, seventeen, eighteen,* Eric counted as it tapped on the final window. Then it was quiet.

Eric listened at the door. He wondered how long he should wait before he left. Half an hour? Two hours? Surely this thing would get bored after a while, and look for easier prey. He started counting the seconds in his head.

There was a deafening crash as the skylight shattered, sending a torrent of glass shards down to the floor below. Eric wasn't standing under the skylight, but he still jumped backward, then crouched with his hands over his head. When he looked up again, he was no longer alone.

A man stood before him, blocking the exit. He wore a formal black suit with crimson accouterments. A long dark cape billowed around his shoulders. His skin was pale and his eyes were blood red. When he smiled, Eric could see that two of his teeth came to sharp points.

"You're... you're a vampire," Eric said.

"And you're an entrée," the vampire replied in an archaic accent.

Eric still crouched on the floor, but now he scooted backward towards the wall. "I don't believe in vampires," he said, more to himself than to the monster he faced.

"Yeah, well, I don't believe they should keep rebooting superhero movies, but guess what opens this Friday," the vampire retorted.

"Y-you're just a guy in a Halloween costume," Eric stammered.

The vampire was in front of him in an instant, on his knees

and nearly nose-to-nose with Eric. "Then I guess there's no reason for you to fight back," he said, opening his mouth unnaturally wide.

"Wait wait wait!" Eric pleaded, making a cross with his fingers.

The vampire backed off, studying Eric with an amused expression. "Yeah, that ought to do it," he said. "I chased you across an entire graveyard and smashed my way into a church, but your crossed fingers drove me off."

"How can you even be in here?" Eric asked, gesturing at the crosses on the wall.

"I'm an atheist," the vampire replied. "Now can I just eat my dinner or do you have more stupid questions?"

"More stupid questions, please," Eric said.

"You're only delaying the inevitable," the vampire said. "You think if you distract me long enough you can run out that door or cannonball out one of those pretty windows, but you'll never make it. I drove you here for a reason. Why do you think the doors were unlocked? I like privacy when I eat."

"Please," Eric said. "I just don't want to die."

"Should've thought of that before you started living," the vampire said. "Everything alive dies eventually, didn't you know?"

"Can't we talk about it first?"

"I suppose I don't have anything better to do," the vampire said, and gestured towards a pew. "Have a seat, meat."

Eric stood and made his way to a pew. He kept stealing glances at the door, but he knew he'd be dead before he made it halfway. He checked the seat for broken glass and carefully sat down.

"So what's on your mind?" the vampire asked, not even

attempting to fake interest.

"What's your name?" Eric asked.

"Francis," the vampire said.

"Francis?" Eric asked incredulously. "*Francis* the Vampire?"

"Well it's not like my parents knew I was going to be a vampire," Francis said.

"Yeah, but still," Eric said. "You could give yourself a new name any time. Something scarier than Francis."

"Names don't really matter to me at this point," Francis said. "I don't really talk to a lot of people. Especially the ones I intend to eat."

"How long have you been a vampire?" Eric asked.

"Two hundred and thirty-six years," Francis replied.

"Why do you dress like that?"

"Like what?" Francis asked, glancing down at his wardrobe.

"Like a regular person trying to look like a vampire," Eric clarified.

"Because you expect it," Francis said. "You recognize it. You fear it. Frightened people make more mistakes. Makes 'em easier to catch."

"Do you… like being a vampire?"

"Oh come *on*," Francis blurted. "Are you about to ask me to turn you? Because the answer's no."

"No, no," Eric said. "Not at all. I can't think of anything I'd like less."

Francis cocked his head. "Really?"

"Do most people ask you to turn them?" Eric asked.

"Well, yes, frankly," Francis said. "If I give them a chance to talk. They've all seen those insipid films – you know, the angsty teen vampire love stories and such. They think it's romantic somehow. Don't you?"

"No," Eric replied. "I don't want to have to kill people to survive. That's just evil."

"Well, there are good vampires," Francis said. "That's one thing the movies got right. You can survive on animal blood, it's just not as tasty. Or you can only kill evil people."

"Evil's subjective," Eric said. "To one person that means only killing murderers. But to others it might mean people who vote differently."

"Oh god, not another philosophy major," Francis muttered. "This is your plan? Keep me talking 'til the sun comes up?" He made a vague gesture toward the skylight.

"No, it's just something I think about," Eric said. "But if you can go after murderers, why did you pick me? I never killed anyone."

"I never said I was one of the good vampires," Francis replied. "But you have piqued my curiosity. Now that you know you don't have to kill people, are you still so afraid of immortality?"

Eric nodded. "I don't want to live forever," he said.

"Well why not?" the vampire asked. "Worried you'll get bored? Afraid you'll miss getting tans? Something about damning your immortal soul?"

"No, it's not any of that," Eric said. "As long as there's books in the world, I can stay entertained. I don't get much sun as it is. And I'm not sure I even believe in souls."

"Then what is it?" Francis asked.

"Look, it's just… I've never told anyone this before," Eric said.

"I'm going to kill you in a minute," Francis said. "Might as well get it off your chest. Dying with untold secrets is just sad."

Eric took a deep breath. He tried to speak, but just couldn't find the words. Then he counted to ten. Counting usually calmed him down.

"Any time," Francis said.

Eric took another deep breath. "I'm transgender."

The vampire nodded, not looking very surprised.

"You know what that means, right? I identify as a woman. I was 'born in the wrong body' or 'assigned male at birth' or whatever they're calling it right now. I don't know what they called it in your time."

"This *is* my time. Just because I'm old doesn't mean I haven't kept up with the world."

"Sorry," Eric said again. "But that's why I'd never want to be immortal. It's hard enough pushing my way through this life as a man. Eternity as a man sounds a lot like hell to me."

Francis frowned. "What's your name?"

"Eric."

"You can be straight with me," Francis said. "What's your real name?"

Eric looked thoughtful. "I was thinking of keeping it simple and going with Erica. But if I'm going to die tonight, I'd like to try out Jess."

"Jess it is," Francis said. "Jess, have you ever noticed how attractive vampires are in the movies? How they're always perfect specimens of the human form? Thin, muscular, never overweight..."

"Are you body-shaming now?" Jess asked.

"I murdered three people this week, but heaven forbid I imply some people are larger than others," Francis said. "Just answer the question."

"I guess so," Jess answered. "But that's Hollywood for you. It's hard to even get an acting job unless you're good-looking. Or funny."

"True as that is, it's also one of the things Hollywood got right," Francis told her.

"You only turn attractive people?" Jess asked. "That seems sort of—"

"Me, I've never turned anyone," Francis interrupted. "But you don't get it. It's not about who gets picked to be a vampire. It's about what vampirism does to you. If you survive the transformation – and not everyone does – your body changes. You become the ideal version of yourself. You become ruggedly handsome or exquisitely beautiful."

"I still wouldn't want to spend eternity as a man, no matter how handsome he was," Jess said.

A flash of exasperation crossed the vampire's face. "I suppose it's my turn to get to the point. Jess, before I became a vampire, I was a woman."

"Wait, what?" Jess asked.

"I spent my entire life hating myself, and I never knew why," Francis said. "It wasn't until my rebirth that I understood who I really was."

Jess couldn't believe her ears. "So you're saying, if you were to turn me, I might become…"

"Only if that's truly who you are on the inside," Francis said. "If you have the soul of a woman, then that's what you'll become. Granted, you don't believe in souls."

"I don't know what I believe anymore," Jess said.

"Then don't worry about it," Francis said. "Perhaps I'm lying. We've already established that I'm evil, so maybe this is just a game I like to play with my food. Maybe I was intrigued by your disinterest in immortality as a male, and I want to see you suffer for an eternity. Maybe this is all just a ruse so you'll let your guard down. If you think I'm going to grant you eternal life in the body you've always wanted, you won't fight back while I drain your blood."

Jess nodded silently.

"Or," Francis continued, "Perhaps I lied about being evil, because I knew you'd only be honest if you thought you were going to die. Maybe I suffered so much in life, that now I seek out fellow spirits so I can grant them relief from their incongruous bodies. Maybe I didn't pick you randomly because you were walking alone at night, but targeted you specifically because I could feel your torment."

Jess looked up and scrutinized the vampire's face. She thought she saw a twinkle in his eyes, like a bright mote of truth peeking out from a pile of twisted lies. But it might have been wishful thinking.

"Or maybe this is all just a dream," Francis concluded. "You're asleep in your bed right now, and none of this really matters. You'll wake up only remembering bits and pieces of our conversation, and it'll all be gone by the time you grab your first cup of coffee. It all comes down to one thing, and one thing only. What do you want to believe?"

"I... I..." Jess began.

Francis held up his hand. "I'm going to give you a choice now. You can walk out that door and I won't chase you. Go home, get a good night's rest, and forget this ever happened. You'll be no worse off than you were this morning."

"You'll just... let me go?" Jess asked.

"If that's what you choose," Francis answered. "Or... you can stay here and learn what's true and what isn't. It's like a game show, isn't it? But the stakes are much higher, no pun intended. Maybe I'll kill you. Maybe you'll get what you've always desired. Or you can walk away, but you'll spend the rest of your life wondering. You might not be able to stand it."

Jess already couldn't stand it. A million thoughts swirled through her mind. She looked around the room, counting the crosses on the walls. Counting often calmed her down, but not this time. She looked down at her hands - her big, mannish hands. *Do I really hate my life so much that I'd risk dying for the chance of eternal happiness?*

"Take your time," Francis told her. "It's a big decision, and there's a few hours yet until dawn. One bite to know the truth. Just one bite... You'll either wake up as a new person, or you won't wake up at all. Or you can tell me to go to hell and walk away with some lovely parting gifts. And by that I mean, a pulse."

If nothing else, this encounter pushed Jess off of the mental fence she'd been straddling. She couldn't go back to living as a man, not after this. She was going to transition. The question was, how? She could still do it the slow way. The hormones, the surgeries, the voice training... and she still might not be satisfied with the results. Or she could risk her life for a shortcut, and live much longer in a more ideal body. She'd never see the sun again, but she would own the night.

After a few more minutes of deliberation, Jess lifted her head and stared back into the vampire's eyes. When she finally spoke, her voice was serious and full of conviction, with more confidence than she'd felt in over two decades.

"Bite me."

True Faces

"You can't say anything anymore!"

I hate Thanksgiving, Gavin thought. *Just don't answer. If nobody responds, maybe he'll drop whatever he's ranting about.* He put his fingers on his temples, preemptively massaging the headache he knew was coming.

"I mean it," Uncle Randy continued. "All those commie socialists have too much power to censor us."

Over on the couch, Cousin Andie looked up from her tablet and cleared her throat.

Don't do it, Gavin thought. All they had to do was wait out the commercial break, and Randy would go back to yelling at the crooked referees. Andie meant well, but she was young and didn't know when someone was a lost cause.

"Usually when someone says that, it's because they want to say something stupid," Andie said.

"Hmmph," Randy said. "The internet tell you to say that, or was it your liberal schoolteachers?"

"Personal experience," Andie said. "What exactly is it you wish you could say?"

Gavin braced himself.

"Well, I'd start by buying a ten-foot high billboard that says the Vesu are all sicko perverts!" Randy's face was turning red.

Gavin relaxed. At least it wasn't the Skeen this time.

"Dad, they're not perverts," Andie said. "They're just different. On their planet, you'd be considered the strange one."

"God made men and women," Randy said, crossing his arms. "I don't know who made these Vesu, but it sure wasn't God. And don't get me started on those Skeen creeps."

"What's wrong with the Skeen?" Andie asked, causing Gavin to cringe.

"Quiet, the game's on," Randy said.

Saved by the bell, Gavin thought. He wasn't sure why he'd even come. Probably just to keep up appearances. If his family ever suspected anything had changed, they might make his life difficult. And that wouldn't end well for anyone.

"You sure I can't talk you into staying for a double shift?" Terry asked.

"You know I'd love to," Lynn said. "I mean it. But I can't be late for my other job."

"The waitressing gig? You'd really rather do that than help me fix a few engines?"

"Sorry," Lynn said. "But the tips are better there."

"They'd have to be," Terry said. "Go on, man, but be back bright and early tomorrow."

"Count on it," Lynn said, and they shook hands. Then Lynn left the garage, drove home, and took a quick shower. He was already running late, but he couldn't show up at

Double Dee's covered in grease.

After he toweled off he stood in front of the mirror and shifted. His hard muscles gave way to graceful curves, his hips widened, his waist narrowed, his bust expanded, and he lost a few inches of height. When the transformation was complete, Lynn gave herself a once over in the mirror, deemed it satisfactory, and put on her waitress uniform.

Gavin was nearly in tears on the drive home. *Why do I let them get to me so much?* he wondered, but he already knew the answer. Even though they weren't technically his family, this body's brain still retained many heartfelt memories of them. Some Skeen remembered more than others. The most fortunate Skeen, in Gavin's opinion, were the ones who had no former memories at all to worry about. It all depended on how the original host died, and the state their brain had been in at the time.

The vast majority of his species remained in the Voidskipper. Thousands of Skeen had managed to board before the evacuation, and they'd hopped to this dimension just ahead of the disaster. There was no going back now. The Entropic Entity would have consumed their planet by now, possibly their entire galaxy. For good or ill, they were stuck here.

The problem was, the Skeen couldn't actually breathe Earth's atmosphere or tolerate the planet's numbing temperatures. On this plane of existence, the only way they could survive outside the Voidskipper was to transfer themselves into human bodies.

Fortunately for the humans, the Skeen had a strong moral code. They refused to take over a body by force. But they also didn't have the ability to inhabit corpses. Nor could they transfer into animals, because a sapient brain was required for them to retain their consciousness.

This left them with a single option. They could take over living human bodies that had been declared brain dead. However, the red tape required for these transfers meant they didn't get a lot of donors. The families had to approve, and the doctors had to confirm that the patient would never wake up. So far only a few hundred of these transfers had taken place, leaving the majority of the surviving Skeen stuck in the Voidskipper.

Gavin had been one of the first to be assigned a human body. He had been transferred into a woman named Beryl, and while he'd appreciated being one of the lucky few to experience this new world, he'd had no love for that body. In his home dimension he'd been male, or at least the Skeen equivalent of male. While Skeen genders were quite different from human ones, he knew he'd have been happier as a male human.

And then the accident happened. Seven months had passed, but Gavin still remembered every detail.

It was mid-April, and Beryl was enjoying a quiet drive on a remote country road. It had been two years since she'd been implanted into this body, and she was still getting used to living among humans. Any time she could find an excuse to be alone, she took it.

As she turned on a sharp curve, she spotted an object in the road. With no time to slow down, her tires thump-thumped over what she belatedly realized was a body. She shrieked and pulled to a stop as soon as she could. Beryl jumped out of the car and examined the figure, barely able to breathe. It was human, male... and fake. Someone had placed a mannequin in the middle of the road. *Maybe it fell off a truck,* she thought.

She was about to return to the car when something grabbed her from behind and stuck something in her neck. Then she blacked out.

The memory still made Gavin furious. Humans were so cruel to each other, even when there wasn't much to gain. It made sense that they fought over resources, as those were necessary for survival. But Beryl's kidnapper had only wanted her for sick pleasure. And to make her think she'd run over someone... The nature of the trap ensured that the victim would be someone with empathy, as opposed to the callous kind of humans who would just drive off after running over a body. The kidnapper had wanted someone kind, because soft hearts were more fun to break.

Beryl had woken up strapped to a table, where she'd endured all manner of indignities and sexual torture. Those memories were thankfully just a blur now. But what happened next would stick with Gavin forever.

"Why are you doing this?" Beryl whimpered. She no longer struggled against her bonds, as her strength was long gone.

The man loomed over her, holding her head still. "So you won't blink," he said, forcing her eyelids open with a set of calipers. It wasn't what Beryl had meant by her question, but he continued anyway. "I want to see the spark fade at the moment of death. If you close your eyes, it just looks like you went to sleep. But I want to stare into your eyes and witness the exact moment your mind slips away."

"Wait," Beryl said. "I don't—"

But then he stabbed her. Beryl could feel her life fading. Even though it wasn't her real body, she would still die as it died unless she acted fast. The kidnapper leaned over her, staring hard, their noses nearly touching. Beryl weakly turned her head to the side, and the kidnapper grabbed her head once again. That bit of skin contact was all she needed.

It was against her core beliefs and it violated Skeen law, but she had no choice. With her life at stake, Beryl transferred her consciousness into the kidnapper's head. The room spun until she found herself looking into her own face.

She was now the killer. As his victim breathed her last breath, the man took a few steps back and studied his surroundings. A battle played out inside his mind, as the Skeen's consciousness edged out the human's. It only took a few moments – the Skeen knew their way around a brain, and had no trouble smothering an existing consciousness when it was necessary for their own survival. If the Skeen had wanted to take over Earth by force, they could have. The humans were lucky they had such a strong moral code.

Disgusted by the torture chamber, the man found a set of stairs and took them to the main floor of the house. He found a bathroom and washed his hands thoroughly. He still felt unclean, so he took a shower and put on some fresh clothes.

It still wasn't enough. This human was disgusting, and Beryl – no, not Beryl, he would never be Beryl again – wondered how such people even came to be. There were no serial killers among the Skeen. The very concept was like something out of bad fiction.

He searched the pants he'd removed and found his host's

wallet. "Gavin Jameson," he said, reading the license out loud. *I guess that's my name now*, he thought. *So where do I go from here?*

It had now been seven months since he'd taken over Gavin's life. He'd had no trouble taking over his host's job. Even though he'd had to choke out Gavin's consciousness, it had still been a healthy brain, so he'd still been able to access all the memories stored within. The worst part had been covering up Beryl's murder. Gavin would have much preferred to turn the monster over to the authorities, but since that version of Gavin was now dead, there was no point in going to jail to serve another man's sentence.

No one was looking for Beryl, so Gavin was in the clear. Using Beryl's accounts, Gavin sent out several e-mails explaining that she was moving overseas. Unfortunately, a tour of Gavin's memories revealed that Beryl hadn't been his first victim, so there was no telling if any of those would be discovered someday. He could remember one victim in particular who had gotten away, but hopefully they'd never run into each other.

Over the past few months, a few of Gavin's coworkers had commented on his personality changes. It was all positive feedback, however, and he got the impression that old Gavin had been a bit antisocial. He was a little worried that people would find the changes suspicious, but that was just paranoia. No one was going to jump from "Gavin's more outgoing" to "Gavin's been possessed by a Skeen."

Despite the worry that he'd be discovered, Gavin was happier than he'd ever been as Beryl. He finally felt like himself, or at least as close to himself as he could feel while wearing human skin. He made good money, he had a nice house - except maybe the basement - and he was really happy to be male again.

Still, sometimes it hit him that he was living a lie. He slept fitfully some nights, hounded by the knowledge that he'd had to kill to get this life. He'd violated Skeen ethics by taking over a living brain. The fact that it had been self-defense didn't make him feel any better. To this day he wondered if he'd have been better off just giving up the ghost.

And then he remembered he'd stopped a serial killer. His act had probably saved future victims. In a way, he was a hero, though no one would ever know. He'd made sure of that. He could just imagine trying to come clean to the cops. "Yes, Gavin killed several women, but I'm not really Gavin, I'm a Skeen." If the police didn't believe him, he'd get the chair. If the police did believe him, he'd be returned to the Voidskipper and punished for performing an unauthorized mind transfer. The extenuating circumstances wouldn't matter to them, as the Skeen bent over backwards to keep the humans from seeing them as the enemy.

No matter how Gavin looked at it, he was stuck playing the role and covering up his former host's past deeds.

As Gavin turned the next corner, his car shuddered for a moment before the "check engine" light came on. "Damn," he muttered, hoping he'd be able to make it home.

Lynn's waitressing shift ended and she went home. A human would have gone straight to bed, but the Vesu only required about two hours of sleep a night, so she stayed up for a while. She changed into something more comfortable - first her form, then her clothing. When she emerged from her bedroom, she was still a woman, but a much less buxom one. This shape felt comfier for relaxing around the house in her pajamas.

Some nights she lounged as a man, and other nights she felt more comfortable as a woman. It wasn't that she didn't have a preference; it was closer to say that she strongly identified with both genders. This was typical of her species, though there were exceptions. Lynn's mother had almost always presented herself as female.

The Vesu had been on Earth for a decade, making them the first off-world beings to officially land on Earth, beating out the Skeen by a good six years. They'd arrived on a generational spaceship that had launched more than ten thousand years earlier. The ship had been on its last legs, and once they'd landed, they'd allowed the Earth's government to dismantle the vessel for research purposes.

In exchange, the government granted them places to live on Earth. This had upset a lot of humans at the time, but it was unlikely that the Vesu would be leaving Earth again.

Lynn cracked open a book and tried reading, but she couldn't get into it. She never talked about books at work, regardless of which job she was working. Her coworkers just weren't into literature. Though it was probably pushing it to refer to her current read as 'literature.' It was a steamy romance novel about a human who fell in love with a shapeshifting alien. Even if her coworkers cared, she would have been too embarrassed to admit that she was into that kind of story.

When she tried to get close to people, they always backed off. Maybe they just didn't trust aliens, but she wasn't about to start lying about that. She didn't think that was the issue anyway. They always seemed fine with the alien thing, but cringed when they saw her eclectic range of hobbies. Her apartment looked like two people lived there, with one wall devoted to collectible dolls, while another was decorated with sports memorabilia. How many people out there were into both car engines and romance novels? How many cried at action movies and laughed at dramas?

She wished she had someone to talk to. To *really* talk to. Lover, friend, she didn't care. She just wanted a connection. Someone she could trust. Someone who she could let inside her head without worrying that they'd judge her.

She just didn't connect with humans very well. She was friendly with her coworkers, but it was an artificial kind of friendliness with no emotional depth. Her own people were scattered across the globe, and she'd yet to encounter one in her city. She wanted a friend who was similar enough to relate to, but they also needed to be different enough that they could spend the rest of their lives learning about each other.

Did such a person even exist?

"So what seems to be the trouble?" The mechanic had white hair and a weathered face, but his smile was almost childlike. He wore a grease-covered jumpsuit with a name patch that said "Terry."

Gavin shrugged. "The idiot light's on, and the engine shudders now and then."

"Wait inside and I'll take a look," Terry said.

Gavin got out, handed Terry the keys, and went into the little waiting room. Even though the room smelled like bleach, it still gave off an unclean vibe, as if a deadly accident had occurred there and the owners had spent all week covering it up. Gavin was oddly reminded of his basement, a room that would never be comfortable to him no matter how many gallons of disinfectant he used.

He sat in a surprisingly comfortable chair with a rusty frame. There were no other customers in the room. A soap opera played on a wall-mounted television, but the sound was muted. The subtitles were on, but they seemed to be about five seconds behind whatever happened on the screen.

Gavin liked soap operas, even though some humans considered them feminine. He also enjoyed romantic movies that some men dismissed as "chick flicks." He didn't feel it made him any less of a man. That sort of gender division was a human value, and it was meaningless to the Skeen.

And yet, his gender was still very important to him. He'd tried to examine why, but the reasons didn't really matter. He was who he was, and he was a man right down to his soul.

Next to Gavin's chair was a small table with a stack of magazines on it. Most were about cars, and all of them were at least two years old. Gavin left the stack alone and stared at his phone instead. He was halfway through an article about the upcoming election when a door opened.

"Gavin Jameson?" a man asked, and Gavin looked up from his phone. This mechanic was younger and had features so perfect he almost looked like a mannequin brought to life. He wore a jumpsuit similar to Terry's, only this man's patch identified him as "Lynn." His eyes were glued to the clipboard he carried.

"That's me," Gavin said, standing.

"We've looked your car over, and..." Lynn looked up from his clipboard and trailed off. As he locked eyes with Gavin, his expression changed from friendly to confused to horrified. "You," he said.

Gavin didn't recognize this man at all, but that expression told him everything he needed to know. This man *knew*. How much he knew, Gavin wasn't sure. But it was enough.

"I'm not him..." Gavin stammered, but he knew that wouldn't convince him.

"Excuse me," Lynn said, turning away. Then he dropped the clipboard and ran.

I've got to get to a phone, Lynn thought. His own phone was in his work locker, where he wouldn't accidentally damage it while wrestling with a stubborn lug nut. But he'd run right past the lockers on his way out the back door. He could hear that customer behind him, his footfalls echoing off the concrete.

"Stop! It's okay!" came Gavin's voice.

Why am I running? I can probably take him, Lynn thought. But when dealing with psychopaths, it wasn't about who was stronger. It was about who was willing to go farther. A man like Gavin would never hold back, would never pull a punch, and would be unpredictable from the first hit to the last. *And of course, he might be armed*, Lynn thought.

Lynn ducked behind a parked car and dropped to the ground. Then he rolled under the car and waited for his pursuer to run past. As the man's footsteps sounded by the car, Lynn rolled back out from under and got to her feet. Now presenting as female, she crept behind a line of cars as the man came to a halt somewhere to her left.

"I'm not who you think I am!" Gavin called.

Yeah, right, Lynn thought. *That's just what a psycho killer would say.* She stayed hidden until she reached the last car in the parking lot, then waited. She peeked through the car's windows, but the customer was nowhere to be seen. She stayed perfectly still, waiting to hear his heavy footsteps again.

Lynn frowned. Was it safer to run or to stay hidden? Should she go back to the auto shop or run across the street? If she ran, would he give chase? She'd changed shape, but she still wore the mechanic coveralls with the "Lynn" patch. She considered slipping out of the coveralls.

"There you are," Gavin said, stepping around the car's side. Then he looked confused for a moment before he understood. "You're a shapeshift—" was all he got out before Lynn tackled him.

"You won't take me again," Lynn growled, sitting on his chest with her hands around his neck. She expected Gavin to fight back, but all he did was try to wrestle her hands away.

"That… wasn't… me…" he said between gasps. Then he reached forward and touched her forehead.

For just a second, Lynn felt a presence inside her mind. Her hands involuntarily released her captive, and she heard Gavin's voice echo through her head. "See? I'm an alien too," he said, and then he left as abruptly as he'd come.

Gavin pulled his hand away from her forehead. "The man who attacked you is dead," he said. "I'm a Skeen. I'm a completely different person now, and I mean you no harm."

"That doesn't mean you weren't already a Skeen when I was attacked," Lynn said, breathing heavily. She shifted her weight and got to her feet. "Maybe I should call the Bureau of Extraterrestrial Affairs and see when your transfer took place."

"Please don't," Gavin said, giving her a pleading look.

"If you don't want me to, that's all the more reason I should," Lynn replied.

"Look, there's…" Gavin said, then paused and took a deep breath. "I'm not a killer, I swear I'm not. But I'll still get in trouble if you make that call."

Lynn was about to turn around and run back to the auto shop, but something about the look on Gavin's face made her reconsider. She had vivid memories of him attacking her a few years earlier, but this man didn't look capable of that kind of violence. Granted, psycho killers were often experts at blending in and fooling the public, but like most of her species, Lynn was unusually adept at reading faces. When your friends wore new faces on a daily basis, you learned how to recognize them by body language and facial expressions. And while this man wore the same face as the one who'd once attacked her, in no other way did he remind her of the attacker.

Lynn relaxed. "The Bureau doesn't know you took over his body, do they?" she asked.

"It's a long story," Gavin said.

"I've got a lunch break coming up," Lynn said.

"I'll buy," Gavin offered.

"So what do you really look like?" Lynn asked, studying Gavin from across the table. They sat in a booth at a burger joint across the street from the auto shop.

"Tiny pinpricks of light," Gavin answered. "Microscopic, actually. The Voidskipper – the ship we used to get here – it's only about the size of a bowling ball. You've heard the story, right?"

"A couple of times," Lynn said. "Your world was burning so you hopped to this one, and your ship appeared in the living room of an elderly couple in Minnesota. Freaked them out. If I remember correctly, one of them chased your ship with a baseball bat before he collapsed from a heart attack."

"The media exaggerated that story," Gavin said, taking a sip of his soda. "He just got winded. Didn't even have to go to the hospital."

"So in your own dimension, did you ride around in other bodies there, too?" Lynn asked. "Or did you just fly around as motes of light?"

"Both," Gavin said. "We had a symbiotic relationship with another species. They were a bit like... I guess the closest creatures here would be raccoons, maybe if you crossed one with a shaved lemur. They had humanlike brains, but they were struck with dementia just a few years after adulthood. That's when we'd take over their bodies. Without us in their minds, they didn't even know how to feed themselves."

"What happened to your world?" Lynn asked.

"Stupidity," Gavin said. "We put the wrong people in charge, and let them lead us into war over resources that would have been plentiful if not for the scarcity caused by the war itself. Then a world-devouring creature arrived - we call it the Entropic Entity - and we had no resources left to fight it."

"I see humans making those same mistakes," Lynn said.

Gavin nodded. "We all took a vow when we came here. No more wars. No killing, no fighting. Hopefully we can teach the humans a better way. But we won't force them. We're guests in this universe, and our hosts get to set the rules."

"But you killed Gavin," Lynn said softly, after looking around to make sure she wouldn't be overheard.

"That was self-defense," Gavin said, then told her the whole story.

"You did what you had to," Lynn said when he was done. She placed her hand on his and looked into his eyes. "You did nothing wrong," she said.

"My people won't see it that way," Gavin said. "They're paranoid about breaking the rules. They're worried that any transgression will turn the Bureau against us and get us evicted from this planet."

"But he killed your old body," Lynn said. "What would they expect you to do?"

"Probably die," Gavin replied. "Better for one of us to perish than for our entire species to suffer." They ate in silence for a few minutes.

Lynn swallowed the last of her veggie burger and took a long sip of water. "I'll keep your secret," she said finally.

"I appreciate it," Gavin said. "But enough about me. What do you look like when you're not copying humans?"

"It doesn't work that way," Lynn said. "It's not like I have to concentrate to maintain my current form. I'm not going to revert into some gray blobby thing when I die. We start out with worm-like bodies, but calling that our 'natural form' is like saying a butterfly's natural form is a caterpillar."

"But what did the Vesu look like before they had humans to copy?" Gavin asked.

"Like, right before we reached Earth?" Lynn asked. "The closest Earth animal I can think of is a crab, but mammalian. But even that wasn't always our most common form. Trends changed from generation to generation, or even family to family. We left our home planet more than ten thousand Earth years ago, and the Vesu back then would be unrecognizable to the Vesu today."

"Do you like being in human form?" Gavin asked.

"It's not bad," Lynn replied. "Versatile, not too bulky.

Manageable number of limbs, and I've always been a fan of opposable thumbs." She held both thumbs up as a demonstration, as well as to show her approval of her human form. "Feels weird walking around in crowds though, where everybody's always relatively the same shape."

"Ah," Gavin said. "I can relate. Walking around humans sometimes feels like being at a costume party."

"Reminds me of a book I'm reading," Lynn said, then quickly shut up. *Don't ask, don't ask, don't ask,* she thought.

Gavin squinted, then his face brightened. "Wait… is it called 'Moon-Crossed Lovers?'"

"You've read it?" Lynn asked, genuinely surprised.

He gave an embarrassed smile. "I loved that book. I mean, yeah, I know, it's not exactly —"

"…literature," they said together, and they both laughed.

Gavin frowned. "The ending is so—"

"Don't spoil it!" Lynn said, holding up her hand.

"Oh, sorry," Gavin said, and decided to change the subject. "When it comes to humans, do you prefer being male or female?" he asked.

"It depends on my mood," she answered.

"So you have no preference?"

"Oh, I have a preference," Lynn clarified. "Sometimes it's a very strong preference. But that preference changes from day to day, sometimes from hour to hour. And some days I just don't care. What about you?"

"I was male before," Gavin said. "I know, 'How can a speck of light be male or female,' but we do have genders. When I first got placed into a human body, it was…" He trailed off when he realized Lynn was no longer listening. Her eyes were on the front door, beyond which a utility truck barreled toward the restaurant at an alarming speed.

"Truck!" Lynn shouted, her voice deep and booming despite her current form.

The other customers barely had time to look up before the vehicle crashed through the glass. The whole building shook and the ceiling collapsed. High-pitched screams mixed with the deafening sounds of crunching metal and shattering glass. In a moment that seemed both instantaneous and bordering on eternity, a glass shard spun through the air like a shuriken in an inexorable path toward Gavin's chest.

Lynn grabbed him by the thigh and pulled him under the table. The rest of the ceiling came crashing down around them, filling the air with dust and smoke. A fire alarm joined the maddening cacophony of groaning metal and cries for help.

"Gavin?" Lynn cried between coughs. It was the middle of the day, but it might as well have been midnight. She felt around herself, pushing rubble aside until she once again found Gavin's thigh. "Gavin!" she shouted again, but he still didn't answer. She moved her hand up his body, working her way up to his face so she could see if he was breathing. She'd reached his neck when she found the shard of glass.

Even if Gavin was still alive, he'd be long gone by the time anyone came for them. Lynn wasn't even sure if she should remove the shard from his neck to apply a tourniquet, or if doing so would cause him to die faster. *There's nothing I can do,* Lynn thought.

Or was there? She traced his body until she found his hand, and she pulled it to her forehead. "Gavin," she said. "If you can hear me, move into my mind until we get out of here." There was no response. Five seconds went by. Ten. Lynn was about to give up when she felt a weird tingle in her mind.

I'm here, Gavin's voice said.

Lynn dropped his hand and then began to unbury herself. She changed back into her male form, and while changing shape didn't actually make him any stronger, the extra bulk helped him push his way out of the detritus. Following the nearest cries, he started to search for other survivors.

"Disaster struck today when a utility vehicle collided with the EveryBurger restaurant on West End Avenue, an accident which caused four deaths and left eight severely injured. It all started when a cherry-picker crew left the keys in their truck while they went to lunch. A fourteen-year-old boy entered the cab and started the engine, then quickly lost control of the vehicle. Our news crew will bring you up-to-the-minute updates as we continue to investigate this incident."

Terry turned off the television and looked Lynn over. "Wow," he said. "I'm surprised you're not in the hospital yourself."

Lynn wore a few bandages but otherwise he looked fine. "We heal pretty fast," he said.

"Even so, you sure you don't want to take a few days off?" Terry asked, scratching his head. "I'd say you've earned a rest."

"No sir," Lynn said. "I'd like to jump right back into things if that's okay."

"Your choice," Terry said, and shrugged.

Lynn gave him a reassuring smile and headed back to the garage. Gavin's car still sat in the bay with the hood open. Lynn grabbed a lug wrench out of his tool belt and bent over the engine. *Now, this is how you remove a carburetor,* he thought.

Can I try this one? Gavin's voice replied.

Sure, why not, Lynn thought, relinquishing his control of their hands.

Gavin took over and began loosening a few bolts, while Lynn gave him instructions. Between the two of them, they had Gavin's car running smoothly by the end of the day.

A human pair would have felt strange cohabitating in a single body, but to Lynn and Gavin, it felt oddly normal. Gavin was already used to thinking of organic bodies as a bit like vehicles, so this was like having a copilot. Lynn had been lonely for a while now, and now he had someone to talk to all the time, someone just as perplexed by the human world as he was.

They would probably look into finding Gavin a new body eventually, but for now, they were content to enjoy each other's company.

Reality Check

I can hold it 'til I get home, Moira thought, putting more items in her shopping cart. The store wasn't very crowded, so she doubted there would be much of a line at the register. She'd be out in ten minutes at the most, then another fifteen minutes to home. That wasn't even half an hour.

Half an hour? her bladder screamed at her. *I'll give you ten minutes, take it or leave it. After that, you can explain the puddle in aisle three.*

Oh, come on, Moira thought. *It's not like we had that much to drink. A small diet soda at lunch, a few sips from the water fountain on the way in. You're being dramatic.*

It's those pills you take, her bladder replied. *They make me jumpy.*

Those pills make me feel like who I really am, Moria thought. *Deal with it; they're not going away.*

Nine minutes and counting, her bladder teased.

"Fine," Moira mumbled. There were two sets of restrooms in the store. The ones up front were closer, but the ones in the back didn't get as much use, so she headed for the back. She abandoned her cart, hoping she'd get back before an employee started putting her items away.

She hesitated when reached the entrance to the restrooms. She'd been living as a woman for more than a year, but public restrooms still made her nervous. The transphobes had turned one of the most basic biological functions into a political act, and the thought of a confrontation terrified her.

She'd looked at herself in the rearview mirror before getting out of the car earlier. She was having a good makeup day. She wasn't exactly a supermodel, but there was no reason to think she'd get clocked. By her estimation, she looked like an ordinary, everyday, average, plain, cis woman.

Or is it wishful thinking? she wondered. Those nagging doubts always set in at the worst possible moments. But she felt it was a valid question. When she looked at herself in the mirror, did she really see herself as she looked, or did she just see the progress she'd made? She pulled a makeup compact out of her purse and tried her hardest to look at herself objectively.

Six minutes, her bladder threatened.

She obviously couldn't go into the men's room, not dressed like this. Especially in this part of the country, where bigotry was rampant and transphobia was the norm. A couple of months earlier she'd been harassed just for carrying a purse with a rainbow on it.

So it wasn't actually a choice between the women's and men's. It was a choice between the women's and walking out of the store immediately, then pissing herself on the drive home.

I'll do it, too, her bladder taunted.

Fine, she thought. *But if someone screams at us, you do the talking*. Steeling her nerves, Moira walked into the women's room.

On the opposite side of the store, Ennie's plan was in motion. He was dressed like a woman from head to toe, though not very convincingly. He'd never tried to perfect his look the way trans women did. He didn't live as a woman day-to-day. He dressed up for one reason and one reason only, and it was one of the sickest reasons imaginable. And yet somehow no one stopped him. Not a single customer or employee so much as turned their head as he passed by the registers and slipped into the women's room.

There was one other woman in the restroom as Moira entered. The lady stood at the sinks, using the mirror to touch up her makeup. She gave Moira an indifferent glance as she entered, then went back to her makeup.

Moira didn't even look at her, she just rushed into one of the stalls, slammed the door, lifted her skirt, and pulled down her underwear. *Finally*, her bladder remarked as relief came.

"Sounds like you made it just in time," a voice said. It had to be the other customer, the woman at the sinks.

It was the first time a stranger had spoken to Moira through a restroom door. *I should say something*, she thought. It would be weird to just ignore her. But she couldn't think of a reply that wouldn't just make it weirder.

"Too much coffee," Moira finally said, and forced a giggle. *Too much!* she thought, cringing at what she'd said. She was suddenly very conscious of her voice. Did it sound too masculine? Did it sound too feminine, like a creepy man trying too hard? She'd been training her voice for years, and even strangers on the phone assumed she was a woman without any prompting. But right this minute she was convinced she was a baritone attempting falsetto.

"Been there," the woman said with a laugh. Then she left the restroom without another word.

Ennie passed two women on his way into the stall. Neither even spared him a look, despite his off-center wig and ragged facial hair. He made sure to look under each stall door before selecting one. *Jackpot,* he thought. He picked a door right between two occupied stalls. He'd be able to listen to them pee in stereo.

He sat down on the toilet, listening closely to the sounds of urination. It didn't sound any different than whenever he pissed, but for some reason knowing it came from women made it erotic.

He lifted his skirt and grabbed himself, stroking hard to the sounds of splashing water. But it wasn't enough. He had to know what these women looked like. He got down on his knees and looked under the wall to his left. The woman just sat there, oblivious to his leering face.

Of course he couldn't see anything scandalous from this angle, just her naked thighs. Still, knowing that her panties were down sent shivers up his spine.

He scooted over to the stall on the right. Somehow this woman didn't see him either. She wasn't quite as fit as the other woman, but Ennie didn't care about looks. It was what was inside that counted, and by that he meant urine.

He slid back into his stall. One of the women started making flatulence noises. *Oh yes,* he thought. There was nothing more arousing than hearing a woman take a shit.

Ennie thought back to all the women he'd sexually assaulted in toilets just like this one. It was a challenge, for sure. Restrooms got more foot traffic than pretty much any other area in the store. There had to be hundreds of safer places to attack a woman. Plus the mechanics of it were difficult. The stalls were too small, and the floors were too sticky. But for some reason, restrooms were the only place that really did it for him.

He continued to stroke until he climaxed, then cleaned himself up and left. He was about to return to his car when he remembered there was another restroom at the back of the store. *Ready to go again so soon?* he asked himself.

Yes, please, his penis answered, and he made a beeline for the far end of the store.

Moira flushed and pulled up her underwear. She peeked out of the stall, making sure no one else had come in, even though she knew she would have heard them. She was tempted to rush out the door without washing her hands, but she'd been raised better than that.

As she stood at the sink, scrubbing vigorously, the door opened. Over the last few years, Moira had helped a several trans women try out makeup for the first time. She'd seen a lot of cosmetic disasters, usually by first-timers who overdid it with their lipstick and blush.

But this woman - if she even identified as a woman - was something else. She looked like a cis man who'd decided to dress as a woman for Halloween, but had only been given five minutes to assemble a costume. Her makeup would have looked garish on a clown, and her wig didn't cover all of her original hair. And Moira didn't want to judge, but she'd never seen so much facial hair on a woman.

"Get on the floor," the newcomer said with a lewd smile.

Moira now knew for sure he was a cis man. Why he was dressed as a woman, she didn't know. It certainly couldn't have helped him gain access to this restroom. But the good news was, she didn't find him the least bit intimidating.

"Nah," Moira said.

The man marched forward until he was almost nose-to-nose with Moira. "I said, get on the floor," he growled.

Moira took a deep breath, then blew into his face. He fell apart, breaking up into pieces of straw that gusted across the restroom.

After all, he'd never actually existed in the first place.

Quarantine

"Why do people fit into boxes?" Gene asked.

"Like coffins?" Emma asked, sounding confused. They were working out in their home gym, with Emma on the bike and Gene on the treadmill.

"No, I mean like... You're anti-choice," Gene said. "Which immediately tells me you're also going to be anti-welfare and anti-LGBT. If they were to hold a vote tomorrow on whether 'In God We Trust' should remain on our money, I wouldn't even have to ask how you were going to vote. Why does the one always lead to the others?"

Emma scowled. "Okay, first off, I'm not 'anti-choice,' I'm pro-life," she said.

"Really?" Gene asked. "All life? Even bugs? Death row inmates? Poor people?"

"No, the movement focuses on the lives of unborn babies," Emma said carefully.

"Then why not 'pro-birth' or something?" Gene asked. "They only picked the name 'pro-life' to give it some emotional 'oomph.'"

"Why 'pro-choice' then?" Emma countered. "Are you for

all choices? The choice to rob banks? The choice to shoot random people in the street?"

"You know which choice we're talking about," Gene said, picking up the pace. He was starting to run out of breath but his rising temper kept him going.

"And you know which lives we're talking about," Emma said. "Organizations have names. They're not always one hundred percent literal."

Gene shook his head. "But that's not even what I wanted to ask. Why is it that - for example - if someone gives me a 'guns don't kill people' speech, I immediately know how they feel about climate change as well?"

"That's probably not the best example to make your point," Emma said. "Not these days."

"Fair," Gene said. He stepped off the treadmill and looked out the window. Hundreds of beady eyes stared back at him.

Hardly anyone was in favor of gun restrictions anymore. Not since the penguins came.

Emma and Jean had known each other all their lives. They met as children and instantly became best friends. They might as well have been sisters, and everyone said so. They grew apart during high school, as Jean became disillusioned with religion and Emma doubled down on her beliefs. But they always stayed friendly with each other, and had no trouble overlooking their political differences. They were seniors in college when mortgage rates soared to an all-time high, and they decided to buy a house together. Their bedrooms were on opposite sides of the house, so they hardly ever got on each other's nerves.

And then Jean came out as transgender. He changed his

name to Gene, saw a therapist weekly, and went on hormone treatments. Emma watched the transition with a scornful eye. To her, it wasn't just a sinful lifestyle choice. It was a betrayal. They'd sworn an oath as kids – they'd promised that they'd always be sisters. It didn't matter if they argued or said hurtful things or even slept with each other's boyfriends. With sisters, nothing was beyond forgiveness.

Except for this. Gene's transition rendered the sister pact null and void. After all, a man could never be a sister.

But they continued to live together, mostly because neither of them could afford to move. Sometimes they fought, other times they avoided each other in a silent truce, and sometimes they bickered like an old married couple.

Until one day when some bio-lab in Wyoming successfully combined the DNA of a penguin with a piranha. No one was quite sure what they'd been trying to accomplish. The lab's entire staff was wiped out by the initial outbreak, and no one had successfully recovered any of their data. These new creatures looked like penguins but they were much deadlier. They could survive anywhere on Earth, from the deserts to the Arctic, on land or underwater.

The world's governments were working on the problem. At least, that's what they kept promising their citizens, over and over. In the meantime, people installed high barriers around their houses, and penguins roamed the streets looking for easy prey. Almost everyone worked from home now, having supplies delivered by drone, and using taxi-drones if they absolutely needed to go anywhere else.

Whether they liked it or not, Emma and Gene were stuck with each other.

"Drone for you, Jean," Emma said, coming back from the window with a package.

"Gene," he corrected as he took the box.

"That's exactly what I said," Emma replied.

"Yeah, but you said it with a J instead of a G," Gene said. "I can tell."

"Whatever," Emma said, rolling her eyes. "What did you get?"

"Just my monthly T pills," Gene said, opening the box of hormone supplements.

"Ugh, I should have thrown it to the penguins," Emma groaned. "You're never even around other people anymore. What difference does it make if you take the pills?"

"It makes me feel like me," Gene replied.

"We had the same childhood. We did everything together," Emma said. "How did you end up like this?"

"Remember when we were kids, how much we loved playing soldiers?"

"We were tomboys," Emma said.

"*You* were a tomboy," Gene said. "I was a boy in denial."

"I will never believe that."

Gene scoffed. "You don't have to believe it, you just have to stop giving me crap about it."

"So make me understand," Emma said. "Convince me. I've got nowhere else to be, I might as well listen."

"We've had this conversation a dozen times," Gene said. "Look... surely you have an ideal picture of yourself in your head? Maybe you're one of the few who don't, but most people look in the mirror at some point in their lives and think, 'I wish I was thinner.' ...Or more muscular, or taller, or maybe they want less acne or a smaller nose."

"I mean, yeah, I've had days like that," Emma admitted.

"So somewhere in your mind, you have a mental image of the perfect version of you. The person you would be if french fries weren't fattening and chewing them burned lots of calories."

"I guess…"

"Well, in my mind, that ideal self is a man," Gene explained. "I didn't choose for that image to be there, it just is."

"So that's all it is?" Emma asked. "A picture in your head you can't live up to?"

"Of course not. If that's all it was, do you think I'd go to all this trouble? There's hundreds of reasons, and the signs have been there all my life."

"I was right there with you, and I never saw any signs," Emma said.

"Because every time I acted too boyish, you made fun of me," Gene said. "Especially when we hit our teens. I quickly learned to hide it. Sometimes I even overcompensated."

"So now you're blaming *me* for your psychosis?" Emma asked.

"No," Gene said. "Just… let's just drop it, okay?"

Emma snorted in an "I just won the argument" sort of way and walked off.

Gene shook his head. Emma would never get it. She would always see Gene as a deluded fool, brainwashed by modern "woke culture." She would fight Gene at every turn, and the worst part was, she would do it thinking she was being helpful. In Emma's mind, Gene was a soul in need of saving, and it was her duty to keep him from making a terrible mistake.

And it was infuriating.

I wish I didn't have to do this, Gene thought as he loaded up the YuFly app and stepped out onto the balcony. Below him, beyond the fence, hundreds of penguins eyed him hungrily. They filled the streets at this time of day, when taxi-drone traffic was at its heaviest. It looked like a scene from a zombie movie, if the zombies all wore tuxedoes and were only three feet tall.

It only took three minutes for the taxi-drone to arrive. A single hanging chair, suspended by four well-protected rotors, flew towards the house and came to a hovering stop next to the balcony. Gene carefully climbed over the railing and into the chair, then strapped himself in. Then he tapped a green button marked "go" near the armrest, and he was on his way. He zoomed over streets and houses, swinging precariously like some ride at the fair. It might have been fun if it wasn't so dangerous.

People rarely left their houses these days. They worked online, they ordered food and supplies by drone, and they postponed appointments in the hopes that the government would fix the penguin problem soon. If they needed home repairs, they looked up tutorials online. If they needed to go to the doctor, they used tele-visits and even learned to draw their own blood.

But when a trip couldn't be avoided, they used the taxi-drones. Today Gene had to visit the hospital as part of his ongoing hormonal therapy. He would be undergoing a variety of tests, both physical and psychological, some of which he'd been putting off for more than six months. People didn't waste trips these days, and he'd made appointments with three different doctors in the same building.

The sun was setting by the time his third appointment was over, and he ordered another taxi-drone from the hospital's roof. Once again his stomach lurched as it took off, flying past the building's outer fence and over the flocks of murderous waterfowl. It was amazing how quickly the penguins had spread across the planet. The surviving humans had barely had time to erect fences around their homes before the birds invaded neighborhoods all over the world. Gene wondered if there had also been rabbit DNA in there, for how quickly the creatures multiplied.

The drone dipped low – a little too low for Gene's comfort – and his feet dangled maybe ten feet over the snapping beaks. Penguins hopped and tried to climb over each other as they attempted to snatch some easy prey from the sky. Then the drone went high again, soaring over the suburban neighborhoods. Gene was constantly amazed at how they survived on so little food. There couldn't be that many stray animals left.

But he'd watched the documentaries, and he knew about their efficient metabolism and how they could store up fat like a hibernating bear. They could survive for weeks on a single meal, and they ate their own dead. While they preferred meat, they could survive on all kinds of foods. Since there was no garbage service anymore, people tended to throw their trash over their fences and into the streets, where the penguins ravaged most of it.

Gene was almost home when one of the rotors began to sputter. Sparks rained down on Gene's head and the rotor started spewing smoke. He lifted his legs in panic as the taxi-drone dipped toward the street. "Holy hell!" Gene shouted as dozens of hungry beaks snapped at him. Then an emergency protocol took over and the taxi-drone rose back into the air, heading for the nearest roof. It set him down on top of a four-bedroom home, about three streets away from his own house.

Gene unhooked his safety harness and carefully stepped away from the drone. A few seconds later, the drone slipped off the roof and clattered to the ground below.

"What's going on up there?" a voice shouted.

Gene moved closer to the edge of the roof. "Engine trouble, sorry to disturb you!"

"You better not cause any damage up there!" the voice replied.

"If I do, bill the YuFly company!" Gene shouted back. Then he pulled his phone out of his pocket and ordered another ride. It arrived within moments and took him the rest of the way home.

"Jean, wake up."

"What are you doing in my room?" Gene mumbled, brushing Emma's hand off his shoulder. He opened one eye and looked at the clock. It was nearly midnight.

"There's a penguin in the yard," Emma said.

Gene reluctantly sat up and rubbed his eyes. "Did you use the chow?"

"I can't find it," Emma said.

"Right, my fault," Gene said, getting out of bed. "I think I put it under the sink instead of the laundry room. I should have told you."

"No problem," Emma said. She turned away when she saw he was in his underwear.

Gene noticed her embarrassment and groaned. "I've known you since we were three. We used to take baths together."

"Things have changed," Emma said.

Gene pulled on a pair of pajama pants and a T-shirt. "You

either believe I'm a guy or you don't," he said. "If you don't, then you can see me in my undies. If you do, stop giving me grief about 'transgender ideology' all the time."

"Come on," Emma said, leading him out of the room. From the upstairs hallway, she opened the door to the second-floor balcony and stepped outside. Then she leaned over the left side and pointed. "It was right there," she said. "But it's gone now."

"Keep looking," Gene said. "I'll get the chow." He went back inside and trudged down the stairs, still not fully awake. He knew it would be at least another hour before he could go back to bed. Random penguin facts buzzed about his sleepy brain, as if prepping him for the upcoming task.

Normal, unmodified penguins were cathemeral, which meant they might be active day or night depending on environmental factors. These genetically altered creatures tended to be active during the day, probably because that was when the most taxi-drones were in the sky. But the occasional penguin roamed the streets at night, hoping to get the jump on some nocturnal prey without having to compete with the other penguins.

A single penguin by itself wasn't much of a threat, though, at least not compared to a pair of humans. Emma and Gene could probably have taken the loner out with their bare hands, but not without getting bitten a couple of times in the process. It was easier and safer to use the chow.

Gene retrieved the box from under the sink, then walked back up the stairs. "Seen it yet?" he asked as he stepped onto the balcony.

"Yeah," Emma said, pointing. "He's over there, pretending to stare at a tree."

That was another one of their more flexible behaviors.

When the penguins fought in packs, they tended to make a lot of noise in order to attract more of their flock. But solo penguins were more subtle. They would often stand perfectly still, feigning interest in something else while watching their prey out of the corner of their eye.

"Oh, he's smooth," Gene said. "He's like, 'Oh, don't mind me, I'm just admiring this fine bark, you go about your business.' Little faker."

Emma laughed. "He'll break character when he sees the chow."

"Let's find out," Gene said, reaching into the box. He pulled out a foul-smelling cube about the size of a biscuit, and tossed it towards their visitor.

The penguin immediately turned toward the balcony and opened its beak, catching the treat before it hit the ground. It gobbled it up and swallowed, then opened its toothy beak again as if requesting more.

"One's all you get," Gene said, closing the box. Then he and Emma stood and watched, waiting for the chow to kick in. After a few minutes the penguin yawned, then began to sway. It took a few wobbly steps toward the house and then fell forward, hitting the ground beak first.

"Lights out," Emma said.

"Get your gun, just in case," Gene said, and the two headed downstairs.

"So why do you hate God?" Emma asked.

"Really? Now?" Gene asked. They stood on their back lawn, carrying some rope and a stepladder. The penguin was still sound asleep. The box of Penguin Chow guaranteed it was effective for a minimum of four hours, but Gene and

Emma weren't about to chance it.

"Might as well talk about something," Emma asked. "What did God ever do to you?"

They pulled their stepladder over to the fence, then worked together to haul the penguin. "Okay, first off, I don't hate god," Gene said, as they looped some rope around the penguin's feet and dragged it toward the ladder. "I can't hate a fictional being." The creature was heavier than it looked, but it didn't give them any trouble. Getting it up the ladder was more difficult, but they managed it. Gene looped the rope around the top of one of the metal fenceposts, and pulled the penguin up the side of the fence.

"Then where did the universe come from?" Emma asked. "Even if evolution's true, something had to put everything in motion."

She steadied the ladder while Gene climbed up backward, one step at a time, one hand on the rope and one on the chain link. Then he grabbed the hanging penguin and worked it over the top of the fence, loosening the rope as it cleared the top. It crashed down on the opposite side, briefly disturbing two other sleeping penguins.

"I don't know," Gene admitted. "But not knowing doesn't mean it has to be some magical being."

They put the stepladder back in the storage shed, and Gene picked up a baseball bat.

"If you don't know, then how can you risk going to Hell?" Emma asked. "If you worship God and he's not real, you've lost nothing. But if you're wrong..."

She grabbed a golf club off of the shed wall. Neither of them had ever played golf, and they weren't even sure where the club had originally come from.

"Because it's not black and white," Gene said. "It's not like atheism and your version of Christianity are the only two choices. What if you're in the wrong religion?"

The two began to walk the perimeter, checking every section of the fence. The fence was eight feet tall, but sometimes penguins just randomly got in. Tonight's intruder might have climbed up a pile of sleeping penguins, or it might have managed to scale the chain link using its beak and flippers. It was rare, but it happened. But it was equally possible that there was a breach in the fence, such as a broken section of chain link, or a divot the penguin could have used to tunnel under. They couldn't go back to bed until they knew for sure.

Emma was quiet for a few minutes before she spoke again. "My religion can't be wrong," she said, tapping the fence with her golf club. "I can feel it in my heart."

"That's euphoria brought on by the acceptance of your church group," Gene said. "You all worship together and the vibe spreads throughout the room. Admit it... you haven't quite felt the same excitement since the quarantine started. That's why you're always trying to get me to pray with you."

"That's not true," Emma said. "I still feel the Lord in my heart every day. And you would too if you would just—"

"Emma, listen," Gene interrupted, then paused, trying to get his thoughts in order. He just wasn't as good at words as she was. He felt like he lost more arguments than he won, even when he knew he was right.

Emma stopped tapping the fence and stared at him, waiting for him to speak.

Gene took a deep breath. "Emma," he said slowly. "You and I have... different points of view."

"Duh," Emma said. "And that's okay. I just want you to

give God a chance before—"

"No, listen," Gene said. "From your point of view, it's like you're in a hotel room. Everything in that room is Christian-themed. People all around you tell you you're in the right room, and you've never heard anything different."

"It's not like I never studied other—"

"Please, let me get this out," Gene said. "I grew up in the same room as you. But after a while it felt like I was in the wrong room, so I stepped out into the hallway. And you know what I found?"

Emma opened her mouth, but Gene didn't give her a chance to say anything.

"Thousands of rooms," Gene said. "Literally thousands of doors marked with words like Presbyterian. Southern Baptist. Episcopal. Seventh-Day Adventist. Thousands of denominations, doctrines, and sects. And that's just the doors on this floor. Other floors have doors representing other gods and their various sects."

"Yes, there's a lot of false religions," Emma said. "So?"

"So now that I'm outside, why would I pick one door over another?" Gene asked. "Every one of them claims it's the only one that leads to the 'good' afterlife, and there's nothing to indicate which one is right. Frankly, I'm happier out here in the hall."

"If you're so happy, why do you need hormones?" Emma asked.

Gene ignored that. "Let me ask you this," he said. "With thousands of rooms, don't you think it's a little convenient that the 'One True Room' is the one you were born in? I mean, what are the odds?"

"I don't believe *all* the others are going to Hell," Emma said. "Just the ones that—"

"It doesn't matter," Gene said. "It would be like winning the lottery just to be born on the right floor. But here's what you really need to understand." He paused.

Emma waited patiently, her head tilted slightly. She absently tapped the fence with her club, but her attention was on her friend.

Gene took another deep breath. "Even if I were to go back into a room, it wouldn't be yours. I wouldn't pick a room that promotes homophobia and transphobia as a virtue. If I was even remotely curious about religion at this point, I'd pick a church that was more accepting than yours. From out here in the hallway, your god doesn't look like one of the good ones. Frankly, he looks more like a devil."

Emma was too stunned to reply. They walked in silence for a few more minutes, occasionally tapping the fence to test its sturdiness.

"Fence looks fine," Gene finally said.

"It must have gotten in some other way," Emma said quietly. "Sorry I had to wake you."

"Had to be done," Gene said, and they went inside.

Had they not been so involved in their discussion, they might have noticed a weak spot in their fence. On the right side of the house, just behind the trash cans, the bottom corner of the chain link was no longer attached to the post. It looked sturdy at a glance, but it would only take an intruder one strong push to breach the fence.

"I have my own theory, you know," Emma said.

"This should be good," Gene muttered, putting down his book. It had been two days since the penguin incident, and they'd mostly been getting along since then.

"We're all gender neutral as kids," Emma said.

"I don't think that's—" Gene said.

But Emma wouldn't be interrupted. "Then you hit puberty, and for the first time you realized just how badly women are treated in this society. And so you—"

"No," Gene said.

"Let me finish," Emma said. "You saw that men had all the power. Why would anybody choose to be a woman if they had the choice?"

"That's not what happened," Gene growled.

"Then you didn't want to give up being a tomboy," Emma said. "You know that's okay, right? Women don't have to wear dresses and look sexy. It doesn't mean you have to run off and get surgery."

"No, I—" Gene said.

"Did you even *try* to just accept yourself as you were?" Emma asked.

"This *is* me accepting myself," Gene said, gesturing toward his body.

"By changing everything that made you who you were?" Emma asked.

"No, by refusing to pretend I'm something I'm not," Gene said.

Emma cocked her head. "But that's the exact opposite of—"

"This is what you need to understand," Gene said. "I know more about this subject than you do."

"Because you browsed a few websites that told you what you wanted to hear," Emma said.

"Is that really what you think happened?" Gene asked, but he didn't give her a chance to answer. "Listen to me. Like a lot of trans people, I started out in denial. I didn't want to be trans. Who *wants* to be trans? It's a life full of closed doors, expensive meds, and angry bigots. You think I chose the sex with the most power, but being trans puts me right back in the disenfranchised pile."

"Yes, but—" Emma said.

"No," Gene continued. "I did research. Not just websites that agreed with me. Because a lot of us start out by trying to prove we're *not* trans. I would have gladly taken any other explanation. But none of them fit. So I searched and searched, and you know what? When I realized I was trans, that was the first time I truly accepted who I was."

Emma put her hands on her hips. "If you have to take pills to be who you are, then that's not really who you are."

"Lots of people have to take pills," Gene said. "For every reason under the sun. Are you 'rejecting your true self' when you take a pain pill for your headache? Or when you take allergy pills for your hay fever?"

"No, but—" Emma said.

"But that's not the point," he continued. "All I'm saying is I've done way more research on this than you have. In fact, I'd wager that *every* trans person knows more about the psychology of being transgender than the average cis person. We're the ones who look at the actual research – first to try to disprove it, and later to understand and accept it. Your side is the one that traditionally cherry-picks the data until you find something you can use against us."

"That's not true," Emma said.

"Then why is it that every major medical and psychological association supports transgender people?" Gene asked.

"Because there's money in it," Emma said.

Gene groaned and swiped his hand down his face.

"No, I mean it," Emma said. "You tell a kid they need to

take pills and get surgery to be happy, then you've got a customer for life."

"So you'll trust a doctor's expertise for the flu or a ruptured spleen," Gene said. "But the minute they say something you don't agree with, suddenly they're all frauds?"

"No, I—" Emma said.

"These guys go to medical school for more than a decade," Gene said. "They know what they're talking about. And they make plenty of money without resorting to hooking patients on treatments. Heck, one of my biggest problems when my egg cracked was finding a therapist who was taking on new patients. But sure, they're so desperate for money that they'd risk malpractice suits and whatnot just to make a few extra bucks."

"When your *what* cracked?" Emma asked.

"Egg," Gene said. "It's kind of a metaphor for when you realize you're trans."

"See?" Emma said. "You have your own language. It's like you're in a cult."

"Says the woman who prays to a magical sky being," Gene said, but he regretted it immediately. He usually tried not to cross that line, but his temper got the better of him.

To Gene's surprise, Emma didn't look angry. She just frowned a bit, then sighed. "I don't know if I can keep doing this," she said.

Gene nodded. "We used to get along so well," he said.

"You changed," Emma said.

"We both did," Gene said. "My changes were just more obvious."

"Remember when we used to sneak into your neighbor's garage and use it as a clubhouse?" Emma asked.

"And we found that mounted boar's head that scared you so much?" Gene added.

"That thing gave me nightmares," Emma said.

"I used to tease you about that," Gene said. "I was such a jerk."

"We were both jerks," Emma said. "Most kids are jerks. But you always had my back when I needed it."

"We had each other's backs," Gene said. "Still do when it matters."

"But are we still friends, though?" Emma asked. "I mean, we can't talk for five minutes without getting in a fight."

"I don't know," Gene replied. "I still love you. I'd still fight anyone who puts you down."

"Your entire ideology puts me down," Emma said.

"And yours doesn't?" Gene asked. "Half your congregation would like to stone me to death."

"And your social group would burn my church to the ground if they could," Emma said. Gene started to object but Emma held up her hand. "Don't. This is what I'm talking about. I can't keep having this fight every day. I think one of us should move out."

"We've talked about that before," Gene said. "Nothing's changed. Neither of us can afford to move, and neither of us can afford this house's mortgage on our own."

"Whoever moves can try to find someone who needs a roommate," Emma said. "And whoever stays can look for a tenant to move in."

"That might take a while," Gene said.

"Then we should start," Emma said. "Because I can't keep having this same fight every day. I'd rather wrestle a penguin bare-handed than have my faith attacked again. And I'm sure you'd like to live with someone who supports your… issues."

Gene nodded. "I guess that's it, then. You stay. I'll look for a place."

"You sure?" Emma asked.

"Most of the furniture's yours," Gene said. "I can fit all my stuff in a few boxes."

They hugged silently, then went to their separate rooms to search the web for potential roommates.

The following morning, Emma was making coffee when her phone buzzed. Another delivery. *Better not be more of Jean's trans crap*, she thought. She set her phone down on the kitchen counter, then climbed the stairs and slid open the doors to the shared second-floor balcony. She cocked her head when she didn't see any packages. *Did Jean already get it?* she wondered, but she could hear him snoring away in his bedroom.

Emma stepped out onto the balcony, then looked over the railing. *There.* The package had landed on the ground below, mere inches from the fence. "I hate drones," she mumbled as she went back down the stairs. She stepped out the kitchen door, turned the corner, and headed for the package. The penguins began to frenzy when they saw her, poking their beaks through the chain-link fence as she carefully bent down to retrieve the box.

Package in hand, she turned back toward the house. She'd only made it a couple of steps when she heard the trash cans fall over. Emma turned her head and screamed at what she saw. A corner of the fence had been pushed inward, and the penguins were getting in.

Gene's dreams were filled with themes of isolation and despair. Over the course of the night he'd been thrown to the penguins, forced to live on the moon by himself, left alone on a deserted island, and chained to a rock near an erupting volcano. Right now he dreamed that he'd been kicked out of prison and was about to go to something called "super prison." But that's when he heard the screaming.

"Jean!" the woman called, over and over. It sounded like Emma.

"It's Gene," he muttered, waking up. As he shook the dreams from his head, he realized he could still hear Emma's voice. *That's real*, he thought, and rolled out of bed. He stood perfectly still, listening for her cries. Then he heard another scream and rushed out his bedroom door.

From the balcony, Gene looked out on a sea of penguins. They'd breached the fence and now filled the yard. Emma squatted on top of the little storage shed next to the fence. Penguins surrounded the shed, hopping up and down to try to reach her. When Emma looked up and saw Gene, she looked relieved for a moment. Then the swarm began rocking the shed, and she had to hold onto to the edge of the roof to keep her balance.

"Do something!" Emma shouted.

Gene wasn't the best in a crisis, and his mind became muddled with conflicting ideas. He thought about tying a rope to the balcony and tossing the other end to her, but there wasn't anything for her to tie her end to. Maybe she could use it to climb her way to the balcony, but she was just as likely to swing into the killer flock. Then he remembered they had a ladder. Would it reach from the balcony to the storage shed? Would they be able to keep it steady enough for her to climb across? And where was the ladder, anyway? *Oh right,* he thought. It was in the storage shed.

"Just call a drone you idiot!" Emma shouted.

"Right," Gene said, and went back inside to get his phone. He came back out a few seconds later, and the drone arrived shortly, hovering by the balcony.

And that was the issue. Customers couldn't directly control the drones. The drones just used GPS coordinates and phone tracking to automatically arrive at specific destinations. To get the drone to go to the shed, Emma would need the phone.

"Emma!" Gene shouted. "Get ready!" He held up his phone to throw to her, and she held her hands ready. Then he tossed her the phone. It bounced out of her hands at first, but she managed to catch it before it fell off the shed. She nearly lost her balance in the process, but just managed to steady herself. Below her, the hungry birds snapped their jaws in anticipation. Finally holding the phone still, she pressed the "Come To My Location" button and the drone moved next to her. Then she sat down and typed in their address as the new destination.

Gene helped her out of the taxi-drone and back onto the safety of the balcony, and the two went back inside.

A call to emergency services brought two aerial crews out to their house. One to fix the fence, and the other to exterminate the birds that had breached it. Gene stood at his bedroom window, watching them work. Drones flew all about their lawn, spraying poisonous gas. Other drones lifted the corpses out of the lawn and dropped them into the street where they would be eaten by others of their kind.

If they can take out the birds so easily, why can't they do it all over? Gene wondered. But he knew the answer. The problem was just too large. Even if it were possible to manufacture that much poison, spraying it around the world would kill more than just the penguins.

There was a knock on his bedroom door. "Come in," he said, and Emma entered.

"It's just me," she said.

"Who else could it be?" Gene asked.

Emma sat down on his bed. "Thank you," she said. "I'm sorry I called you an idiot. You did great out there."

"I just did what you told me," Gene said, and sat down next to her.

"Listen, Gene," she said. "And I am saying Gene with a G, I swear... Maybe you don't have to move. I know I've been judgy of your lifestyle, but I can tone it down. You saved me today. Maybe that was God's way of telling me I should give our friendship another chance."

"Thanks," Gene said, patting her on the back. "But no. You were right. We're holding each other back, and I think we'll both be happier if we go our own ways. I will always love you, and I will always be your friend. But it's time we move on."

Emma nodded, and they sat on the bed together for a long time.

Four months later...

"Guess what guess what guess what?" Emma asked excitedly.

Even though the video feed was grainy, Gene could see her vibrating with joy. "You got the puppy?" Gene asked.

"Yes!" Emma said, her face practically glowing. Then she reached down and came back up with a beautiful Pomeranian in her arms. She held it up to the camera for Gene to see. "Say hello to Diddles."

"Adorable!" Gene said. He liked dogs, but their fur made his throat close up. He'd always felt a little guilty that his allergies had kept Emma from having one. Seeing her so happy brightened his entire day. "So where'd you get him?"

"She's a she," Emma corrected. "I got her through church. They sponsor an animal shelter."

"Nice," Gene said. "How's the new church going?"

"Oh you'd love them," Emma said. "They're so much more open-minded than the old one. We even have a lesbian pastor. I've come around on a lot of things."

"That's great," Gene said.

"If you want to join us Sunday for virtual service, I'm sure they'd love to have you."

"Still an atheist," Gene replied. "But thanks. I appreciate the offer. I really do."

"So how's your new roommate?" Emma asked. "You two still just friends, or are you… you know… *roommates?*"

Gene laughed. "We're just friends, silly. He's really great. You two wouldn't get along, but he's just what I needed right now."

"Glad to hear it," Emma said. "Well, I have to run. Diddles needs her walkies. Call me soon!"

"Later," Gene said, and logged off. He couldn't stop smiling. The last few conversations with Emma had been some of their best in years. They hadn't gotten along this well since they were kids. It was odd, but splitting up was the best thing they could have done for their relationship. It seemed counterintuitive, but the distance had brought them closer together.

Some friendships were just stronger that way.

Legal Battle

The courtroom didn't look much different from those back in the twenty-first century. The judge still sat behind a large wooden desk, and he still wore long black robes and wielded a gavel. The Accuser and the Accused sat behind separate tables across from the bench, and a stoic-faced bailiff stood to the judge's left. The two biggest changes were the massive audience that surrounded the court floor on all sides, and the rectangular mat that covered the floor between the bench and the attorney tables.

A lawyer stood on each side of the mat, decked out in heavy padding like a football player. Each brandished a meter-long steel baton, currently at rest by their side. The Defendist – the lawyer appointed to represent the Accused – stood to the judge's right. The Offendant stood on the opposite side of the mat, to the judge's left. The lawyers locked eyes with each other and tried to get under each other's skin.

Lights flickered on around the courtroom. White neon stripes moved around the border of the mat. The audience ceased their murmuring and began to cheer. Some chanted

"Lock him up" while a few others booed.

"The Court of Public Opinion is now in session," the judge said, banging his gavel to quiet the audience. "Charges?"

The bailiff read from a transparent tablet. "Your honor, the Accused is one Anthony Jones, a.k.a. Tonya. The Accuser is Nera Krenn. Krenn claims she was changing in a locker room and caught Jones watching her. Krenn believes that Jones had no right to be in that locker room. Jones claims that he was only there to change clothes, and while he may have accidentally glanced in Krenn's direction for a moment, he had no intention of watching her change clothes."

"Your honor," the Defendist said, raising her baton. The judge nodded, granting her permission to speak. "My client would appreciate it if we could use female pronouns from here on out. She has been living as a woman for more than five years now."

"Denied," the judge replied. "If he wants to be treated as a woman, he will have to justify his gender identity, just like any other Accused."

"Acknowledged," the Defendist said, lowering her baton.

"I will now hear opening arguments," the judge said. "Offendant, since you won the coin toss earlier, you get to speak first."

The Offendant raised his baton and pointed it at the Accused. "Your honor, that man is a pervert. He wears women's clothing in order to sneak into women's spaces and spy on them. If he is allowed to continue, someone will get raped. It is our recommendation that his access to such spaces be restricted, and that he submit to state-sponsored therapy. I would even recommend—"

Just then a light turned red on the judge's bench, and a short alarm sounded. "Time's up," the judge said, as the

Offendant lowered his baton. "Defense?"

The Defendist raised her baton. "Your honor, my client simply wants to live her life and be left alone. She has no desire to intrude on anyone's rights, but she can't live fully as a woman and continue to use the men's room. The Offendant's accusations are pure conjecture and rank hyperbolism. She has never entered a women's locker room with any intention other than to get in, change clothes, and get out as quickly as—" The alarm sounded again, and she lowered her baton.

"First strike goes to you, Offendant," the judge said. The two lawyers took a few steps towards each other, until they were about ten feet apart. The judge raised his gavel, then brought it down hard. "Fight!" he shouted.

"Men don't belong in women's spaces!" the Offendant shouted, swinging his baton. The Defendist brought up her weapon just in time to block the blow. "Gender is fiction!" the Offendant screamed, swinging again, just grazing his target's arm. "If he has a penis, he's a man!" the Offendant yelled, then made a low swipe. This strike found its mark, hitting the Defendist on her left thigh.

"Divide," the judge ordered, and they stepped apart. "Lock in your votes," he ordered the audience. Thousands of court fans pressed buttons on their keypads, giving the Offendant's arguments a score of one to ten.

"Seven," the bailiff said, reading the average score. "Plus a one-point hit on the arm, and a solid hit on the thigh for five points. Six strike points multiplied by seven votes equals forty-two."

"Your turn, Defendist," the judge said, and the lawyers stepped forward again.

"My client lives as a woman full-time," the Defendist said,

feinting low, then swinging high. The baton hit the Offendant in the shoulder. "She's been in gender therapy for more than two years," she said, her next blow blocked by her opponent's baton. "You can't expect her to out herself by using the men's locker room!" she shouted, then thrust straight at the Offendant's torso. She scored a direct hit to the middle of his chest.

"Divide," the judge said. The audience voted again, judging the Defendist's arguments.

"Four," the bailiff said, reading the results from his tablet. "Two points for the shoulder, ten for the heart. Twelve strike points times four votes is forty-eight."

A scoreboard on the front of the judge's desk lit up and displayed:

OFF 42 – DEF 48

Despite being in the lead, the Defendist shook her head. *It shouldn't be this close*, she thought. It barely mattered what she said, as the uneducated audience voted based on their prejudices rather than the facts. Attention spans were almost non-existent these days. If she was going to win this case, she'd have to make every blow count.

"Powerup time," the judge announced.

The lawyers stood with their arms stretched wide. All over their padded suits, embedded piping began to glow. The overhead lights dimmed until only the piping could be seen. The lawyers now looked like a pair of wireframe models, with the Offendant in red and the Defendist in blue. They held their now-glowing batons high and faced each other, ready for round two.

"This round is a free-for-all," the judge said. "Attorneys will no longer take turns." He paused for a moment, then ordered them to fight.

"Eighty percent of trans people detransition," the Offendant said, thrusting forward. His red glowing armor now enhanced his speed and reflexes, and he moved like a crimson blur. His thrust hit the Defendist square in the face, and she fell backward onto the floor. The Offendant raised his baton high, then brought it down hard.

"That number is a lie," the Defendist countered, using her heightened reflexes to roll out of his way. "Less than one percent detransition," she said, swinging her baton again. Her blow barely grazed his shin. Still on the ground, she pounced forward and thrust at his stomach. The blow landed, and he staggered backward. "And of those who do detransition, most do it due to lack of support, rather than transition regret."

"Divide," the judge said. A medic approached the Defendist and pressed a cold compress against her bloody nose.

The bailiff cleared his throat. "Offendant gets ten points for the face..."

"Objection," the Defendist interrupted, waving her medic away. "Requesting a fact check. His detransition stats were questionable."

A team of court statisticians quickly researched the detransition stats. "Defendist is correct," they reported. "The regret rate for transitioning is less than one percent. For comparison, the regret rate for marriage is forty percent. The regret rate for..."

"We don't need the full report," the judge said. "Offendant scores half points for the blow."

"Offendant receives five points for the face," the bailiff corrected. "The Defendist gets no points for the shin, and four points for the stomach. Audience, please vote now."

A few seconds passed while the audience voted. The Defendist wiped more blood from her nose and braced herself for the bad news.

"Offendant gets eight points from the audience. Five strike points times eight votes is forty, bringing him up to eighty-two. Defendist receives four points from the audience. Four strike points times four votes is sixteen, bringing her up to sixty-four."

The scoreboard now read:

OFF 82 - DEF 64

Not good, the Defendist thought, but it wasn't surprising. Once again the audience cared more for spectacle than facts. *That blow to the face must have looked spectacular from the stands,* she thought as she wiped her throbbing nose.

"Final round," the judge said.

"Your honor, I'd like to Double Down," the Defendist said.

"Request granted," the judge said. "Offendant, do you wish to do the same?"

"No, your honor," the Offendant replied.

"Ten-minute recess while you prepare," the judge told the Defendist.

I must be crazy to try this, the Defendist thought. In her six years as an attorney, she'd only Doubled Down twice. Not only was it risky, but it made her feel dirty to pander to the audience that way. But she was eighteen points behind and headed into the final round. Her audience was clearly biased, and they were more interested in a flashy show than credible facts.

The Defendist believed in her client and supported trans rights. It seemed like every case against a trans person ended up being about trans people as whole. This case would be used as precedent for hundreds of future trials. She had to win, whatever the cost.

If they want a circus, that's what they're going to get, the Defendist thought as she removed her armor.

"This is the final round," the judge announced. "Lawyers, please take your positions."

The Offendant stood at the ready, his reflex-enhancing armor nearly doubling his bulk. The Defendist looked much smaller in contrast. She wore a low-cut leotard, covered in silver sequins. Gripping her baton tight, she sized up her opponent and prepared her defense. She'd be going into this fight without the benefit of enhanced speed or protective padding. His strikes were going to hurt.

Last chance to chicken out, she thought. But she knew that wasn't an option. Changing her mind now would be disastrous for her case. The audience would feel cheated, and that would be reflected in their votes. No, she had to see this through.

"Fight," the judge said.

The Offendant didn't waste any time. Charging forward like a rhino, he shouted, "Trans ideology is a new age scam!" Holding his baton with two hands, he swiped it in a downward arc. The Defendist brought her baton up in time to block his blow, but he hit so hard it still drove her to her knees. When the Offendant pulled back for another swing, the Defendist rolled to the side and got to her feet.

"Trans people have existed all throughout history," she retorted, then dove forward. She ducked under his swipe and scraped his upper thigh with her baton. Then she rolled between his legs and stood up on the other side. "The science supports trans people," she added, before striking him in the back.

"It's just a delusion," the Offendant said, spinning around to face her. He moved impossibly fast for someone with so much padding. He swung low, and the Defendist attempted to drop to the floor to avoid the swipe. Unfortunately she was too slow, and the baton hit her in the side. There was a loud crack that could only have been her ribs.

The Offendant took a couple of steps back, worried that if he pressed the advantage, the crowd might view him as cruel. Then he heard their chants of "Finish her!" and raised his baton again. *Better give them what they want,* he thought.

But that hesitation was all the Defendist had needed. Clutching her side with her left hand, she thrust forward with her right, hitting him in the knee. From her low angle, the tip of her baton hit him underneath the padding, striking him hard in the tendon. "Trans rights are human rights," she said.

The Offendant cried out and lost his balance. "They *aren't* human," he wailed, but he didn't have a leg to stand on. The Defendist scooted out of the way as her opponent toppled forward onto his face.

"Divide," the judge said. Both lawyers had to be helped to their feet by the court medics. "Bailiff?" he asked, while the audience voted.

"The Offendant receives eight points for the solid hit to the ribs," the bailiff said. "The audience awards him ten points. Eight strike points times ten votes is eighty, which brings his final score to one sixty-two."

The Defendist winced. With her current score of sixty-four, she'd need ninety-nine points to win.

"The Defendist scored three hits," the bailiff continued. "A glancing hit to the thigh worth one point, a solid blow to the back for four, and the crippling knee strike was worth five, for a total of ten. With the Double Down bonus that becomes twenty," the bailiff said. "She received an audience score of five. Five votes times twenty strike points is one hundred. This brings her total score to one sixty-four," the bailiff said.

"Judgment goes to the Accused with a final score of one sixty-four to one sixty-two," the judge said. "Ms. Jones, you're free to go."

The final score flashed repeatedly on the judge's desk, and the audience erupted in a cacophony of boos and cheers. Ms. Jones stood and shook hands with the Defendist, while Ms. Krenn gave them an angry glare. The Offendant gave his client a shrug that seemed to say, "You win some, you lose some." Then he grimaced and limped out of the courtroom.

The Defendist, however, had to leave on a stretcher. As the medics carried her down the hallway towards an awaiting ambulance, she wondered it if was all worth it. The legal system was broken, and the uninformed masses had too much power over the lives of innocents. Today's audience had consisted of bloodthirsty bigots who just wanted to see a show. She hoped they didn't represent the public at large, but they probably did.

She hated that she'd had to fight dirty. It didn't matter that her arguments had been more accurate than the Offendant's. She'd arrived with a briefcase full of stats and research and citations, but the fast-paced nature of the modern court system had prevented her from presenting a proper case.

Given the opportunity, she could have delivered an hour-long speech on advanced biology, sex and gender diversity, and the psychological validity of transgender people. But none of those arguments could be condensed into one-sentence sound bites. The audience always wanted catchy slogans, not facts. All her preparation had been for nothing.

So was it worth it?

As they loaded her into the ambulance, she caught a glimpse of her client. Tonya Jones waved at her, tears of happiness in her eyes.

Yes, the Defendist thought finally. *It's definitely worth it.*

The Loner

ED.02480.09.13

"When the police can't help you, when the IGP ignores you, when the case is so dangerous even bounty hunters won't take the job, there's only one man you can call. Skiff Kilzit, Space Hero."

The video screen floated in midair, the three-dimensional images projected from an emitter on the ceiling. The picture was a little grainy – Datan's parents bought everything used – but his imagination filled the gaps. On the show, a man in high-tech armor fought wave after wave of generic bad guys, using a combination of martial arts and an array of fancy gadgets.

It was a remake of a reboot of a reimagining of a character more than a century old, but it was all new to eight-year-old Datan Taush. He was up to season three, and while his friends had all abandoned the show midway through the second season, Datan was still enthralled.

In this episode, Skiff had infiltrated the lair of a band of weapons smugglers. He'd used his stealth shield to sneak past the security sensors, then hacked the front door using his index finger. He'd lost his right hand way back in the first episode, only to have it replaced with a robotic prosthesis. That hand was Skiff's secret weapon, an almost magical device that seemed to have new functions in every episode.

But it wasn't going to save him this time. Despite Skiff's stealth tech, one of the bad guys had spotted him and hit the hero with his only weakness – an EMP device, designed to fry all electronics in a hundred-meter radius. Suddenly most of Skiff's gadgets were useless – hand included – and he had to rely on his fighting skills alone. But given Skiff's prowess in that area, Datan still liked his odds.

Except the villains didn't fight fair. The bad guy – the big bad, Lord Darkmind, CEO of EvilCorp Incorporated - didn't give Skiff a chance to fight. Instead he launched an electric net from his wrist, pinning Skiff to the wall. *Why didn't the EMP short out Darkmind's own gadgets?* Datan thought briefly. It wasn't the first time he'd noticed a plot hole on this show, and the fun wasn't in spotting them but in justifying them. *Of course Darkmind's immune to his own EMP*, Datan rationalized. *I bet all his gadgets are shielded somehow.*

Now Skiff was defenseless, his back against the wall and his arms stuck to his sides. Six of Darkmind's elite minions marched into the room, their laser rifles drawn. "You won't win," Skiff snarled, straining against the electric web.

"Skiff Kilzit," the villain said smoothly. "I'm so glad we could dance this one last time. But I'm afraid you're too late. I've already launched the missile that will destroy the moon. Oh, I'm sure you could still stop it if only you could get back to your ship, but that's not very likely, given that you're about to die."

"Darkmind, you venomous space lizard!" Skiff yelled. "Destroying the moon will have devastating effects on the tides!"

"But of course," Lord Darkmind cackled. "But that's just step one of my plan. Too bad you won't be alive to see the rest." Then, turning to his henchmen, he ordered, "Execute him."

The minions raised their rifles again, and the screen cut to black. "Zarg it!" Datan shouted as the first commercial came on.

"Watch your language!" The voice came from somewhere else in the house, most likely the laundry room.

"Sorry Mom," Datan mumbled, rolling his eyes.

After an interminably long commercial break, the show started right where it left off. The henchmen were about to fire their rifles when a woman's voice interrupted them. "Hey, boys," the woman said, causing all the henchmen to look up in the air. They spotted the newcomer, a woman in armor similar to Skiff's, except hers was bright red instead of black. "Mind if I join the party?"

"Ava!" Skiff and Datan shouted together. Skiff's sister was Datan's favorite character on the show. She'd been introduced early in season two, and while Datan's friends weren't fond of her, she was the biggest reason he continued to watch the show.

"You don't know what you're missing," Datan often told them.

"She ruined the show," they always replied.

But to Datan, she *was* the show. He watched every week waiting for her appearance, and he hoped she'd get her own spin-off.

Ava hopped down from a catwalk and fought the goons while Darkmind fled. Then she released her brother and the two stole a spaceship, pursued the missile, and destroyed it just in the nick of time. Datan cheered as the missile exploded mere meters from the lunar surface. Ava and her brother had saved the day once again.

Datan's mother walked through the holographic display as the credits rolled. "Mom!" Datan shouted.

"What?" she asked. "I waited until the show was over." She wore an oversized T-shirt and held a laundry basket against her left hip.

"I like the credits," Datan said. His mother moved aside, and a slideshow of the episode's most exciting scenes appeared behind the names of the cast and crew.

"Have you done your chores?" she asked.

"Most of them," Datan replied.

"Well I was just in your room and it looks like a hovercar exploded in there," his mom replied.

"I was building something," Datan said. "I'll clean it up before bedtime."

"See that you do," his mom ordered.

Just then a commercial came on, advertising Skiff Kilzit's line of action figures. Datan stared with his mouth open. "Mom," he said absently, "Can I get the Ava figure?"

"Not until your birthday," she replied. "And you don't even have Skiff yet. Why do you want Ava before Skiff?"

"She's so much cooler," Datan said.

His mom shook her head and left the room to finish the laundry. As she put a load in the washer, she thought, *It's just a phase. Kids are weird. One week they want to be a dinosaur. The next they want to be a spaceship.*

But on some level she knew it was more than that. Most whims came and went, but some seemed like a core part of Datan's personality. He always glommed onto the female characters. Her theory was that it was because he spent more time with her than with his father. *I've got to change that,* she thought. *He needs more masculine role models in his life, or he's going to grow up to be...*

ED.02482.07.22

"...such a wuss," Nirt said. "You only want to be the blue one because he has more armor."

"He's the leader of the team," Taka replied. "That makes him the best."

"But you always get to be the blue one," Nirt said.

"My house, my pick," Taka said. "I'm blue. You be red."

"Fine," Nirt said. "Gimme red."

Datan held his tongue. He knew what was coming.

"I call yellow," Ferrin said quickly.

"Orange," Erran said, only a second behind his twin brother.

"Guess I'm stuck with pink," Datan said, forcing himself to look disappointed.

"You snooze you lose," Ferrin said.

Vulpestriker was the latest video game craze, a five-player cooperative shooter based on the anime of the same name. Each player piloted one of five robotic foxes, which would combine to form a giant robot during boss battles.

The ten-year-olds crowded onto the U-shaped couch in Taka's den. They played video games at Taka's house because he always had the newest equipment. And he always bought five of everything, since it was more fun to play with his friends.

Taka handed a lightweight pair of VR glasses to each of his friends, and they quickly slipped them on. The living room melted away. Suddenly they sat at the controls of their respective foxes, ready to take on the forces of the vile

Emperor Hunglore.

From their starting positions outside Castle Vulpestra, they could already see Hunglore's armies approaching from across the barren wastelands. Everything looked just like it did in the cartoon, and the little details were amazing. Wisps of sand blew by in the wind, light reflected off their canopies, and if you looked hard enough, you could even see the tiny rivets in the vehicles' metal plating. The players reached out and gripped their flight yokes, launching their foxes forward into battle.

Taka's father watched them from his office doorway, shaking his head. Five boys wearing sunglasses and turning imaginary steering wheels. *Some things never change*, he thought. Then he got an important phone call and shut the office door.

It may have looked silly to an observer, but behind the digital glasses it seemed all too real. Gleaming black spidertanks fired at them from all sides, and the only defense was to take out as many as you could before you took too much damage.

"I've got one on my tail!" Nirt shouted, and it wasn't just an expression. According to his control panel, a chomper mine had latched onto his vehicle's tail, and it would explode at any moment.

"I've got you," Datan said as he changed course. His fox turned and galloped until it was just behind Nirt. He couldn't blast the mine without setting it off, but he had an idea. It was a risky move because the mine was already flashing red, but it was too cool not to try. He pulled a lever and his vehicle's fox-shaped head carefully bit the mine off of Nirt's tail. Then he whipped the head to the side while releasing the mine. It flew into an oncoming spidertank right as it exploded.

"Great shot, Datan!" Nirt shouted.

But the more spidertanks they destroyed, the tougher they got. Just as Datan trained his eye lasers on a new foe, a barrage of cannon fire hit him in the side. "Zarg!" he shouted as his shields dropped to fifty percent.

"Boys, can you keep it down in there? I'm on the comm!" The voice sounded so distant it might as well have been from another planet.

"Sorry, Dad," Taka replied, and everyone hushed a bit.

Datan bounded forward and bit the cannon off of a spidertank, then fired his eye lasers through its canopy.

"Watch out, Datan!" Taka shouted, then remembered his father's request. "Missile on your six," he whispered.

Datan leaped out of the way, but not quickly enough. The missile exploded on his left flank, taking out the rest of his shields. Inside the cockpit, the lights flickered and sparks flew from his control panel. For just a moment he could see himself reflected in the canopy.

Except, of course, it wasn't Datan he saw in the reflection. It was Princess Sheila, who piloted the pink fox in the cartoon. It was just one more immersive detail that made this game so fun. The hands that gripped the flight yoke, while they mimicked Datan's movements perfectly, were the delicate hands of a princess. When the other players looked in Datan's direction, they didn't see Datan through the canopy, but Sheila.

This was why his friends didn't like playing the pink one. It was one thing to play a female character in a normal video game. After all, games were just that - games. But when the game was this realistic, this involved, this all-encompassing, it no longer felt like you were just controlling a character on a screen. It felt like you *were* that character for a while. And stepping into Princess Sheila's skin that way creeped most boys out.

But not Datan. He looked forward to getting "stuck" with the pink fox every weekend, for reasons he couldn't quite articulate. He always let the other boys pick first, knowing he'd end up with the fox he wanted. But he couldn't let them think he'd done it on purpose. If they found out he actually *liked* pretending to be Princess Sheila, they'd tease him mercilessly. Or worse, they'd think he was weird and wouldn't want to hang out anymore.

And maybe he *was* weird. Was that such a bad thing? He didn't think so. What was so wrong with being different? History wasn't made by "normal" people; it was always the oddballs and outcasts who changed the universe.

Except... Datan didn't want to be an outcast. He liked hanging out with his friends. His pragmatic side said it was because Taka had the best video games, but deep down he knew it was more than that. People needed people. The last thing Datan wanted was to be some loner.

"Wake up, Datan," Taka said. "It's time to take out the boss."

"Right," Datan said, and formed up with the team. They'd wiped out the rest of the spidertanks while he was lost in thought, and now a giant gorilla-bot charged at them.

On Taka's command, they combined into the titular Vulpestriker. The pink and red foxes transformed into arms, while the orange and yellow foxes became the legs. Then the limbs attached to the blue fox, which had reformed into a torso and head.

Their control panels reconfigured for the boss fight. Taka now fully controlled the robot, and from his perspective it was like playing a first-person arena fighting game. As the arms, Nirt and Datan operated the robot's shoulder cannons, doing their best to weaken the robo-ape's shields so Taka's punches could do more damage. Down in the legs, the twins played something more akin to a resource management puzzle game, diverting Vulpestriker's power to where it was most needed at the time.

While some of the jobs were more exciting than others, all five positions were necessary to defeat the ape. Thanks to their communication and cooperation, they vanquished the boss in record time. "Nice teamwork," Taka said as they advanced to the next level.

Teamwork, Datan thought. That's why it was important to be accepted, to be liked. Working alone was for losers. To really get ahead in the universe, you needed a strong team. And that's why he would never tell his friends he actually enjoyed playing as the pink fox.

They can never know, Datan resolved. *I don't care if I have to lie to them forever. I never want to be...*

ED.02488.08.04

...Alone, Detanna thought. She sat on the roof of a video arcade. It was pouring rain, but she didn't care. Next to the bruises and the sting of betrayal, a little rain was nothing. Refreshing, even. In a way, it felt like it was washing her pain away. But she still felt very alone, and very scared.

She was sixteen. She'd run away from home three times this year, but it looked like this time it was going to stick. She'd spent the past month in the company of a gang called the "Scud Hackers," but now she was on her own once again.

All because she'd told them her secret. The Big Secret, the one that had caused so much upheaval in her home. The one that had caused her father to leave. The one that had provoked endless lectures from her mother.

She'd thought the gang was different. They'd always stuck up for each other in the past. It was the gang motto. "Pain is easier when shared." They'd probably stolen the quote from a celebrity or something, but they usually lived up to it. If a gang member had a problem, they worked together to fix it.

That's why Detanna had felt so comfortable telling her secret to one of her new friends. "I think I'm really a girl," she'd said. "Can you start calling me Detanna?"

She knew he'd be confused, and thought maybe he'd ask her a bunch of questions before finally hugging her and telling her it was all going to be okay. Instead he started calling her a bunch of really nasty words, then blabbed her secret to the rest of the gang. They beat her pretty badly on the way out the door, but at least she'd made it out. A couple of them had chased her for a few blocks, their AON daggers glowing and ready for blood.

From her vantage point on the roof, she watched a couple of her ex-friends walk down the sidewalk. It looked like they'd given up the search and were heading home.

I need to get out of here, Detanna thought. It wasn't just a whim or a way to get some distance from the gang. She needed a fresh start, a new direction, and most of all, she wanted to see the galaxy. *There's nothing for me here*, she thought. *I've got to get...*

ED.02492.05.12

...off this planet, Detanna thought, watching the pirate ship blast into the sky. Detanna climbed to the top of an ice dune and studied her surroundings. Frozen wasteland stretched

in every direction. The clouds flashed red and blue as IGP ships arrived on the scene. *How am I going to get out of this one?* Detanna wondered.

She was back to square one. She had no money, minimal supplies, and the nearest settlement was over fifty kilometers away. *On the bright side,* Detanna thought, *If I survive this, I can survive anything.*

She'd joined the pirates with three goals: to see the stars, to live a life of adventure, and to pick up some new skills. She'd hit the jackpot where that last goal was concerned. The pirate crew was packed with highly skilled individuals, most of whom had been more than happy to show off. During their lessons she'd developed a camaraderie with them, not unlike the bonds she'd formed with the Scud Hackers.

But she'd had to hide her true self. The pirates were almost all men, and sexist ones at that. Detanna wasn't sure how they felt about trans people, but seeing how they treated women in general had been more than enough to still her tongue. It also hadn't taken her long to realize that piracy was a career with no future. Maybe she'd have worked her way up to captain someday, but she was more likely to have wound up dead or in prison.

Unfortunately, the pirates didn't allow deserters. Once you were a pirate, you were a pirate until you died. And now she was, at least as far as they were concerned. Faking her death hadn't been easy, but she'd managed it, and by using skills that they'd taught her.

Earlier...

"Come on, you can fight better than that," Drallak said, easily dodging the swipe of Detanna's dagger.

"Just lulling you into a false sense of... Oof!" Detanna grunted as Drallak kicked her in the stomach. She staggered backward until her back was against a crate.

"Quit holding back," Drallak said, his dagger against her throat.

"Kicking's against the rules," Detanna grunted, lowering her weapon.

"Are you going to complain about 'the rules' when an IGP officer has a gun in your face?" Drallak asked. "Are you going to call 'no fair' when some stupid bounty hunter blindsides you?"

"Point taken," Detanna said. "And I wasn't holding back, Drallak. I just didn't want to accidentally hurt you."

"You couldn't if you tried," Drallak said with a smug grin. "These practice knives can't even break the skin." He poked the dull ceramic blade into Detanna's chest a couple of times to make his point.

"We have guns," Detanna said. "You really think I'm going to get in a lot of knife fights?"

"You'd be surprised," Drallak said. "Guns can malfunction. Run dry. Get knocked out of your hand. But you'll always have a knife on you somewhere, and sometimes it's all you'll have."

Detanna wasn't convinced, but she was ready to go again. They both assumed battle stances, eyes locked, each daring the other to go first. Finally Drallak feinted left, then thrust right. But Detanna was used to that ploy by now, and she dodged nimbly to the side, then swiped her dagger across Drallak's arm.

"Hey!" Drallak said, feeling his wound. Detanna backed off while her opponent recovered. There was a small rip in Drallak's sleeve, and a tiny trickle of blood. "Did you switch out daggers?" he asked.

Detanna examined her blade. Earlier in the fight she'd missed Drallak with a thrust and hit the metal wall. Now it appeared that she'd chipped the tip of the ceramic blade, leaving a jagged edge. "Whoops," she apologized. "I'll get another one." They'd picked up an entire crate of decorative ceramic daggers during a raid on Cytrine Delta, and they'd almost dumped them as worthless. It was Drallak who had convinced the captain that they might be useful for training purposes.

"Don't bother, Skiff," Drallak said. "You won't get another hit in anyway."

Detanna bristled at the name, though to be fair, it was the one she'd given them. When she'd signed on, she'd had to come up with a fake name on the spot, so she'd picked one of her childhood heroes. She regretted it now, but it was too late to change it. As far as the pirates knew, she was a cis man named Skiff. But in her head she called herself Detanna, and she yearned for a day when others would call her that as well.

They faced off once again, and this time Detanna moved first. Taking a cue from Drallak, she feinted left, then feinted right, then tricked him into lunging forward. As she darted to the side, time seemed to slow down for a moment. Detanna analyzed Drallak's entire body, head to toe, picking the best weak point. In the space of a second she considered throwing her dagger at his neck (too fatal), kicking him in the stomach (not painful enough), and stabbing him in the back of the knee (best not to leave a lasting injury during training).

Finally she picked the most humiliating option. She kicked Drallak in the rump as he passed by, knocking him face-first into a crate. Drallak's dagger shattered as it hit the floor, and by the time he turned around, Detanna had her dagger in his face.

They locked eyes again. For the first time, Drallak recognized just how far his trainee had come. *He passed up several opportunities to seriously hurt me*, Drallak realized. *How long has he been pulling his punches? Weeks? Months?*

"I think we're done for today," Drallak said.

Detanna nodded and watched him leave the storage room. She sat on a crate, worried that she'd shown her hand too early. She'd always been a fast learner, and the pirates had been teaching her everything they knew – hacking, fighting, piloting, and much more. But they couldn't have known she'd pick up their skills so quickly.

There was no future for her with the pirates. She needed to leave. But if she was going to escape, it would be easier if they underestimated her. Now Drallak would be suspicious. Now he'd keep an eye on her. Now he'd…

Detanna shook her head. It didn't matter. By the end of the day, she'd either be free or dead. Either way, she'd never see the pirates again.

The weapons storage facility was huge. Well-hidden in the snowcaps of Glayss, the white building was virtually invisible from a distance. The facility was completely automated, with no breathers – that's what the pirates called living humanoid people – anywhere on site.

The mission was simple. First, jam any outgoing signals. Second, send a single pirate inside to disable the security. Then the rest of the landing party would load up all the weapons they could haul, and be long gone before anyone noticed there'd been a break-in.

Detanna volunteered to go in first. It took a bit of convincing. At twenty, she was the youngest of the lot, and she'd only been with them for two years. She'd yet to work unsupervised on a mission. But she was also the fastest hacker they had. It wasn't like she'd cut and run here, in the middle of a frozen continent. Besides, all the pirates wore bodycams so the captain could monitor their progress. They'd know if she tried to double-cross them.

Detanna had to fight three security robots on her way into the warehouse. She defeated the final one with her dagger – and didn't she just hate it when Drallak was right – and then she hacked her way into the security systems. The first thing she did was deactivate the cameras and motion sensors, along with the remaining robots. Then she began toying with her bodycam feed.

"Skiff, are you there? Your feed cut out." Captain Flemm always monitored the missions personally.

"Must be getting interference from something," Skiff replied.

The captain scowled. He had no reason to distrust Skiff, but the kid was still pretty green. Maybe it was interference, or maybe he was about to pull something. He was about to run out of patience when the feed came back. But instead of a bank of security computers, the display showed a wall of explosives.

"What are you doing there?" Flemm demanded. "You're supposed to be disabling security!"

"I heard a noise," Skiff answered. "I think there's someone here."

"Be careful," Flemm said. "I'll send in the others."

"No, don't," Skiff said. "I don't have all the sensors down yet. They'll set off the—" There was a high-pitched noise, like the whine of several energy pistols coming online.

"What's that?" the captain asked. "Do you see something?"

"They've found me," Skiff said, his voice tinged with panic. "No! Don't fire at the explosives!"

Just then there was a boom. The screen went bright white, then black.

"Captain!" It was Drallak's voice. "There's been an explosion! Half the facility's gone!"

"Damn!" the captain cursed. "Get out of there before the IGP shows up."

"What about Skiff?" Drallak asked.

"Forget him," Flemm replied. There was no way Skiff could have survived that. It was a pity, he'd shown a lot of promise. But piracy always had its dangers, and Captain Flemm had learned long ago not to form attachments. He'd raise a glass to the kid that night when the crew was together. One final toast to celebrate Skiff's bravery. After that, the kid would be forgotten.

Now well-hidden and at a safe distance away, Detanna watched as the IGP ships gave chase to the pirate vessel. *Good,* Detanna thought. *That should keep them busy for a while.*

Even if they escaped the IGP, they wouldn't come looking for her. They had no way of knowing that she'd reactivated the security bots under her control, and that the final footage they'd seen had actually come from a bot's camera.

Skiff was dead. For that matter, so was Datan. *Long live Detanna,* she thought. It was a funny thought, given her current predicament - stranded in a frozen tundra with a long, dangerous trek ahead. But she knew she'd survive. Friendships were fragile and alliances fell through, but Detanna could always count on one person... herself.

Maybe teamwork just isn't for me, she thought. *Maybe I'm stronger by myself. If I'm going to make it in this galaxy, I need to become a...*

ED.02499.07.23

...Teddy bear, Detanna thought. *That's where he's keeping the stone.* She spotted her target getting out of a hovercab, carrying a small stuffed bear. The man was human, in his late twenties, with a balding pate and an eye patch. *Probably needs the money for a new eye*, Detanna thought. *Too bad. That money's not yours.*

She'd tracked him for ten kilometers. She'd had no trouble keeping up, despite being on foot. Traffic was stop-and-go, and what should have been a ten-minute drive had taken nearly an hour.

Tightly clutching the stuffed bear in the crook of his left elbow, Savnirt pulled a suitcase out of the hovercab's trunk. Detanna touched the frame of her sunglasses, and the image zoomed in.

There was something about the way Savnirt held the objects, a subtle bit of body language that gave away his priorities. The suitcase almost seemed like an afterthought, just part of the disguise. Just one of thousands of business travelers who passed through those doors twenty-six hours a day. But he clutched the bear in a desperate, animalistic way, the way a poisoned man would clutch a bag of antidote while pushing through a hurricane.

Once, when Detanna was a child, she'd convinced her mother to take her to a haunted house. Her mother had hated getting scared, but little Datan had begged and begged until she'd relented. They'd held hands at first, but something in the second room spooked Datan's mother, and she grabbed her child around the waist and bolted. Detanna still remembered that vise-like grip, that almost supernatural strength her mother had never exhibited before or since. She remembered seeing the rest of the house in fast-forward at a forty-five-degree angle, feeling strangely like a football as her mother charged toward the goalposts.

And that was how Savnirt held the stuffed bear now. It was possible he was just nervous about flying, but Detanna doubted it. Savnirt's priors included several smuggling charges, most of which had involved traveling between planets. Interplanetary smuggling wasn't typically a career choice for aerophobics.

No, the stone – a stolen relic worth hundreds of thousands of credits – had to be in the bear. It was cliché, like something from a low-budget detective movie, but since when were smugglers creative? *At least I won't have to fish it out of his butt,* Detanna thought.

Savnirt climbed the stairs to the terminal entrance, walking at a normal pace. But the way he moved told Detanna that he was holding himself back. He wanted to run. He had his own goalposts in mind, and it was taking every ounce of his energy to keep from charging. Because he knew, as did Detanna, that running through a spaceport would draw too much attention.

Being careful to keep her distance, Detanna shoved her sunglasses into her pocket and followed him through the huge automatic doors.

"I'm sorry sir, you'll need to run the stuffed animal through the conveyor."

At the security officer's demand, Savnirt set the bear on the belt. He'd already handed off his suitcase at check-in, and it was on its way to being loaded into the belly of the spacecraft. Savnirt's heart was in his throat as he watched the bear slide down a little ramp into a scanning device. He barely noticed the other officers patting him down and waving sensor wands over his body. He craned his neck to look at the computer screen. If he was going to run into trouble, it would be now.

The scanner's operator studied the bear's insides, frowned a little, then waved Savnirt over. "You know that seam's busted," the operator said, pointing to a spot on the screen. "If you're giving it to a child, you might want to sew that up first." Then the bear emerged from the scanner and Savnirt took it back. Clutching it tight, he resumed his forced mosey to the terminal.

The operator had been right. The seams had come undone from when Savnirt placed the stone into the bear. *It just has to hold together until takeoff,* Savnirt thought. *Then I'll be in the clear.*

Savnirt had stuffed the stone into a blackout sack before putting it in the bear. The sack was made of materials that made it invisible to most sensors. Acquiring the sack hadn't been easy, as it used technology not yet available to the public. The tiny sack had cost him ten thousand credits. Expensive, yes, but chump change compared to what he'd get for the stone.

Detanna usually carried a lot more gear when bounty hunting. Her signature outfit sported a space helmet and body armor, along with all manner of high-tech gadgets and embedded weaponry. But it was difficult to wear it without calling attention to herself, and wearing it through spaceport security would have been a nightmare. Now Detanna stood impatiently in line, waiting for her turn to pass through the weapons check. She'd lost sight of Savnirt, but she knew which direction he was heading. She could only hope she'd catch up to him before his flight left.

She was now twenty-seven, and she'd been working full-time as a bounty hunter for several years now. She'd first tried it out of desperation. She'd needed some quick money, and she'd actually been preparing to hack an online bank when she'd seen a wanted poster. Unable to resist a good puzzle, she'd deduced the fugitive's location, fought them, subdued them, and collected the reward. All in just a few hours.

And she'd been a bounty hunter ever since. Life offers very few perfect matches. Even those who land their dream job often struggle with the minutia of their chosen occupation. An artist or author might have difficulty promoting their work. An IGP officer might dread the paperwork they have to complete each day. Even a CEO might come to despise all the company meetings. But Detanna had adjusted to bounty hunting like an AON dagger sliding into a custom sheath. It was a perfect fit.

"You're all clear, Ma'am," the security officer said, waving her by. Of course she was. She'd left all her gadgets in a rented locker near the entrance. There were a couple of devices that she might have managed to sneak past security, but it hadn't been worth the gamble. A delay at the security checkpoint could have made the difference between catching Savnirt and watching his ship vanish into the sky.

Weaponless and lacking any tech, Detanna pushed through the crowds, searching for a man and his teddy bear.

Hurry up and let us board, Savnirt thought, watching the arrivals and departures on the big screen. He stared at his flight number – 2308 – his gaze threatening to burn a hole in the screen. Any minute now, the yellow STANDBY would turn into a friendly green NOW BOARDING, and he'd be one step closer to payday. He glared at the board as if he could change it by sheer will. And then, suddenly, the status changed. The digital sign now displayed "2308 DELAYED."

"Zarg blammit!" Savnirt cursed. Several of the other passengers let out groans and curses as well. Savnirt stood and approached the boarding attendant's desk. He gave her a quick look before speaking. The attendant was taller than Savnirt. She had brown skin and purple hair, and she wore a bright pink spaceline jacket which looked way too small on her. Her nametag identified her as Courtney.

"May I help you, sir?" Courtney asked. Her smile seemed genuine, but her eyes scrutinized Savnirt from head to toe as if scanning him for weapons.

"How long is the delay?" Savnirt said.

"It's hard to say," Courtney said. "The captain spontaneously combusted, and we're looking for someone to fill his position. Have you ever flown a commercial spacecraft?" Savnirt shook his head. "If you like, I can go ahead and put your belongings on board," Courtney added, reaching for the bear.

"No, thank you," Savnirt said, half-turning away and clutching the bear even tighter. His voice seemed to rise an octave when he spoke again. "Are there any other flights I could transfer to?"

"Sure, I can help you with that," Courtney said. She tapped a few keys on a tablet, then held it up so Savnirt could see. "Which flight would you like?"

Savnirt leaned in closer, squinting at the tiny writing on the screen. Then Courtney punched him in the face. Her hand moved so quickly that none of the passers-by saw a thing.

Even Savnirt was unsure of what had just happened. Stunned, he raised a hand to his nose. It came away bloody. "Buh... Blood?" he asked in a slurred voice.

"Stone," Courtney demanded, holding out her hand.

Savnirt came to his senses instantly. He turned and ran. Detanna wasted a couple of seconds moving out from behind the desk, then pursued him through the terminal. She passed the real Courtney as she ran.

Courtney had been talking to a security guard, but now she pointed at Detanna. "That's her!" she shouted, and the guard turned and gave chase.

Savnirt turned a corner, then another, then another. The spaceport was huge and mazelike. If he could just get a big enough lead, he knew he could shake off his pursuer. *Just who was that woman, anyway?* he wondered. He was certain he'd never seen her before, but at the same time, she seemed oddly familiar.

As he ran, he reached into the bear and transferred the stone into his pocket. He turned down a small hallway marked "Employees Only." It ended with two doors. The one on the right was labeled "Lockers" and the left door sported a sign that read "Roof Access." With only a split second to decide, he dropped the bear so that it landed in front of the door to the right, then entered the door on the left.

Detanna saw him go into the hallway, but he was gone by the time she reached it. She immediately spotted the discarded bear. There was no reason to search it; there was no way Savnirt would have parted with it if it still held the stone. She was about to check the right door when she heard the left door click shut. Inspired by Savnirt's ruse, Detanna kicked the right door open and threw Courtney's jacket to where the door would close on it. With any luck, that would buy her some time before the security guards showed up. Then she entered the left door and slammed it shut behind her.

A ladder led to the roof, and the hatch was still open. Detanna climbed out into the sunlight and looked around. Savnirt was about twenty meters away, trying to open another hatch. He bolted when he spotted Detanna. The two ran across the spaceport roof, Detanna gradually gaining on her prey.

Realizing he wasn't going to get away, Savnirt ran for the roof's edge. He stopped to look down, then turned around. "Don't come any closer," he said, backing towards the edge.

Detanna skidded to a stop, about six meters away from him. "There's nowhere to run, Savnirt," she said.

"See, that's where you're wrong," Savnirt said, glancing behind himself again. He reached into his pocket and retrieved the stone, then held it out over the edge.

"If you drop it, I'll just find it," Detanna said.

"And while you're looking, I'll run free," Savnirt replied.

"Not if I knock you out first," Detanna said.

"Are you really going to waste time with me while the stone's down there, where anybody can find it?"

Good point, Detanna thought. The stone was far more valuable than Savnirt. Detanna knew she could wipe the floor with him in a fight, but that would waste time better spent recovering the stone. If she had to choose between the two...

"Fine," Detanna said. "If you're willing to go that far, then just toss me the stone and go. I won't chase you."

"And I'm supposed to take the word of a bounty hunter?" Savnirt asked.

Detanna let out a long, slow breath before she replied. "I always had your back before, Nirt."

Savnirt looked confused. He spent a few seconds lost in thought. Finally his eyes widened. "Datan?" he asked.

"Not anymore," Detanna replied.

"But you're..." Savnirt said, then stopped. Neither of them spoke for a few seconds. "I knew you picked the pink one on purpose," Savnirt finally said.

Detanna chuckled. "The stone?" she asked, holding out her hand.

"Can't you just let me hold onto it for old time's sake?" Savnirt asked. When Detanna shook her head, he shrugged and tossed her the stone. "Can't fault me for trying," Savnirt said, then walked away. Detanna did not pursue him.

A few minutes later, Detanna climbed down a ladder and returned to the terminal. She ran into a couple of security guards on her way out. She explained to them that she was on official bounty hunter business, and showed them her BHR license – one of two such licenses she kept on her person. After a brief statement they allowed her to leave.

Detanna returned the stone to its rightful owners, and a reward was posted to her BHR account. Naturally, the reward was substantially less than she would have received if she'd just found an illegal buyer for the stone. She could have, too – she had plenty of contacts, "guys who knew guys who knew guys" who could have found her a buyer, someone willing to pay a hundred times the reward she received for doing her job.

But that wasn't how she wanted to live her life. At least, not anymore. She enjoyed bounty hunting. It didn't take much to piss off the Bounty Hunter Registry, and she wasn't about to risk a promising career for some quick credits.

Why rock the boat? Detanna found herself thinking as she took a shuttle home. *This is the life I've always wanted. I no longer have to rely on the unreliable, counting on so-called teammates who are just as likely to stab you in the back as they are to help. I'm just better alone. I don't need a team, I don't need friends, and I don't need…*

ED.02502.03.25

…Family, Detanna thought, surveying her team. For once, they'd all beaten her to the bridge. Now they stared at her, waiting for her orders. *That's what they are. It's more than a crew, it's a family. I never wanted this… or did I?*

The thought had taken longer to sink in than it should have. Detanna was a quick learner when it came to weapons and technology and new ways of punching someone in the face, but she was a bit stunted on the subject of friendship. She'd often looked at her crew as if they were just more weapons in her armory. But now she'd been with them for more than two years, and she had to admit they'd grown on her.

They were more than just a crew. More than just friends. They really were…

"Where to?" Raven asked, standing at the navigation console. Detanna's silent stare seemed to be making her uncomfortable.

"Set a course for Enceladus," Detanna finally ordered. "It's a moon of—"

"Saturn, got it," Raven answered, tapping a few keys on the control panel. "I'm from that solar system, remember?"

"Doesn't mean you know every moon," Detanna muttered.

"Have you *met* Raven?" Vik quipped, leaning against a wall. "Hey, since we're so close to Earth, think maybe we could pop by and say 'Hi' when we're done? I have some friends I'd like to see."

"No promises," Detanna said. "This one might take a while. Our target is a master of disguise. So good he could probably give Dervish a run for her money, and he's not even a shapeshifter."

Dervish looked up from her position at the communications console, her expression a mix of surprise and concern.

"But I'm certain if we all work together, we can find him," Detanna said. She looked over her crew.

Two scientists – one a human with robotic limbs, the other a green-skinned telepath. An ex-cop with gravity-altering implants. A former pirate who could change into a fiery form. An unusually large panther. A powerful shapeshifter with self-esteem issues. And finally the shadowy martial artist who meant more to Detanna than the rest of the crew put together.

They had their disagreements from time to time, but together they were a powerful team. Three years ago, Detanna couldn't have imagined leading such a group. Or any group for that matter. She'd always felt that connections led to betrayal, and 'friends' were just enemies who hadn't shown their true colors yet.

But she trusted these people. They'd proven their loyalty time and time again. She wasn't used to trusting people, but this group had earned it. If one of them were to betray her now, it would crush her soul. But that wasn't going to happen. She knew their secrets, and they knew hers. As long as they were together, there was nothing they couldn't accomplish.

"Leez was spotted at the Saturn Springs Mall," Detanna

told them. "By now he's had time to pick a new identity. He could be anywhere or anyone. If we're going to find him, it's going to require…"

ED.02522.10.15

"Awesome teamwork," Aria said, as the final boss exploded into shrapnel. Vulpestriker struck a victory pose as the end credits floated across the stars. Aria took off their VR glasses as their friends cheered.

Standing in the doorway, Detanna watched her child celebrate. She was so proud of them. Not for beating a forty-year-old video game, but for everything else. Their good grades, their computer skills, their fighting prowess, and for having the guts to be honest with themself.

It was Aria's fourteenth birthday. Just that morning, Aria had come out to Detanna as non-binary. It had been a bit of a shock, but not an unwelcome one. At fourteen years old, Aria understood themself more than Detanna ever had at their age. Now that Detanna thought about it, Aria had always rejected gender roles. They had always been the kind of kid who would put a doll's dress on a toy hovertruck. Aria didn't so much "march to the beat of a different drummer" – it was closer to say they eschewed the drums entirely and constructed brand-new musical instruments out of materials no one had ever considered.

That's a labored metaphor, Detanna thought, but it was accurate. *I wonder if it's just a phase,* she considered. She was sure her parents had wondered the same of her when she was Aria's age. Detanna's mother had often caught her doing feminine things, such as trying on makeup. The memories still made Detanna's butt hurt.

But it didn't matter. Maybe it was a phase, maybe it was forever. As far as Detanna was concerned, Aria was free to experiment with gender however they wanted. Detanna grew up in a household where "different" was discouraged – sometimes violently – and she refused to subject her child to the same trauma. As Aria's mother – well, one of them – it was her duty to help Aria find themself, and support them every step of the way.

Be who you were meant to be, Detanna thought, turning back through the doorway. *Whoever you become, I will always...*

Love you, Aria thought, watching their mother leave the room. Then they put their VR glasses back on and started up another game with their friends.

Game Face

SESSION ONE

The fluorescent lights came on, one by one, illuminating six long tables. A small crowd filed into the room, some people laughing and cracking jokes, others looking like they were about to go to war. They took their seats, set down their backpacks, and unpacked their supplies. Soon the tables were covered with maps, pencils, paper, and most importantly, dice.

Brant took his place at the head of a table, as his friends took their usual spots. A new face sat to his right, a young man who kept staring at the floor. "Before we get started," Brant said, "I want to welcome our newest player, Nathan."

All eyes fell on Nate, and while the other players seemed friendly enough, he didn't like being in the spotlight. They looked like they expected him to say something, but he had no idea what.

"Hi, Nathan, I'm Sharon," one woman said. She looked like she was the oldest member of the group, probably in her late thirties.

"I'm Dot," another woman said. She was in her mid-twenties, and easily had the most distinctive look in the group. The left side of her face was covered with freckles, so dense in some places that they almost looked like one giant freckle. Nate struggled to maintain eye contact.

"Rita," said the woman next to her. She was muscular and wore a plaid button-up shirt. The way she kept touching Dot's arm, Nate had a feeling the two were more than just friends.

"Robert," said a man to Rita's left. "Good to meet you, Nathan."

"Nate's fine," he mumbled, looking up briefly before his gaze dropped back to the table. Nate had always had trouble looking people in the eyes. He spent most of his time staring at his shoes when talking to people. In recent years he'd tried to break the habit, forcing himself to look up during conversations. But no matter how hard he tried, his natural instincts pulled his chin back down. Sometimes this resulted in splitting the difference, with Nate looking the other person in the chest – a compromise that was particularly problematic when talking to women.

"Have you played Blaggards and Blades before, Nate?" Sharon asked, trying to draw him out with her smile.

"Yeah, I mean, no," Nate replied. "I mean, I've played some of the video games. But I know the rules, sort of."

"It's pretty easy to pick up," Brant said. "Since we're close to finishing up the current campaign, I was hoping you'd run one of the NPCs today, is that cool?"

"Sure," Nate said, and Brant handed him a character sheet. Nate studied it carefully, happy to have an excuse to look away from everyone's faces.

Brant gave him a short recap of the storyline so far, and Nate listened intently. The party had spent the last few months collecting eight magical keys. The ninth and final key belonged to the leader of a thieves guild called the Deep Dragons. It was basically a medieval mafia, and the party was close to locating the big boss, Don Drakyss. Nate was to play Veezil, a former member of the guild who had seen the error of his ways, and now acted as the party's guide through the guild's base.

Brant also slipped him another piece of paper. It was a map of the guild hideout, with guard posts and traps labeled, and an X showing their destination. Underneath the map was written, "Don't show this to the other players. Veezil is actually still working for the thieves guild. Don Drakyss is paying him to lead the party into a trap." Nate's eyes widened at this, and he glanced up at Brant for confirmation. Brant gave him a subtle nod.

Yikes, Nate thought. He'd just met these people, and now he was supposed to betray them? He wasn't very good at lying, and he wasn't sure he could keep up the deception without blowing his cover. It was definitely going to be a challenge.

But then, the whole day was about overcoming challenges. Nate didn't get out much. He wasn't good at making friends, and while he still kept in touch with some former classmates on social media, he rarely saw any of them in person. The lack of human contact was finally getting to him. A few weeks ago he'd resolved to work an in-person social activity into his life. He'd always loved playing computer RPGs, so joining a tabletop group seemed like a good choice.

Brant unrolled a gridded battle map. The dry-erase markings were still there from the previous session, depicting the hallways and rooms they'd been through so far. The other players pulled out their miniatures and put them in the room where they'd left off. Brant placed an additional mini in the room to represent Veezil.

Nate examined the miniature, which looked pretty close to the sketch on Veezil's character sheet. He wore a black hood and had rat-like facial features. *Why would anybody trust this person?* Nate thought. He hated to judge anybody based on their appearance, but this character was obviously designed to look evil. He wondered how the party had ever come to ally with him.

"At the end of last session," Brant said, "You took a brief rest in a supply room."

Rita spoke up. "Before we get moving again, Bjertha could use a little healing. I want to make sure I'm in good shape before we fight the boss."

"Skorn's at full health," Sharon said. "So she'll watch the door while the others patch Bjertha up."

"Veritas uses 'Soothing Hands' for... sixteen points," Robert said, rolling some dice. "Does that max you?"

"Seven short," Rita said. "But good enough, thanks."

"You sure?" Dot asked. "Venus can sing you a healing tune."

"Save 'em," Rita said. "I mean, how tough can Drakyss be? Veezil said we'd catch him by surprise. With a little luck, we'll find him in bed. Or on the chamber pot. That'd be funny."

Nate opened his mouth to say something, but then closed it.

"Let's get moving then," Sharon said. "Lead on, Veezil."

"Follow me," Nate said, his mouth a little dry. Using the map Brant had given him, Nate led the party through the guild's lowest tunnels, avoiding guards and sidestepping traps.

"It's just through here," Veezil said, leading them through a large door. They went through a short tunnel that came out in a huge, oval arena. Above them, the stands were filled with dozens of black-clad spectators. At the far end of the arena, Don Drakyss relaxed on an ornate throne, clad in purple robes and an oversized crown.

"What is this?" Veritas asked, as the gate slammed shut behind them.

"We're trapped!" Skorn said, drawing her wand. She fired a magic blast at Drakyss, but the projectile was nullified by an invisible barrier surrounding the arena floor.

Bjertha grabbed Veezil by the collar and pulled him close to her face. "Is this your doing?" Veezil was more than a foot taller than the dwarf, but he still shrank away from her intimidating physique.

Venus put her hand on Bjertha's shoulder. "We don't know that," she said. "Maybe he was tricked by Drakyss."

"Impudent fools," Drakyss said, his magically-amplified voice booming throughout the arena. "Veezil was working for me the entire time. Now come, my loyal servant, and take your place by my side so we can watch their demise together." Drakyss snapped his fingers, and Veezil was teleported past the barrier to stand next to his master.

"Get down here and face us, Drakyss," Bjertha growled. "You and me, right now."

"While that would certainly be amusing," Drakyss said, "I already have entertainment planned." With another snap of his fingers, a gate opened beneath the throne. This gate was much larger than the one the party had come through, and Bjertha spotted six glowing eyes approaching in the darkness.

Brant reached into his bag and pulled out a monster that stretched the limits of the word "miniature." The players gasped as he set it on the table. Its six-by-six inch base took up nearly a quarter of the arena.

"How much did you spend on that?" Robert asked.

"More than I should have," Brant said. "In fact, maybe don't mention it to my wife. Everybody roll initiative."

A three-headed dragon burst through the gate, with gleaming black scales and fangs as long as a greatsword.

Standing by his master's throne, Veezil watched as the doomed captives charged into battle. *Not my fault*, Veezil thought, as the dragon stomped on Veritas and took Bjertha into its jaws. *They should have known better than to trust me.*

"A little healing would be nice!" Bjertha shouted, hacking at the dragon's face with her greataxe. The monster's teeth were boring into her platemail, and she now dangled halfway out of its mouth, trying desperately to get a good hit in.

"I'm all out," Veritas grunted. The dragon's massive foot kept him pinned to the ground, constricting his armor and making it hard to breathe. Nearby, Venus played a song of protection on her harp. Skorn fired blast after blast at the dragon, but most of her shots bounced harmlessly off of the creature's scales.

Drakyss stood and took a step forward. "Yes," he hissed. "Yes, kill them. Kill them and I will bring the world to ruin!"

Veezil knew the truth of his master's words. The paladin Veritas held eight of the nine Keys of Kuthiz, having quested for them over the past year. Drakyss held the final key, which was why the party had come to bring down his criminal empire. Once the party was defeated, Drakyss would possess all nine keys, and would use them to destroy the world.

And I'll be his right-hand man, Veezil thought. *Second-in-command to the ruler of the world… or what's left of it.*

Veezil winced as the dragon bit down hard, his powerful jaws cutting Bjertha in half.

"Aw man," Rita said. "I've been running that character for three campaigns now."

"Sorry," Nate said.

"Don't sweat it," Rita said, suddenly smiling. "It's actually kind of cool. I just got bitten in half by a dragon. I couldn't ask for a more epic death. Her clan will be writing songs about her final battle."

"They'll have to get in line," Dot said. "Venus is already composing one as we speak."

"You might want to concentrate on the battle at hand," Robert told her.

"I'm not sure it matters at this point," Sharon said. "With Bjertha down, we're headed for a TPK."

"I stab Drakyss in the back," Nate said softly.

"Don't give up yet, Sharon," Robert said. "We can still win this. I'm going to—"

"Hold up," Rita interrupted, looking at Nate. "What did you say?"

"Veezil realizes the error of his ways, and stabs Drakyss in the back," Nate said.

"I'm not sure Veezil would do that," Brant said. "I don't want to tell you how to play your character, but Veezil being an NPC and all…"

"He knows his master plans to use those keys to destroy the world," Nate said. "You know, the world Veezil lives on? Or… maybe he just wants the power for himself. If he kills Drakyss right now, he can collect the keys and become all-powerful, instead of… you know, just a lackey." It was the most words he'd spoken since the session began, and his cheeks began to turn red.

"That sounds more like Veezil," Brant said. "Roll your attack."

Everyone held their breath as Nate rolled a twenty-sided die. "Crit!" Nate shouted, unable to believe his eyes.

"Huh," Brant said, doing the math. "And Drakyss wasn't expecting it, so you'll get your backstab bonus… and Veezil uses a poison dagger… You do forty-seven points of damage. Not quite enough to kill him, I'm afraid. He turns around to face you, and he doesn't look happy."

"Uh oh," Nate said.

"Does a thirty-three hit your AC?"

Nate laughed nervously. "Uh, yeah, by a good bit."

"Drakyss is so angry, he isn't even thinking straight," Brant said. "He burns all three of his Torment Tokens. His hand turns into a blade of white fire. And…" Brant rolled some dice. "Make a save against decapitation."

"Six," Nate said.

"Your head goes flying across the room," Brant said. "But… that shield around the arena? Drakyss was doing that. When he attacked you, he lost his concentration. The shield goes down."

"Ooh! I fire a Ray of Randomness at Drakyss," Sharon said.

"He fails his save," Brant said. "What's the effect?"

"Come on six," Sharon said, rolling a six-sided die. "Darn.

Two. He's paralyzed."

"I sing Ballad of Befuddlement to the dragon," Dot said.

"One of his heads makes the save," Brant said. "But the other two are befuddled. They each pick a new target at random, and the dragon runs up into the stands to attack some of the guild members. The scene devolves into total chaos as the audience flees in every direction. Veritas, you're no longer pinned."

"I get to my feet and use Prayer of Damnation on Drakyss," Robert said.

"You know you can only use it once per level," Brant warned.

"I know, I've been saving it for Drakyss."

"A beam of holy light comes down from the heavens and envelopes Don Drakyss," Brant said. "He fails his save, and he was down to three hit points, so he's pretty much disintegrated. The magic items he was carrying fall to the floor, including the ninth Key of Kuthis."

"I use Planar Hop to reach the throne," Sharon said. "Then I'll grab the key and whatever else he dropped."

"And as soon as Sharon's close enough, I sing Anthem of Escape to get us out of here," Dot said.

"That about wraps things up, then," Brant said. "You escape with the artifact, and return the complete set to the Council of Protectors for disposal. The Deep Dragons thieves guild is dissolved, and city guards are sent into their base to capture any survivors. Bjertha's clan throws her a funeral the likes of which you've never seen, with a week-long party that none of you can remember afterward. Roll credits."

"Great campaign," Rita said.

"So what's next week?" Robert asked.

"Before we start our next full campaign, I thought we'd try

something different," Brant said. "I have a horror module I'd like to run. It shouldn't take more than two or three sessions to get through."

"I'm game," Sharon said. "Will you be joining us next week, Nate?"

"Probably," Nate said, though he didn't look very sure.

Nate got home and took a seat on his couch. He spent several minutes staring at the television, even though it wasn't turned on. He sat perfectly still, but his brain was like a busy airport, with too many thoughts to process flying in every direction. Of all the players at that table, he'd spoken the least, and yet his throat was sore. And he was exhausted, more tired than he would have been if he'd run the ten miles home instead of driven.

It had taken every ounce of his energy to be social, and he really didn't feel like he'd contributed that much to the story. In a sense he'd saved the day, but he'd also gotten another character killed, so the two canceled each other out. He hoped Rita wasn't mad at him. She'd sounded happy with how things ended, but she could have been trying to spare Nate's feelings.

He considered whether to go back next week. He'd had fun, but it had come at a cost. A thousand voices bickered in his head, replaying every interaction, telling him what he should have said. Snappy comebacks he could have made. Things he should have apologized for. Jokes he didn't get until just now.

Why are you such a freak? he asked himself. Surely the other players weren't staring at a blank TV screen right now, obsessing over the day's conversations. He wasn't sure his ego could take another session. It didn't matter if things went well, his brain would find a way to berate him for every word that did or didn't come out of his mouth. It was a lot to endure just to play a game.

It sure was fun, though.

Nate lay down on his side, turned away from the television, and took a nap.

That evening Brant messaged the group, excluding Nate.

<u>Brant</u>: What do you think of Nate?

<u>Robert</u>: Seems harmless

<u>Rita</u>: So did Tyler.

<u>Robert</u>: We should frisk new players for weapons

<u>Rita</u>: Don't go overboard. We'll just all wear bulletproof vests.

<u>Dot</u>: Haha

<u>Brant</u>: I can vouch for Nate. He's not dangerous.

<u>Rita</u>: He killed Bjertha but I'll let it slide this time ;)

<u>Robert</u>: There's not much to say - didn't talk much

<u>Dot</u>: Just needs to get used to us maybe.

<u>Sharon</u>: Seemed really shy.

<u>Brant</u>: I know. Always has been. I've been trying to draw him out.

<u>Dot</u>: Careful. Been there. Some people hate the spotlight. Might drive him off.

<u>Brant</u>: Understood.

On Wednesday after work, Nate got home and loaded up an RPG on his computer. He usually preferred single-player games to multiplayer. Even with the anonymity that came with online gaming, he was just as shy on MMOs as he was in real life. Plus, he just didn't have as much free time as most players. Every time he found a decent group to play with, they'd be twenty levels ahead of him by the next time he logged on.

With single-player games, he didn't have to worry about all that. Plus the plots were deeper, like he was reading an interactive book. The MMOs he'd tried always seemed to be about leveling up your character and maxing out your gear. Sure they had plots, but few of the players cared. Nobody spoke in character, and if they did, it came across more Monty Python than J. R. R. Tolkien. He didn't expect the other players to be Shakespearian actors, but at least they could act like they cared about more than loot and experience points.

But even though they weren't his favorite, he'd tried his share of online RPGs. There was a MUD he'd gotten addicted to back in college... But he quickly pushed that memory aside. He'd screwed up and hurt someone's feelings. It was one more reason he didn't like playing online. Those games came with temptations. Nate just couldn't resist lying about... *Forget it,* he thought. *Never again. Those days are over.*

Single-player games were just better. And yet, when Nate loaded up his save and resumed his exploration of his favorite virtual world, something felt empty about the experience. Something was missing. A quote kept bouncing around his head. "The unexamined life is not worth living." *Who said that?* he wondered. *Was it Socrates?*

In the game, he found a secret enclave of bandits and fought his way through to the boss. It was a tough battle, but Nate had come prepared. Overprepared, even. He finished off the boss with a firebomb he'd looted from an ogre chieftain. Usually he saved those firebombs for later in the game, as they were pretty rare. In fact, he often held onto rare items so long that they became useless, even going as far as to beat the game with an inventory full of powerful, unused weapons.

As the head bandit crumpled to the ground, an achievement popped up. This would automatically be posted to Nate's profile, a badge of honor that no one would ever actually read. How often did gamers actually root through their friends' achievement lists? "If no one sees you do something, did you really do it?" he asked aloud.

He still wasn't sure if he'd return to Brant's game on Saturday. He'd spent last Saturday evening sick with embarrassment, even though he hadn't done anything to be embarrassed about. Even today the occasional random memory made his cheeks flush.

Get over it, he told himself, as if it were really that easy. *You're never going to overcome your shyness unless you get used to people. At least they're doing something you love.*

But what if I say something stupid? he retorted.

Then they'll laugh, you'll laugh, and you'll all get on with your lives, he thought. *Life is too short to spend it in hiding. Go make some friends.*

All right, he replied to himself. *But if I spend next Saturday night cringing at all the dumb things I said, I'm blaming you.*

Deal, he thought back. It was settled. He would show up on Saturday and try the horror game.

Probably.

SESSION TWO

"So, the module is called 'Frozen Terror.' You're playing as a team of scientists who've set up a research base on a frozen moon, when something bad happens. But a couple of you have secret agendas, so you might find yourself working against the other players. It uses pregens, which you'll be picking at random."

"We don't get to build our characters?" Dot asked.

"No, that's part of the fun," Brant said. "You won't know until you see your character's agenda if they're going to be an asset or a hindrance to the party. And there's a whole stack of characters, so if you get killed, you just draw another one."

"Hey," Nate said, taking a seat by Brant.

"Just in time," Brant said. "I wasn't sure you'd make it." Brant held out a small stack of character cards, and everyone drew one. "Don't show them to each other," Brant said.

"What did you say about agendas?" Nate asked.

"Usually it's just something that slows the party down," Brant said. "Maybe you don't mention your fear of heights until the party has to run across a narrow scaffold. But it could be something major, like, um... like if this was a zombie game, you might hide that you've been bitten."

Everyone took a moment to study their cards. A couple of "Hmms" and "Huhs" could be heard as they got down to the agendas section.

"So what did everyone end up with?" Dot asked.

"Let's go around the table," Brant suggested. "Just don't read that bottom box."

"Rakesh Becker, Biological Studies," Rita read. "He's a serious scientist, but he's mostly in it for the money. He hopes they'll make a big discovery here so he can get a bonus."

"Carl Blake, security," Dot said. "He's not particularly deep. He's used to being the biggest person in the room, so he feels a need to protect people. He's also an expert in hand-to-hand combat as well as dozens of weapons."

"Can we switch?" Rita asked. "He seems more like the kind of character I usually play."

"Nope," Brant said. "Get out of your comfort zone. Try something new. What did you get, Sharon?"

"Durant Fontaine," Sharon said. "He's a climatologist. He hopes that by studying the weather on this moon, he can create computer models that help predict climate patterns."

"And I'm Alena Kitt," Robert said. "She's an engineer. It says here that she's better at talking to machines than to people."

"And Nate?" Brant asked.

Nate looked over his card. "Yolanda Kale, Commanding Officer," he said. "Her fondest desire is to discover extraterrestrial life." He didn't read it to the others, but in the box marked "Private Agenda," the card read, "Yolanda is dying of an incurable disease. She has approximately six months before the symptoms begin to show, and less than a year to live. She refuses to tell anyone, or to let it slow her down. She hopes to get her name in the history books by finding alien life." *This should be interesting*, Nate thought.

"You outrank us?" Robert asked.

"Guess you're in charge," Sharon added.

Oh, Nate thought. He hadn't considered that. He didn't like the thought of having to make decisions for the party. He wanted to draw a different character, but Brant had already told Rita no, and he didn't want to make a fuss.

"Wait, did everyone end up drawing the opposite sex?" Sharon asked.

"Looks like it," Dot said.

"Neat," Brant said. "Now let's begin. It's the year 2159. Your team works at a research base on Europa, a moon of Jupiter. The moon is covered in ice, with constant snowstorms and hail."

"I'm not sure Europa actually gets snow," Robert said.

"I wouldn't look too closely at the science in this module," Brant said. "There are fourteen of you on the research base. You were sent because an earlier probe found readings that could indicate the presence of ancient microbes under the ice. This would be the first extraterrestrial life found in our solar system. But it hasn't been easy. You've been there for three months, and so far you haven't learned much. Your equipment keeps breaking due to the frigid temperatures. It's so cold, you can't survive outdoors for more than a minute without special heated suits. You don't think you're making any progress, when one day…"

"We've got a reading!" shouted Becker.

Kale didn't want to get her hopes up again, but the prospect of finding life – even long-frozen, microscopic life – was too exciting to stay calm. "Where?" she asked, pulling her chair up alongside Becker's workstation.

"Third quadrant," Becker said, pointing at his monitor. The screen showed a map of the surrounding area, and a red icon flashed on the lower right-hand side of the screen. "One of the drones detected something buried in the ice. Right before it froze up. Find that drone, and we'll find our microbes."

"Looks like it's only a couple of kilometers away," Kale said.

"I'll get a team together," Becker said.

Ten minutes later, Blake, Becker, and Fontaine pushed their

way through the waist-high snow. They were decked out from head to toe in heated snowsuits. Blake led the way, using a heat blower to forge a path for the rest to follow. Their spiked snowshoes crunched on the icy ground. Visibility was poor even with their enhanced goggles. Harsh winds and heavy snowfall ensured that the path quickly filled in behind them.

"It's like being inside a snow globe," Fontaine remarked. His mask's transmitter relayed his voice to the rest of the team.

"More like being in an ice machine," Becker replied. "Specifically, the kind that makes crushed ice."

"What's the matter, Becker?" Kale asked. "Not enjoying the weather?" She leaned forward in her office chair, following the field crew's progress on her screen. They were nearly a third of the way to their target.

"Why don't you join us?" Becker asked. "We'll make snow angels."

"You'd know I'd love to be there, but Blake wouldn't let me," Kale said.

"Don't you outrank him?" Fontaine asked.

"Not when it comes to security," Blake said.

"What, you're afraid we're going to run into a psycho killer out here on Europa?" Fontaine asked. "Maybe a vacationing walrus with a grudge?"

"I don't speculate," Blake said. "I just do my job."

"Fun, isn't he?" Kale asked.

"You three talk too much," Blake said. "I can barely concentrate as it is. I think I'm picking up some movement…"

"Wait, I've got it too," Fontaine said, studying the motion detector strapped to his left wrist. "The snow is causing all sorts of false readings, but there's something big… half a kilometer that way."

"Too big," Blake added. "This can't be our target. Aren't you looking for bacteria?"

"Frozen bacteria," Becker reminded him. "Whatever's moving, it's not why we're here."

"Can't be an animal," Fontaine said. "Maybe another science crew landed?"

"Without telling us?" Kale asked. "I'll raise hell if it is. We paid for exclusive rights. If those thieves at VivaSource sent their own team, we'll sue."

"I don't think it's an animal," Becker said. "Too big. I think this is seismic activity."

"Can't be," Fontaine said. "We have data nodes planted all around the compound. If there were going to be quakes today, we'd have known hours ago."

"It's stopped," Becker said.

"I don't feel right about this," Kale said. "Maybe you should head back, and we'll try again in a few hours."

"I said it stopped," Becker said. "And we're more than halfway. We'll be back before you know it."

Kale wasn't so sure. Her instincts told her to order them back. But she was just as excited as they were at the prospect of finding new life. Probably more so. With less than a year to live, this could be her big chance to contribute to the universe. Future generations would see Kale's name in their history books. Yolanda Kale. Leader of the team who discovered alien life on Europa. Her body would wither away, but her name would live on forever.

"Fine," she finally said. "But at the first sign of danger, you *will* turn around."

"You don't have to tell us twice," Fontaine replied.

Another kilometer passed, and their sensors picked up the

fallen drone. It had gone down near the base of a mountain. Though it had only been a couple of hours since it crashed, it was already buried under a meter of snow. Blake blasted the site with his blower, melting a tunnel to the drone.

Back at the base, the power flickered a couple of times, then the lights went out. "Um… Kitt?" Kale called out. Her headset no longer worked, so she looked around for her walkie-talkie. She had just about reached it when the power came back on. "Kitt," she said into her headset. "What was that?"

"Sorry," Kitt replied over the transmitter. "Generator's being a little twitchy today. I'll try to keep the heat on."

Through her headset, Kale could hear the machinery running in the background. Instead of pounding rhythmically, the generator shuddered and thumped and made random grinding noises. "Do you need me to send you some help?" Kale asked.

"They'd just be in the way," Kitt said. "Don't worry, I've got this."

"Just keep me in the loop," Kale said, and cut the channel. Then she reconnected to Blake's team and asked for a status update.

"We are, indeed, detecting microbes in the ice," Becker reported. "We're cutting through now. I should have a sample in about five minutes." Becker used a vibrating saw to cut a square around the sample, so they could bring it back to base without thawing the microbes.

"I'm getting more movement," Blake said.

"Seismic?" Fontaine asked.

"Most likely, but it's hard to tell," Blake said.

"Get out of there, now," Kale told them.

"Just another minute," Becker said.

"Now," Kale repeated, trying to sound as threatening as possible.

"I've almost g—" Becker said, then screamed.

"What's going on?" Kale asked, and then the power went out again. Kale cursed, then grabbed the walkie-talkie. "Kitt, report!"

"Main genny threw a rod," Kitt said. "I've almost got the backup on, but it's not good for much. It'll keep us warm and give us emergency lights, but I can't get the computers up until I fix the main."

"How long?" Kale asked.

"Ten minutes? Twenty at most," Kitt offered apologetically.

"I need communications ASAP," Kale ordered.

"On it," Kitt said.

Just then the backup lights came on. Kale tried her headset but it still didn't work. The walkie-talkies didn't work outside, as there was too much interference. She considered getting a second team together to find the first, but she didn't want to put more lives at risk. If communications didn't come up within the next ten minutes, she'd put on a heat suit herself. Blake wouldn't like it, but he wasn't here to stop her, either.

She stood and started packing a gearbag. As she rooted through a supply cabinet, a few scientists trickled into the command room. "What's going on?" one asked. Her name was Rayla Fleeke, and she was an expert on arctic survival.

"Blake's in trouble," Kale said. "I may need you to accompany me on an excursion."

"Of course," Fleeke said. "But I'd rather take my own team. You shouldn't put yourself at risk."

If one more person says that to me, Kale thought. "Your objection is noted," she said. "But I'm—" The computers came back up again. Kale immediately put on her headset and shouted, "Blake?"

"We're fine," he reported. "It was an avalanche. I'm pulling Becker out now."

"He got your sample," Fontaine added.

"Get back here right away," Kale said.

"No arguments here," Fontaine replied.

By the time they returned to base, the main generator was running smoothly. They took the sample to the lab and placed it in a refrigerated case. While the computers ran their scans, Kale held a meeting with Becker, Fontaine, and Blake.

"Next time I give you an order, I expect it to be obeyed," Kale said.

"Understood," Becker said. "But I just—"

"Don't," Kale interrupted. "I don't care. This moon is a block of ice. Nothing on it is going anywhere. Risking your life like that was just irresponsible. You should have just recorded the location and gone back when conditions were safer."

"I apologize," Becker said. "It won't happen again."

"I take full responsibility," Blake added. "I was leading the mission. I should have made him follow orders. I will accept any punishment you deem necessary."

"Nobody's getting punished," Kale said. "At least, not this time. Besides, I'm too excited about our discovery. Do you have an ETA on when we'll get some readings?"

"We should have some preliminary data in about four hours," Becker said. "And a full analysis by tomorrow morning."

Brant's phone buzzed. "Hold on," he said, reading the text. He glanced up and locked eyes with Rita for a second, then gave a slight nod. Then he typed something back.

Now Rita's phone dinged, and she took a quick look at the message. She smiled slightly and nodded, then put the phone down.

Nate looked from Brant to Rita, one eyebrow raised. "Don't worry about it," Brant told him, and they got back to the game.

The preliminary reports didn't tell them much, but they confirmed that the specimen did indeed contain life. Even more exciting was the fact that the microbes were unlike anything found on Earth. They left the scanners running overnight and went to bed.

Security Chief Blake returned to his quarters to find a bottle of whiskey sitting prominently on his desk. There was a note taped to it which read, "Great job today!"

Has Kale been saving this all this time? he wondered. He removed the note and studied the label. It was a bottle of Argyle's Best Whiskey, a favorite of his when he was younger. He reluctantly set the bottle down. He'd been sober for two years now, and his body still ached daily with the need for a drink. One of the reasons he'd taken this job was to get alcohol out of the picture. After all, the best way to keep from having a relapse was to make it physically impossible to access a drink.

He picked up the bottle again, then quickly set it down. *I should pour this down the sink,* he thought. Kale couldn't possibly know about his addiction. He'd never told anyone on the base. He'd pour it out, then thank Kale for a lovely gift. She'd never have to know he didn't want it.

But he did want it. He stared longingly at the bottle, imagining the exquisite taste and the numbness it would bring. He'd missed that numbness. *One bottle won't cause me to relapse,* he rationalized. Even if today's discovery turned out to be the real deal, it would still be months before Blake saw Earth again. Months without access to alcohol. Whatever progress he lost by succumbing to this bottle's allure, he'd gain it right back. Logically speaking, it was impossible for him to become an alcoholic again, even if he drank this entire bottle in one sitting.

But you are an alcoholic, he told himself. He would always be an alcoholic, regardless of whether he ever drank again. That's what they'd always told him at the meetings. *But if I'm an alcoholic either way, then there's no reason not to drink this,* he thought, picking up the bottle again.

He started to twist off the cap, then stopped himself. *How am I going to feel about myself in the morning?* he wondered. That two-year streak would be broken, and he'd have to start counting from zero once again. All for one night of pleasure. And it wasn't even pleasure, so much as a short break from that constant yearning. That maddening craving could be sated right now. All he had to do was twist off the cap and take a sip.

He knew he was about to give in. Suddenly furious with himself, he nearly hurled the bottle at the wall. But his hand simply wouldn't let go.

Fine, he thought. *Just one sip.* He sat down at his desk and twisted off the cap.

Early the following morning, Commander Kale woke up to a knock on her door. "Come in," she said, squinting at her clock. The door opened, and Fontaine stepped through.

"Big problem," Fontaine said. "The sample is gone."

Kale cursed as she rolled out of bed. She was in her underwear, but she didn't care. The research crew was like one big, dysfunctional family. "How?" she demanded.

"I don't know, I came to you first," Fontaine said.

"Find Blake," Kale said, reaching for her robe. "I want everyone in the lab in five minutes."

The research base housed a crew of fourteen, but only eleven were currently assembled in the lab. Fontaine, Becker, and Blake were the only ones who hadn't shown up yet. Kale was about to call them on the intercom when Fontaine yelled from down the hallway.

"I need medical here, now!" he shouted. Three of the assembled personnel rushed to Fontaine's aid. Kale followed them to Blake's room.

Kale gasped when she looked in on the scene. As the three medics worked to revive Blake, Fontaine reached down and picked up a nearly empty bottle of whiskey. Most of the bottle's contents had spilled onto the floor, but there was a little bit left at the bottom.

"I'm going to have this tested for poison," Fontaine said as he brushed by the commander on his way out the door.

"Is he going to make it?" Kale asked the medics. They were too busy to answer her, but they didn't have to. Kale could tell by looking that Blake had been dead for hours.

"I think that's the first time I've had to roll a save against alcoholism," Dot said.

"Was that Blake's secret agenda?" Robert asked.

Dot nodded. "His goal was to stay sober, and to keep others from finding out about his addiction. Should I draw another character?"

"Let's hold off on that," Brant said. "I think we're close to a stopping point for the week."

"We found a note in his room," Fontaine said. "It said 'Great job today.' Was that from you?"

Kale shook her head. "I need Becker found," she ordered. "Now." The two remaining security officers immediately turned and left the lab. Blake had been pronounced dead, and they had found trace amounts of poison in the bottle of whiskey.

"I just tried calling him again," Fontaine said. "He's not answering. You don't think—"

"Either he killed Blake, or he's a victim too," Kale said. "Have they finished going through the security logs?"

"Kitt's looking at them now," Fontaine said. "It shouldn't take too—"

Just then Kale's transmitter beeped. "Kitt?" she asked, putting on her headset.

"It's me," Kitt confirmed. "The security logs have been erased. Not just from last night, either. All of it's gone. Even the backups."

Kale cursed. "They must have been afraid of an investi—"

"Sorry to interrupt," Kitt said. "But there's more. A lot of our research data is gone, too. The preliminary scans we took last night, as well as all the sensor data since the last backup.

I'm still looking into the extent of it."

"Keep at it," Kale said. "Call me back when you know more." She was about to remove her headset when it beeped again.

It was Arvid Morris, one of the computer techs. "Commander, we've detected movement outside," he said.

"Becker," Kale said. "Has to be. Widen the scan. See if any other ships have landed in the area. If Becker's working for someone else, he might be taking the sample to another ship."

"On it," Morris said, and cut the call.

"Suit up," Kale told Fontaine. "We're going for a walk."

Becker pushed his way through the snow, holding a heat blower in one hand and a metal briefcase in the other. The snow was now more than two meters high, and the tunnel he made collapsed behind him as he walked. *Good, I won't be followed,* Becker thought. With the snowfall as heavy as it was, any trail he left would be covered within minutes.

He couldn't see where he was going. All he could do was follow his instruments, which told him that his rendezvous was less than a kilometer away. The VivaSource ship used an encrypted signal that only Becker's instruments could translate. To the equipment back at the base, it would just look like white noise.

Becker couldn't wait to get off this frozen hellscape. VivaSource was going to pay him twice what BioFinders had promised, and he'd finally get to go back to Earth for good. The red dot blipped more rapidly. He was getting close. Twenty meters... ten meters... five...

Becker burst into a clearing, a snowless divot created by the heat from the VivaSource shuttle. The ship's white exterior blended with the snow, and for a moment all Becker could make out was the open hatch. He closed the gap, then grabbed the handrail and climbed the three steps that led into the ship's interior.

Something didn't look right. The ship's interior lights were off, and no one greeted him as he entered. "Hello?" he shouted into the darkness, then turned toward the forward cabin. He tripped over something and fell face-first onto the deck, dropping his equipment. He turned and discovered that he'd tripped over a body. He had to remove his goggles to get a better look.

The man was frozen solid. Becker took off one of his gloves and touched the corpse. It was as if it were a statue carved from solid ice. Becker looked around in a panic. "Hello?" he called. "Anyone here?" No answer came.

Leaving his equipment behind, he got to his feet and ran to the cockpit. The pilot and co-pilot sat at their stations, similarly frozen solid. *I've got to get out of here,* he thought. He looked over the instrument panel, wondering if he could get the ship going by himself. He tried to push the pilot's body aside, but it was frozen to the seat. A light blinked on the control panel, indicating movement outside the ship.

Several humanoid-sized blips approached. At first there were four, then eight, and then twenty. Whatever they were, they had the ship surrounded, and they were closing in fast. *It can't be the crew from the base,* Becker thought. He took a step back as the number of blips more than doubled. And that was when he felt an icy hand grip his shoulder from behind.

"Make a save against cold," Brant said.

"Fourteen," Rita said. "Is that enough?"

Brant shook his head. "You feel a biting cold spreading through your body, like icy needles poking every inch of your skin. Within seconds you're frozen solid."

"Serves you right for pulling a Nedry on us," Sharon said.

"Hey, I was just following the agenda on my character sheet," Rita said, handing the card back to Brant.

Back at the base, Kale and Fontaine had just finished putting on their heat suits. A security officer named Li accompanied them out of the hatch and into the cold. The base was a prefabricated metal building, designed to be dropped onto a planet or moon and abandoned once it was no longer in use. It had external heat radiators placed around the structure, which kept the snow from gathering too close to the building's walls. This resulted in a clear path around the building, roughly three to four meters wide. Beyond that, the snow piled high, higher than the building itself in places.

Kale, Fontaine, and Li walked the perimeter of the building, looking for any trace of Becker's exit path. "This *could* be a collapsed tunnel," Fontaine said, pointing his light at a section of the snow that looked fresher than the rest.

"Yeah, but so could that," Li said, indicating another part of the snowbank.

"We're wasting our time," Kale said. "Becker won. He's long gone, probably already taken off. Our only hope is to find another sample, and maybe we can fight it out in court. Let's head back in."

"I'll get a crew ready for another excursion," Fontaine said. "It shouldn't be too hard to get another sample. I've still got the location of the last one bookmarked."

They trundled back toward the main entrance. As they

turned the corner, however, Li picked up some movement on his scanner. "Something's coming," he said.

"Surely Becker wouldn't come back," Kale said.

"I'm getting multiple signals," Li said.

"I think we should get inside," Fontaine suggested. They were only a few meters from the door now.

Li kept looking from his scanner to the snowbank. "The signal keeps multiplying," he said. "It was three or four. Now there's at least fifteen."

"Did Becker come back with an army?" Kale asked.

They reached the front doors. Fontaine and Kale stepped inside, while Li did one last scan. Suddenly a frozen projectile burst from the snowbank. The icicle hit Li in the eye, and he crumpled to the icy ground.

"Li!" Kale shouted, ready to run back outside. Fontaine grabbed her by the arm and pulled her back in. Dozens more icicles flew out of the snow, a barrage of frozen bolts, most shattering against the side of the building. Fontaine slammed the "close" button and the doors slid shut.

Kale looked through a transparent steel window. Outside, humanoid shapes emerged from the snow. They were mostly featureless and white, as if the snow itself had assumed human form. They stood right at the edge of the snowbank, seemingly unable to come any closer. Then they stepped backward, vanishing back into the snow.

"What *are* those?" Fontaine asked.

"I don't know, but they killed Li," Kale said. "Call Kitt. Have her divert more power to the outer radiators. I don't know if they can get in, but I'm not taking any chances. Let's keep those things as far away from the building as possible."

And then the power went out.

"That looks like a good place to stop for the week," Brant said. All around the table, the players stared at him like he'd just strangled a puppy. Brant loved that look. It meant he was doing his job right. "Act two is worth waiting for, trust me."

Everyone packed up their things and left the store.

That evening they sent another round of texts.

<u>Sharon</u>: I think Nate's starting to warm up to us.

<u>Brant</u>: Noticed that. Came out of his shell today.

<u>Robert</u>: Really got into character

<u>Rita</u>: More eye contact, too.

<u>Dot</u>: *nods vigorously*

<u>Robert</u>: I don't feel like I got to do much

<u>Brant</u>: I'll give Kitt more screen time next week. You liking the story?

<u>Rita</u>: Great story. 10/10

<u>Robert</u>: Reminds me of that Wilford Brimley movie

<u>Dot</u>: Cocoon?

<u>Robert</u>: No

<u>Brant</u>: Gives me an idea for a future one-shot tho.

<u>Rita</u>: Did Rob just refer to John Carpenter's masterpiece as "that Wilford Brimley movie?" :P

<u>Robert</u>: Couldn't remember title sorry

<u>Rita</u>: If only there were some THING on your phone you could use to look up movie titles ;)

<u>Dot</u>: That is a THING you could do.

<u>Robert</u>: Nah it'll come to me

Nate got home feeling energized. He'd had such a good time that he hadn't wanted the game to end. He couldn't wait until next week. *What's so different this time?* he wondered. After the previous week's self-flagellation and nap, he'd been certain he just wasn't meant to be social. But now? He felt like going out to a karaoke bar. Or whatever cool people did these days.

He couldn't put his finger on why, but he'd felt comfortable today, in a way he usually didn't feel around people. He'd spent most of the gaming session talking in character. It had felt oddly like a shield. No one had spoken to Nate or put him on the spot; they'd directed all their questions to Commander Kale. Nate hadn't felt any reason to feel embarrassed or shy, because any missteps he'd made were Kale's missteps.

So how was that so different from the week before? Why was Kale such an easier fit than Veezil? On some level he thought he knew why, but he blocked those thoughts from his mind.

The last time he'd felt this way had been back in his college days, when he used to play MUDs. Those were the first online games he'd played. No graphics, no voice chat, just simple, text-based RPGs with players from all over the world. He wasn't a dinosaur; plenty of graphical MMOs had also existed at the time. But he'd done most of his gaming in the computer labs, where you couldn't install your own software. Plus the lack of graphics had made it much easier to hide what you were doing from passing professors.

He'd gotten addicted to those games, and his grades had suffered for it. He'd also ruined a few potential friendships along the way. He'd had to quit MUDs cold turkey, and he'd promised himself he'd never touch them again. But tonight he was tempted. He needed to know what was so special about those MUDs that he'd found them more addictive than single-player RPGs. He needed to know why it was so similar to how he felt today.

He sat down at his laptop and did a quick search. Most of the MUDs he'd played back then were long gone, but one of his favorites was still running. QuestixMUD was set in a medieval fantasy universe with loads of anachronisms and dated pop culture references.

Nate still remembered his old username and password, but they no longer worked. It wasn't surprising. There had probably been more than a dozen server wipes since college. He created a new account, then remade the same character he'd played back then, Zephyr the female thief. He scrolled through a couple of pages of server rules, then entered the newbie area where he would spend the first four levels.

The game hadn't changed much. He still remembered all the commands, and he still had a mental map of the starting city. He got right to work, fighting and resting and fighting again, killing weak monsters for xp. So far he wasn't quite sure why he'd found it so addictive. When compared to modern games, it didn't have much going for it. But in a way, it felt like coming home. He could almost smell the coffee machine in the college's computer lab.

He reached level five within an hour, and could now integrate into the rest of the game's population. It didn't seem to be too busy. Other characters walked by now and then, but nobody spoke to him. They all had their own missions, and only passed through town to sell whatever loot they'd found.

Zephyr sat down near the fountain in the town square. It had once been a popular place to wait for parties to form. He didn't have much hope of joining a party tonight, though.

The server seemed too dead.

A ranger entered the area, then left to the north. He returned a few seconds later and sat down next to Zephyr. After a minute he asked, "A/S/L?"

Nate's fingers hovered over the keyboard, but he hesitated. The other player was asking for his real-life age, sex, and location. Back in college, he'd always lied about the middle one. At the time, he'd told himself it was just for fun, so he could laugh at how many guys hit on him. But now he wasn't so sure. He thought about answering honestly, but he simply couldn't make himself type that 'M' key. It wasn't enough to play a female character, he had to let the other player think he was 'F' in real life as well.

He logged off immediately. *What was that about?* he wondered. And then it hit him. He'd never been addicted to the MUD's gameplay. He'd been addicted to being seen as a woman. And today he'd spent four hours pretending to be the opposite sex. So had the other players, so he'd fit right in. But for Nate, it had meant so much more. He'd spoken as a woman, and the others had responded. They'd participated in his little fantasy, a fantasy that included being a woman.

Does this mean I'm...? Nate wondered.

No, of course not, he told himself.

And yet... the way he'd felt at that game today... it was the best he'd felt in years. The best he'd felt since... well, since all that time he'd wasted playing games in college.

It would be a crime not to explore the possibility.

No, Nate thought. *I have a good life. A stable job. I'm happy. Well... maybe not happy, but I've got more than most people get. If I pursue this, my family will hate me, my friends will stop talking to me, and I might even lose my job. I know they can't legally fire me for that, but they'll make up a reason. Why make my life more complicated?*

He paced around his house, looking at all the little collectibles that brought him joy. On one shelf, a set of "Sergeant Napalm" action figures stared back at him. He still remembered the day he started that collection. He'd been nine years old. The first run had consisted of seven characters, five good guys and two bad guys. One of the good "guys" had been Lady Rouge, an absolute badass secret agent who mostly fought hand-to-hand. To this day, she was still Nate's favorite member of the team.

He thought back to the Christmas he started his collection. He'd asked his parents for the entire set. He'd told them it was because he wanted to collect them all, but the truth was, he hadn't cared about most of the characters. If he could have asked for Lady Rouge by herself, he would have. But he hadn't wanted his parents to think he was into girl toys.

Still, his parents had to have noticed that he played with Lady Rouge more than the other figures. His friends sure did. One of his friends even called him a sissy. After that, Nate was more careful about which figures he played with. At least when certain friends were around.

Was I really just playing back then, or was I expressing my true identity through toys? Nate wondered. *And is that what I'm doing now, with Brant and the others?*

I was happier before I opened this can of worms, Nate thought. *Wasn't I?*

Nate sat down. He thought about the last few years of his life. He couldn't honestly say he'd been happy, but at the very least he'd been content. Or if not content, he'd been…

Not sad, Nate thought. But was that enough? Was "not sad" the best he could hope for?

If I pursue this line of thinking, it's going to make my life difficult, Nate thought. *I have to remove the temptation.*

If I don't at least explore my feelings, I'll wonder about it the rest of my life, Nate thought back.

He stood up again and paced some more. Within the space of a few minutes, he experienced grief, anger, denial, hope, and more anger. Once again he wound up standing in front of his shelf of action figures. He stared longingly at Lady Rouge, wondering what it would be like to step into her shoes.

"Screw it!" he shouted, then swiped the shelf with the back of his hand, knocking all the toys onto the floor. Then he sat down and put his head in his hands.

The following morning Nate sent Brant a text.

Nate: I don't think I can make it this Sat.

Brant: You feeling ok?

Nate: I'm fine. Just busy.

Brant: It's cool. If things change, feel free to show up.

On Friday evening, Nate returned home from work and sat on his couch. Throughout the week, hundreds of suppressed memories had come rushing back to him. He now recalled several instances of asking his mother for a girl's toy, only to be told no. He remembered his father chastising him for "standing like a girl" and using feminine hand gestures. He remembered how much easier it had been to make friends with girls in elementary school.

He remembered dozens of cartoons he'd watched as a kid - he'd always focused on the female characters. He remembered all the video games he'd grown up playing. He'd always been drawn to games where you could play as a woman.

He remembered playing dress up in his mother's clothes. He remembered trying on her makeup. He remembered being jealous of the girls' roles in the school plays. He remembered playing with dolls at his cousin's house, and wishing he could stay longer because her toys were so much better than his.

On their own, none of these memories meant a damn thing. Kids did funny things. They explored their identities without all the hang-ups that came later in life. Not every boy who tried on his mom's high heels was transgender. In fact, most of them weren't.

None of these signs meant anything on their own. But combined, surely they had to add up to *something*.

SESSION THREE

"Okay, looks like Nate's not going to be here today, so somebody else will need to run Commander Kale." Brant held up the character card. Dot and Rita both held out their hands, then both withdrew.

"You can take it," Dot said.

"Nah, maybe I'll get lucky and draw something good," Rita said.

"If you're sure," Dot said, reaching for the card.

"Yoink!" Another hand grabbed it from Dot's closing fingers. All heads turned to see Nate standing by the table. "Sorry I'm late," he said. "I thought I had a thing, but I don't."

Rita smirked like he'd said something dirty. Dot picked up on her thought and rolled her eyes, laughing.

"Glad you made it," Brant said with a smile. As Nate sat down and unpacked his things, Brant gave the group a recap.

"So… Becker betrayed the others and poisoned Security Chief Blake. Then Becker was killed by snow creatures. Now more of those creatures have surrounded the research base, and the power's gone out. Dot and Rita, you can draw new characters now." He held out a selection of pregens.

Rita grabbed a character card and read it to the others. "Ora Vane. Medic. It says she's easily frightened and hates violence. This should be interesting."

"Killian Rocke," Dot said. "Software engineer. He lost an eye when he was a kid, and now he wears a prosthetic eye that he designed himself. Cool, it says I can see in the dark."

Brant nodded. "So, there's eleven of you left, altogether. Everyone's gathered in the main lab, except for Kitt, who's still trying to get the generator online."

"Rocke, see if Kitt needs any help," Kale ordered. "Everyone else, I need ideas. Now." The room was lit by round, portable lamps which cast eerie shadows on the walls.

Fontaine spoke up. "Those things… whatever they are… look like they're made of the snow itself. If they're native to this moon, they have to have evolved to live in the cold. They're probably vulnerable to heat."

"Gather up every one of those heat blowers you can find," Kale ordered, and a couple of her subordinates left. "Does this base have any flamethrowers?"

"No, but we could probably rig something," Fontaine said.

"You two," Kale said, pointing at a pair of engineers. "Work on assembling flame weapons."

"What about de-icing chemicals?" Fontaine asked. "Like salting a sidewalk, we could try surrounding the base with a chemical barrier."

"Good, good," Kale said. She nodded at another pair of scientists, and they took off to take stock of the lab's chemicals. "Everyone else," Kale said, "We need to work on survival. It's going to get very cold in here, very quickly. We need to stay together, preferably here in the lab. I want you to gather up blankets, rations, and medical supplies, and bring them back here. Then we need—"

The lights flickered on for a second. Then there was a loud boom in the distance, which shook the entire building. The lights turned off again, and the smell of smoke filled the lab. Kale grabbed her walkie-talkie. "Kitt! Status report!"

"We're right here, Commander," Rocke said, as he and Kitt entered the room. Black smoke billowed in behind them.

Kitt walked with a limp, and leaned on Rocke for support. Vane rushed over to examine her injuries. "It was definitely sabotage," Kitt said. "Someone installed incendiary devices in both the main and backup generators."

"Nearly killed us," Rocke added. "We got lucky. But those generators are gone for good."

"Becker," Kale fumed, shaking her head. "When I get my hands on him…"

"Not if I see him first," Fontaine said, cracking his knuckles.

"So what's our plan?" Vane asked as she wrapped gauze around Kitt's thigh.

"Evacuate," Rocke said. "If we stay here, we'll freeze."

"Leave?" Fontaine asked. "With those things out there? No way. I saw what they did to Li. I say we stay, get a transmitter working, and call for help."

"Wait for another ship?" Rocke asked. "Why? We already have a ship. We just have to make it to the hangar."

"It's outside," Fontaine whined. "Past those… *things*."

"We can make it," Rocke said. "It's not even a five-minute walk."

"And what if Becker also sabotaged the ship?" Rocke asked.

"Even if it can't fly, we'll be safe there," Fontaine said. "It has supplies. It'll be warmer in the shuttle than it is in here. And we can use its transmitter to call for help."

"Behind the compound's rear exit, about a hundred meters away, lies the hangar with your escape ship," Brant explained. "But as you peer out the windows, you find that hundreds of those snow creatures stand between you and the hangar."

"Why wouldn't they have an interior hall that goes straight to the hangar?" Robert asked.

"Probably because the ship puts out fumes or something," Rita suggested.

"Sure, we'll go with that," Brant said, unsure if the module had even bothered to explain it.

"How many flamethrowers have they been able to assemble?" Nate asked.

"Just three so far," Brant said. "Each has a range of about two meters, and has enough fuel for maybe fifty short bursts."

"I want to take a small team out to the hangar," Nate said.

"Why not just take everyone?" Sharon asked.

"Because we could be heading into a death trap," Nate replied. "Are there any security officers left?"

"Just one," Brant said. "Kiana Holt."

"Give her a flamethrower," Nate said, looking Brant in the eyes. "I'll also take Fontaine, Rocke, Kitt, and Vane."

"Kitt's injury might slow you down," Brant suggested.

"I know," Nate replied. "But I don't want to split the party. Besides, if the ship has any damage, we might need Kitt to fix it. Once we get there, we'll send out a distress signal from the ship. When we confirm the ship is fully functional and flight-worthy, we'll use the ship's transmitter to inform the other scientists, and they can join us for the escape."

"Sounds like a plan," Robert said.

"Who gets the other flamethrowers?" Rita asked.

"Uh, Rocke and Fontaine," Nate said, ignoring the disappointed look on Rita's face. But Rita was currently playing a pacifist, and Nate doubted her character had the stats to use a flamethrower properly.

Kale and her team stood by the rear doors of the compound. Through tiny rectangular windows, they could see at least two dozen snowmen standing between the doors and the hangar. Kale ordered everyone to perform equipment checks. Her team – Holt, Rocke, Fontaine, Vane, and Kitt – patted their snowsuits and made sure their supply packs were full. Fontaine, Rocke, and Holt all held flamethrowers, while Kale, Vane, and Kitt carried heat blowers.

Behind them, the five remaining team members worked on constructing more weapons and supply kits. They'd need all the help they could get if those creatures somehow breached the compound.

The doors weren't even open yet, and Kale could already see her breath in the air. Soon it would be as cold inside the base as it was outside. "Kitt," she said. "How long until you can power the door?"

"Almost there, Commander," Kitt replied. She had her heat

blower braced under her armpit, and she leaned on it like it was a crutch while she configured some wiring. She had hooked up a spare shuttle battery to an electrical panel on the wall, and now she worked on adjustments to make sure it wouldn't short out.

"Once we're outside, will we be able to communicate with the base?" Fontaine asked.

"The walkie-talkies are still a no-go," Rocke said. "But I've rigged a portable radio that should let the base communicate with our headsets. As long as we're not more than a kilometer away, anyway."

"Good work," Kale said.

"Stand back for a second," Kitt said, as she shielded her eyes and flipped a breaker switch. A couple of sparks flew from the jury-rigged connection. They heard a distant hum from beyond the door. "Southern heat generators back online," Kitt reported.

Kale looked out a frost-covered window. Outside, the snow people started backing away from the walls. "Good job," Kale said. "And the doors?"

"Just say when," Kitt said. "It won't last forever, though, so we'd best hustle once the doors open."

"The second we're clear, shut the doors," Kale ordered, addressing the five who were to remain behind. They didn't look like they needed convincing. "This is it, then," Kale said, taking a deep breath. "Everyone ready?" She looked at her five companions, each of whom nodded. "Let's go."

Kitt flipped another switch, causing a few more sparks, and then the group rushed out the door. Outside, the creatures had backed off enough to give them a clear path to the hangar – at least for the first fifty meters or so. The whirling snow made it difficult to see much past that. The wind howled around them, blocking out all other noise.

Though the exterior heat poles did a good job of keeping the creatures at a distance, Kale got a good look at them for the first time. They looked like exquisitely crafted snow sculptures of human beings, some more detailed than others. While a few of the monsters were relatively formless, with blank faces and fingerless hands, the majority of them looked as if they'd intentionally copied existing people. In fact, several of them reminded Kale of that traitor Becker.

As Kale watched, one of the more formless creatures stared directly at her. Bits of snow flaked off of its form, or were blown off by the wind. But as more snow landed on the creature, new features began to take shape. It was as if the wind itself was sculpting the monster before Kale's eyes. After a few seconds, it came to resemble Kale herself. It was especially unsettling since Kale currently wore a facemask, so the creature couldn't have seen her face to copy it.

Maybe it's trying to communicate, Kale thought. Then the creature raised its right arm as if to wave hi. A huge gust of wind blew the outer layers of snow off of its arm, revealing a sharp icicle underneath. The creature turned away, drawing back its arm, then swept forward like a pitcher throwing a fastball. The icicle detached from the creature at the elbow, and flew toward Kale's face.

Kale dove to the ground, just barely avoiding impalement. Rocke and Vane helped her back to her feet, while Holt fired a blast of flame in the creature's direction. The creature backed off, along with a few of its companions, and they once again merged into the snowbank. More creatures continued to watch from a distance, but none of them attempted to attack.

A line of heating poles, each spaced about three meters apart, led to the hangars. This path wasn't quite as wide as the one around the compound, so they had to stick to the middle to stay away from the creatures. The farther they got from the compound, the less heat the poles radiated, and therefore the tighter the path became. As the snowbanks encroached on them from the sides, the six of them became more and more on edge. They held their flamethrowers and heat blowers at the ready, jumping at every movement.

But no attack came. As they got closer to the hangar, the snowbank came within a meter of them. Kale expected a frosty hand to burst from the bank at any moment, but still there was nothing. The wind carried with it a distant scream, and Kale turned around to see if she'd imagined it.

For just a moment the air cleared of snow, and Kale was able to see the base. It was now nearly a hundred meters away, and a mass of snow people lurched their way toward the compound. The doors were still open for some reason, just wide enough for a human to step through. Kale spoke into her facemask's transmitter, shouting, "Base, report. You've got incoming. Why are the doors still open?" No answer came.

"Keep moving!" Holt shouted, her voice barely rising above the wind. "We're almost there!"

Kale reluctantly resumed the hike. Even if they turned back now, they'd be too late to be of any help. Their only hope was that the crew members inside would find a safe room the creatures couldn't breach.

They reached the hangar and slid open the door. The shuttle still sat inside, seemingly untouched. Once they were safely inside the ship, Kale tried calling the base again. "Come in! What's going on?"

"Commander," someone replied. "This is Yava - we've barricaded ourselves in the lab. The outer door shorted out before it was completely shut. We've got... they're getting in!"

Kale heard several screams followed by static. "We've got to go back," she said.

"You're kidding, right?" Rocke asked.

"Commander," Fontaine said. "With all due respect, we can't help them. Even with our flamethrowers, there's just too many of those creatures."

"Engines online," Kitt said, tapping several buttons on an instrument panel. "Running a diagnostic."

"We can at least save some of them," Kale said. "We'll land the shuttle closer to the compound. If anyone's still alive, they can come to us."

"Is there any way to hook the base up to this ship's engines?" Fontaine asked. "Maybe give the compound enough power to turn the heat back on? That might scare off the creatures."

"It would drain the ship's power," Rocke said. "Even if we rescued them, we wouldn't be able to take off after that. We need to get off this moon and get some help."

"Diagnostic complete," Kitt said. "We're ready for takeoff. What'll it be, Commander?"

Kale took a deep breath. "First, send out a distress signal," she said. "Then fly us toward the base, and set us down as close to the back doors as possible." As the ship lifted off the ground, Kale spoke into the transmitter again. "If anyone can still hear me, head for the south doors. We'll be there shortly to pick you up." There was no reply.

"Uh oh," Kitt said, reading a diagnostic screen. "We're leaking fuel."

"I thought this thing was electric," Rocke said.

"Then we're leaking electricity," Kitt said. "I think it's a software problem... it's not diverting enough power to the engines."

"Let me take a look," Rocke said, taking a seat next to Kitt's piloting station. He tapped a few keys. "This isn't our operating system. It's designed to look like it, but—"

The ship shook violently, then took a nosedive. Kitt and Rocke grabbed the flight yoke together, struggling to keep the ship in the air.

"What the hell is happening?" Kale asked. She tried to stand up and approach Kitt's station, but another shudder knocked her against the wall, and she crumpled to the floor.

"Commander!" Vane shouted. She tried to get up, but Holt grabbed her arm.

"Wait 'til we're stable," Holt said.

"The ship bucks like a bronco," Brant said, demonstrating with his hand. "It spins and jerks, flying in random directions. Finally it crashes into a large snowbank, several kilometers north of the base. It was a relatively soft landing, but you still got a little banged up from knocking around the cabin. Everyone takes eight damage, or four if you made your save."

"Ouch, Kale rolled a one," Nate reported.

"As soon as Vane can move, she starts treating everyone's wounds," Rita said.

"You'll want to start with Kale," Brant said. "She's unconscious and bleeding."

"If the computer still works, Rocke will see if he can reinstall the OS from backup," Dot said.

"Kitt looks to see if the ship is damaged," Robert said.

"And Fontaine?" Brant asked.

"I guess I'll help Vane with Kale," Sharon said.

"Good," Brant said. "And Holt takes a look out the windows to see if there's any danger nearby."

"I forgot she was still here," Dot said.

"We'll probably appreciate her more in a minute," Rita said.

"Rocke gets a twenty-two to fix the software," Dot said. "Do I figure anything out?"

"Yes," Brant said. "The OS that was running was actually a virus, but not a particularly complicated one. Once you shut it down, you're able to reboot to the standard operating system."

"Can I tell who installed the virus?" Dot asked.

"Like it could possibly be anybody but Becker," Nate said. Rita whistled innocently, and everyone laughed.

"You can't tell, but you have your suspicions," Brant said.

"How bad's the ship?" Robert asked.

"Well, it'll probably never fly again," Brant said.

"Great," Nate said. "Am I awake yet?"

"Yes," Brant replied. "Vane patches you up and you come to your senses. You have a bit of a headache but you're okay."

"Scan the area for life signs," Kale said.

"On it," Rocke said, tapping a few buttons. "It's hard to say... The heavy snowfall is making it hard to detect movement. And we don't even know if those creatures have heat signatures. But there is something..." He got quiet, a puzzled look on his face.

"What is it?" Kale asked.

"I think it's... another ship," Rocke said.

"How far?" Kale asked.

"One point five kilometers," Rocke answered.

"That's closer than the base," Fontaine said. "Should we..."

"Well, we can't stay here," Kitt said. "That virus knocked out most of this ship's power cells. We'll be lucky if the heat lasts another hour."

"The other ship, then," Kale said. "If it works, we can still use it to look for survivors back at the base. Everybody gear up, we'll leave as soon as we're ready."

Twenty minutes later the ship's side hatch opened. Holt and Kale stepped out into the snow. Kale cleared a path with her heat blower while Holt kept an eye out for snow monsters. Once they determined the coast was clear, Fontaine, Kitt, Rocke, and Vane followed them out into the cold.

It was even colder than before, and their heated snowsuits could barely keep up with the frigid temperatures. The snow was more than four meters high, and they had to blow out each section of the tunnel twice – once to make the tunnel, and again when the tunnel's ceiling inevitably collapsed and had to be cleared again. It was a slow trudge, but at least the tunnel walls blocked most of the wind.

They walked for nearly a kilometer when Kitt suddenly shrieked. "Commander," she said, tapping Kale on the shoulder. She held a makeshift motion detector that she'd cobbled together from parts salvaged from the shuttle. "Something's coming towards us."

"Which direction?" Kale asked, taking a closer look at Kitt's device.

"All around us," Kitt said.

Holt turned around, her flamethrower ready, looking up and down the tunnel. She thought she saw a section of the tunnel wall move, and she gestured for the others to stay back. Aiming her weapon at the wall of snow, she backed away from it, ready to fire as soon as anything emerged.

Suddenly a pair of arms thrust out from the wall behind her, pulling her into the snow.

"Holt!" Kale shouted, running towards where she'd disappeared. Then a blast of flame burst from the wall, nearly igniting Kale's snowsuit. The hole in the wall widened as the surrounding snow melted. The rest of the team kept their distance so they wouldn't catch fire, but beyond the wall they could see several of the snow creatures ripping into Holt's body. Though her finger continued to squeeze the trigger of her flamethrower, she was long past saving.

Soon the flamethrower ran out of fuel, and the jet of flame diminished until it was gone. Thanks to the fiery blasts, the tunnel now ended in a large triangular room. More snow people began emerging from the walls.

"Run!" Kale ordered, though her team needed no encouragement. Unfortunately it was easier said than done, as their heavy snowgear and the uneven ground made it difficult to move much faster than a shuffle. Kitt still walked with a limp, and had to lean on Vane for support.

Fontaine and Rocke were the only two who still held flamethrowers. The other three attempted to use their heat blowers against the creatures, but they barely had any effect. Rocke stepped ahead of the group, making the creatures back off with short bursts of flame. Fontaine moved to the back of the group to fire at anything that might approach them from behind.

Kale stood just behind Rocke, using her heat blower to forge a tunnel. "How much farther?" she asked.

"Almost there," Kitt reported, looking at a device on her

wrist.

"Look!" Rocke said, pointing ahead. Where Kale's blower had just cleared a large patch of snow, a wall of shiny white metal was now visible. "We've found it! Look for a hatch and I'll— URK!" A meter-long shard of ice now protruded from his side.

Kale caught Rocke's flamethrower before he even hit the ground, and she used it to blast the creature that had impaled him. The snowman briefly took on the visage of Rocke's face before it melted from the heat. "Find the hatch!" Kale ordered, dropping her heat blower so she could get a better grip on her weapon. Three more monsters emerged from the tunnel walls, but she forced them to flee.

Vane and Kitt used their blowers to work their way around the sides of the snow-buried ship. They soon found the hatch, which was already open. Snow had piled up inside the ship as well, and had to be melted before they could get all the way inside. Kale and Rocke held off the attacking monsters while Kitt and Vane cleared a path into the ship.

"Go," Kale told Fontaine, once the entrance was clear. He turned and ran, and Kale backed her way into the ship, firing one last burst at some oncoming creatures before closing the hatch. "Kitt!" she shouted, dropping the flamethrower. "Can you get this thing running?"

Instead of answering the question, Kitt screamed. Kale grabbed the flamethrower again and turned toward the others. A short hallway led from the entrance to the cockpit. A man made of solid ice stood in the hallway, blocking the doorway to the cockpit.

"Get behind me," Kale said, raising the flamethrower. Vane and Kitt ducked below her line of fire, crawling past

Kale and crouching near the hatch. Fontaine stayed where he was, directly between Kale and the creature. "I said move!" Kale ordered, but Fontaine remained still. Only then did Kale notice the icicle protruding from his back. Fontaine crumpled to the floor and lay still.

Now Kale could see the creature clearly for the first time. It looked like a living ice sculpture of Becker, except it had sharp blades of ice instead of hands. Kale didn't waste any time, and fired her flamethrower right at the thing's face. This caused the ice creature to convulse and scream, but it didn't back away. Its facial features now half-melted, it glared at Kale and charged.

Kale squeezed the trigger on her flamethrower, but nothing happened. The previous blast had drained the last of her fuel. She spotted Fontaine's flamethrower on the floor, but there was no time to reach for it. The creature was now upon her. It swiped downward with one bladed arm, and Kale instinctively blocked the blow with her forearm. The slice cut deeply into her arm, stopping at the bone. Then the creature thrust its other arm forward, puncturing Kale in the stomach.

Small nozzles then opened up in the ceiling, and a chemical spray burst forth, drenching everything in the hallway. The ice monster yowled and began melting away, diminishing until it was nothing but a misshapen lump of slush. And then it was gone.

Kitt stood by a control panel at the back of the ship. Vane turned from the bodies to stare at her. "What did you do?"

"Simple, really," Kitt said, breathing heavily. "I rerouted the exterior de-icing system through the fire suppression pipes."

Vane rushed into the hallway to help the injured.

"You probably only have time to save one of them," Brant said. "And even then, you'll have to roll pretty high. You going for Fontaine or Kale?"

"Can I tell whose injury is worse?" Rita asked.

"They both look pretty close to death," Brant said. "And you don't really have time to go by more than instinct."

"Am I conscious?" Nate asked.

"Barely," Brant said.

"If I can speak, I order her to save Fontaine," Nate said.

"I'll allow it," Brant said.

"Ten-four," Rita said, and rolled a die.

"Good enough," Brant said, seeing the seventeen on the die. "He'll still need constant care for a while, but he's got a fighting chance. But while you're tending to Fontaine, Kale breathes her last breath."

"At least she can die knowing she found proof of alien life," Nate said. "It's what she always wanted."

"Can the ship still fly?" Robert asked.

"Make a repair roll," Brant said, and Robert rolled a die. "Yes. You make some minor repairs, and soon you've got it running. With Kitt at the helm, the ship bursts forth from the snow and takes to the air."

"Let's swing by the base real quick before we fly off for good," Robert said.

"When you reach the base, you see three scientists on the roof, waving at you," Brant said. "More of the snow creatures are attempting to climb up the sides of the building."

"I set down on the roof," Robert said.

"You manage to rescue the remaining scientists and get

away easily," Brant said. "The three you rescued inform you that everyone else is dead, so there's no reason to stick around. You fly off into space and set a course for Earth. Oh, and you also find Becker's briefcase on the shuttle. The frozen sample is still intact. And… that's pretty much it!"

"Great game," Rita said. "Good and scary."

"You might even say chilling," Dot added, and Rita rolled her eyes.

"What'd you think, Nate?" Brant asked.

"I've never felt more alive," he answered.

"Seems a bit much but I'll take it," Brant said. "So you'll be back next week? We'll be starting a new B&B campaign."

"Definitely," Nate said.

The group packed up their things, said their goodbyes, and went home.

A few months later…

It was another busy day in the back room of the gaming store. Brant's table was in great spirits. The party had just taken down a massive two-headed ogre, and the resulting reward would be more than enough to finish constructing their stronghold.

Rita's minotaur barbarian did a little victory dance, spiking one of the ogre's heads like it was a football. Dot's sorcerer congratulated the barbarian for delivering the final death blow. Robert's cleric tended to the minotaur's wounds while Sharon's rogue searched the ogre's lair for hidden treasure. And all the while, Natalie's bard sang an impromptu ballad about their triumph.

Brant couldn't help but stare at Natalie's smile. He'd never seen her as happy as she'd been these last few months. She was still the same person she'd always been, with the same interests and sense of humor, but this infectious new exuberance brought joy to every room she entered. The act of putting on makeup and a dress had actually removed her old disguise, and Brant was seeing the real person for the first time.

It's like she's been released from prison, Brant thought, watching Natalie trade quips with the other players. *I hope she never has to hide again.*

And she never did.

Author's Notes

This is the third in a series of short story collections, which started with Geek Cutes and continued with Rainbow Nightmares. Since most of the stories are unrelated, it's not necessary to read these collections in any particular order. Though if you enjoyed "Game Face," the other collections also contain stories starring Brant's gaming group.

These stories are very personal to me, but in no way do they represent all transgender people. I am well aware that some trans readers will finish these stories and think, "No, that's not how it felt to me at all." And that's okay. I've done my best to represent a variety of trans experiences, but ultimately the only story I can tell with complete accuracy is my own. If you're transgender but you don't relate to my characters, rest assured that you are still valid and I support you.

The Opposite of Magic

I love fantasy stories where magic has unusual rules. Maybe all magic requires the loss of blood, whether it's the caster's or that of the shackled captives he leads into the dungeon. Maybe magic comes from a long-dead fairy goddess, whose final spell diffused her powers to all those in her bloodline. Or perhaps the magic comes from microscopic insects that live on our skin. The rules don't have to make sense as long as they're consistent.

Power Play

This started out as two separate short stories, but they each felt a little bland on their own. The stoned customer is based on an actual customer I served while working for a sandwich shop.

Bubbles

I wrote this one for a contest, but I didn't finish it by the deadline. It's just as well; I didn't quite follow the rules anyway.

Consequences

This story is based on a meme about an injured hero who seeks out their arch-enemy for help. This was my second attempt to adapt that meme, the first was Quarantine. Both attempts veered way off-course the more I wrote, but Consequences stays closer to the original meme... albeit with the roles reversed. Oh well, maybe someday I'll get it right.

Lest anyone accuse me of picking on a certain author, allow me to state for the record: Cazandra is not a direct reference to any one actual person. She's a satirical amalgamation of several public figures.

Jealousy

Another author self-insert. I've felt the exact same emotions when shopping with my wife.

* * *

Meanwhile

This story takes place in the same universe as my Bloodhunters series. Bits of this story had been percolating in my brain for a while. It bothered me that we never really see the aftermath of the explosion in Bloodhunters. We're told that the police are too short-staffed to pursue the terrorist, but then we're whisked off to other planets to watch the bounty hunters do their work. I wanted to show the same event as seen by another set of eyes, a POV story from someone more directly affected by the disaster.

Midnight Snack

The original ending was more ambiguous: "Jess looked back into the vampire's eyes and made her choice." The final ending is technically also ambiguous, but in a less serious way. Is the final line a request to be turned, or an attempt to insult the vampire?

True Faces

Plot twist: Gavin's people are actually human souls. When people die on Earth, they transcend to Gavin's dimension where they live on as motes of light, with no memory of their life on Earth. Except now that Gavin's home planet has been destroyed, the nature of the afterlife has changed. From now on when people die, their souls end up in an old mop bucket in a long-abandoned mall in Akron, Ohio. Aren't you glad you read the author's notes?

Reality Check

Ennie is called by his initials, "N. E.," which stands for Nobody Ever. I realize parts of this story are gross and offensive, and I debated on whether to include it in this collection. But I wanted to show just how ridiculous some of the arguments for anti-trans bathroom laws are.

To clarify: I'm not claiming that no woman has ever been assaulted in a restroom. There are eight billion people on this planet, so if something can happen, it probably has. Somewhere, sometime, a cis man has dressed up as a woman to commit sexual assault.

But so? Don't punish trans women for the crimes of cis men. Anti-trans bathroom laws do nothing to protect women. If some asshole disguises himself so he can attack women in a bathroom, he's not going to be deterred by an extra law. All those laws do is make it harder for trans people to exist.

Quarantine

This has to be the biggest dialogue-to-story ratio I've ever written. Change a few details and their discourse could almost be teenage me talking to adult me. The penguins are a metaphor for all the barriers life throws at you that prevent you from moving forward, such as financial troubles, depression, unjust laws... Nah, not really, I just thought killer penguins would be funny.

Legal Battle

I suppose this is a satire of our broken legal system, with a bit of social commentary about short attention spans and how bigots don't care about facts. But honestly? I just really like worldbuilding. It's fun to speculate about alien courtrooms and future laws. And the best part is I didn't have to do any research. Did I get a legal detail wrong? Well, that's just how the justice system works in the future, nyahh

nyahh.

The Loner

This one also takes place in the Bloodhunters universe. But unlike "Meanwhile," which introduced entirely new characters, "The Loner" stars one of the more important characters in the Bloodhunters series. It does contain a couple of minor spoilers, but nothing that's likely to ruin Bloodhunters for you if you decide to read that next. Which you should – bounty hunters are cool, and reading about them will make you cool as well. Plus I could really use the money.

Game Face

This is probably the most autobiographical story I've written yet. Especially the part about fighting alien snowmen on a distant moon.

Special Thanks to Kaius.

About The Author

Xine Fury is not: Pretending, delusional, insane, confused, going through a phase, playing dress-up, having a mid-life crisis, dangerous, a fetishist, a pervert.

Xine Fury is: A valid human being, and so are you.

Also By Xine Fury

The following books are also available:
    Bloodhunters v1: Bad Blood
    Bloodhunters v2: Blue Blood
    Bloodhunters v3: New Blood
    Blood Samples (A Bloodhunters Prequel)
    Geek Cutes
    Rainbow Nightmares
    Side Quests
    Nomads of Zyden

Get them here:
  bit.ly/XineFury

www.ingramcontent.com/pod-product-compliance
Lightning Source LLC
Chambersburg PA
CBHW071415300726
48976CB00006B/2108